"I Don't Know When I've Enjoyed an Evening More."

He sighed contentedly. "Good food, good beer, a good woman. Who could ask for more?"

She smiled. "I could. Tell me something."

"Anything you want to know." He lay back and put an arm around her shoulders, drawing her with him.

His shirt was open, and she rested her face against his strong chest. "Every time you spoke to me when we made love, you said the words in French. They sounded beautiful, and I want to know what you said."

He chuckled softly. "I think you already do."

KATHRYN GORSHA THIELS

has "roots" that reach back to the genteel society of the Deep South. Her family is of French extraction and settled in Acadiana (South Louisiana) after migrating from France. Ms. Thiels makes her home in Alexandria, Louisiana.

Dear Reader:

Romance readers have been enthusiastic about Silhouette Special Editions for years. And that's not by accident: Special Editions were the first of their kind and continue to feature realistic stories with heightened romantic tension.

The longer stories, sophisticated style, greater sensual detail and variety that made Special Editions popular are the same elements that will make you want to read book after book.

We hope that you enjoy this Special Edition today, and will enjoy many more.

The Editors at Silhouette Books

KATHRYN THIELS

An Acquired Taste

Silhouette Special Edition
Published by Silhouette Books New York
America's Publisher of Contemporary Romance

Silhouette Books by Kathryn Thiels

Texas Rose (SE #10)
Alternate Arrangements (IM #51)
An Acquired Taste (SE #234)

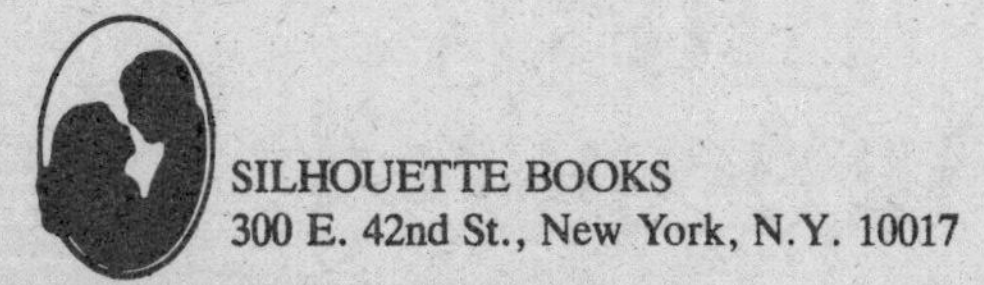

SILHOUETTE BOOKS
300 E. 42nd St., New York, N.Y. 10017

Distributed by Pocket Books

ISBN: 0-373-09234-2

First Silhouette Books printing April, 1985

10 9 8 7 6 5 4 3 2 1

Map by Ray Lundgren

Printed in the U.S.A.

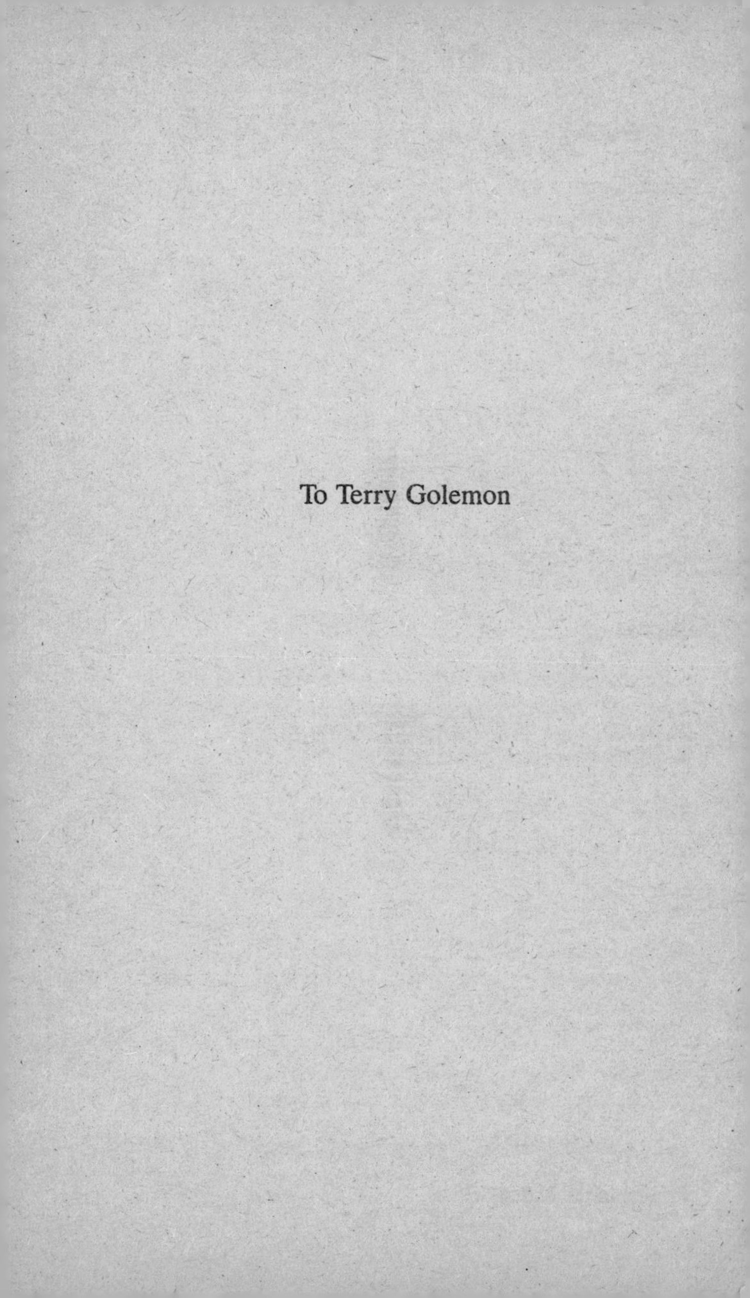

To Terry Golemon

An Acquired Taste

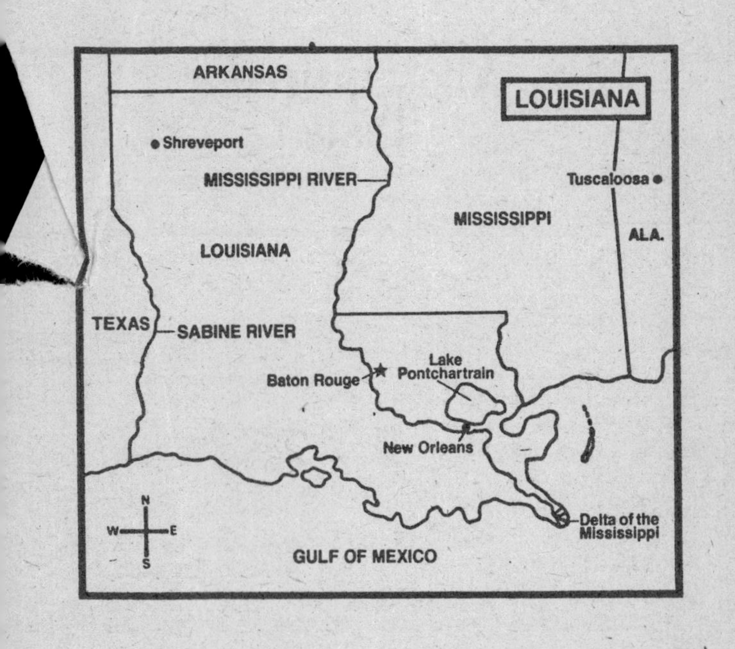
LOUISIANA
ARKANSAS
Shreveport
MISSISSIPPI RIVER
Tuscaloosa
MISSISSIPPI
ALA.
LOUISIANA
TEXAS
SABINE RIVER
Lake Pontchartrain
Baton Rouge
New Orleans
N
W
E
S
Delta of the Mississippi
GULF OF MEXICO

Chapter One

A summer dust devil blew slowly across the yellow-brown grasses of the Tuscaloosa Trend as a team of drillers tended to the finishing touches of securing a new rig. With chrome and steel latticework gleaming in the hot June sun, it reached skyward better than sixty feet, like hundreds of others scattered along the Louisiana countryside.

The workers buzzed around the lofty derrick like bees, but slowly, and at first not apparent to the naked eye, it began to show signs of weakness.

When an underground pressure groaned ominously and made the foundation tremble, the crew stopped and took serious notice. They watched as pilings shifted slightly. The structure strained to hold a disaster at bay, but it was no use.

A drilling engineer sensed trouble and sounded a warning with "She's going to blow. Clear out!" It was suddenly every man for himself as the force of a billion cubic feet of crude oil and natural gas propelled the ironwork high into the heavens like a rocket.

Seconds later a gigantic explosion shook the countryside. Fire shot upward over a quarter mile as a newly drilled well ignited. The dreaded blowout had occurred, and everyone stood by helplessly as it claimed over twelve million dollars' worth of back-breaking toil.

The fire was devastating. A huge orange column of flame swirled fat and greedy in all directions, belching ropes of gray-black smoke into a clear blue sky. Roaring and groaning, it displayed an awesome power, melting the steel that only minutes ago had formed an invincible cage.

Hours later, a quick survey was taken of the area, and it was discovered that no injury or mishap had befallen any of the valued team of drillers. The oil company executives then made the unanimous decision to call in one of a handful of professional men who capped such fires. The best around were Brad Steiner and Quinn Chennault of Wild Wells Limited, and a call was placed to their base of operations in the crescent city of New Orleans.

As the sole passenger in a helicopter bearing the insignia of Wild Wells Limited, Mallory Steiner stared pensively through the glass bubble that surrounded the cockpit. She was on her way to a Baton Rouge hospital, and the ride seemed rough as the chopper flew low and fast.

In the distance she saw titanic flames and black pillars of smoke. They snaked from an uncontrollable blaze in the Judson Field near the small Southern town of Denham Springs, Louisiana. That one parcel of land comprised only a minute portion of the giant Tuscaloosa Trend, a section of Louisiana that ribboned from the western boundary of the Sabine River to Lake Pontchartrain and beyond. From that point, and spanning the entire girth of Louisiana, lay mineral-rich deposits waiting for geological geniuses to tap their hidden ebony treasures. The mutinous occurrence of an unruly fire represented millions of dollars lost to oil companies, as well as an untold amount of lost energy.

Although the explosion and related contingencies were given national coverage through the media for days, Mallory hadn't paid much attention until a broadcast announced that her brother and part-owner of Wild Wells Limited, Brad Steiner, was seriously injured when he and his team had attempted to cap the wayward well.

Mallory currently resided in Houston and worked as an oil broker on an independent basis. At twenty-nine she had quite a reputation as a shrewd businesswoman, and prided herself in wheeling and dealing with some of the most powerful oil people in the world.

Today, though, she felt rather small and helpless as she contemplated Brad's accident. She prayed that the media had exaggerated conditions concerning the blowout, but she highly doubted it in this particular case as she witnessed evidence of the holocaust for herself.

Along with feelings of concern, Mallory experienced a deep-seated anger at Brad for embracing such a dangerous, unpredictable line of work in the first place. It certainly wasn't as if they needed the money.

Sixteen years her senior, Brad had become both mother and father to her after they had lost their parents. And from the beginning, Mallory felt that he had assumed his roles too zealously, in the oil fields as well as at home. He was too overprotective, she was too headstrong; but they didn't love each other any less because of it.

Mallory was in her early teens when Brad uprooted them in Shreveport, near the northwest border of Louisiana, and relocated in New Orleans to be closer to his work. There he met and married Elissa Devereaux, a purebred Southern lady from an old, wealthy New Orleans family.

From the time she was small, Mallory always heard Brad preach: "We're the last of our line, remember that. We're considered the elite when it comes to high society, and we set examples for our peers. It's up to you and me to carry on the Steiner name and keep our heritage pure."

He followed his own words by finding a Southern belle who met his standards, and he promptly married her. For Brad, love appeared to be a secondary consideration, and it seemed a lucky blessing that Elissa fairly worshipped him. The marriage was a good one. Mallory was happy for them, but she often felt like she was in the way. The couple needed time for themselves, time to adjust, so after going away to school, Mallory began spending most of the year abroad. She visited New Orleans only during summer vacations. Guesting at Brad's town house was pleasant, for the most part, although there was little time to spend with her only blood relative, since his work required a great deal of travel.

Over the years each learned little about the other, even though that underlying bond of strong affection and pride continued to exist.

All her life Mallory had adored her brother, sometimes finding herself in awe of what he stood for. He was a powerful man, one of the few left who felt compelled to seek adventure and danger in order to live life to the fullest. He walked, talked, and breathed power, an undisputed king in his vast empire. Those closest to him knew never to show resistance or go against his wishes. That is, all except for Mallory. She flatly refused to be pushed around, and more than once their disagreements threatened to turn into out-and-out warfare.

Always the buffer, Elissa would discreetly step in and

patch things up. It was in her mind to set an example for Mallory. She considered Brad's sister to be an obstinate child. When would Mallory learn, ran the accepted wisdom, that women were born and bred to be members of the gentry, expected to keep home and hearth warm while the husband was away earning fortunes and risking his life for the excitement of it?

It just didn't wash with Mallory, and she found herself with little respect for women intent on acting so subservient to men. It was a great big world. Excitement could be as alluring to the female of the species as it was to the male. One's life should be shared, not sacrificed for a husband, but there was no getting through to Elissa. Too many generations of "good breeding" stood in the way.

Although not the primary cause, this was one reason why four years earlier Mallory had decided to strike out on her own and live her life the way she saw fit. Always in defiance of Brad, she had to show him that she didn't intend to be ruled by any man, that she was too old to stay under her brother's thumb.

For a time Brad humored her, knowing she was too spoiled and accustomed to the wealth she had grown up with to stay away for very long. Only after repeated refusals to accept his "recommendations" did he realize just how far she intended to go. In retaliation Brad tried every tactic he could, going so far as to snip the purse strings to the Steiner fortunes and seeing her without a cent so she would return home where she belonged.

Undaunted, Mallory set up residence in Houston and began the hard work of lining up clients for an independent oil brokerage. She hadn't gone to schools all over the world for nothing, she declared privately, and it was time to put her education to work.

Establishing a brokerage entailed endless visits to oil companies and zealously wrangling contracts for representation when there were none to be had. But she persevered and proved her worth when it came to finding spot oil for buyers. Mallory always came through with the specified deliveries. In return for her services, she received a generous percentage of the transaction premiums, making her bankroll grow quickly. She had done well and could afford to pat herself on the back for managing on her own resources.

Although Mallory no longer harbored ill feelings about the split with her brother, she didn't often make an overture to get in touch with him. Contact over four years was sparse, and it was like talking to a stranger when she did speak to him. But now old arguments and wounds were forgotten and forgiven as she made her way to her brother's side. She just hoped he felt the same way and would accept her for herself.

The imposing structure of the hospital came into view as the pilot slowed their horizontal course. For a few seconds they hovered in the air, floating above the ground like a giant hummingbird. Below was a heliport. The chopper lowered as it geared into a landing position. From the landing pad it was a short walk to an entrance, and then an elevator.

By the time Mallory reached Brad's suite of rooms on the fifth floor, butterflies flitted wildly in her stomach. Actually, they felt more like dive bombers. She didn't like hospitals to begin with, and the sterile, antiseptic smells did little to calm her nerves. The halls were deceptively quiet. The clacking of her heels on the terrazzo floor sounded deafening as she walked toward the threshold of room 542.

Looking down at herself, she straightened her traveling suit of brown tweed slacks and matching blazer before turning the handle and sauntering in. It just wouldn't do for anyone to know how apprehensive she was, so she hid it behind a cool expression.

The door opened to a small sitting room. Mallory paused silently as Elissa relaxed on a corner couch and read a novel. Elissa often seemed to pay little attention to things around her, but it was a deceptive mannerism. Her air of quiet sophistication gave one the impression that she kept herself under cool control, which she definitely did at all times.

As her glance flickered up, she didn't act the least bit surprised to see Mallory. Pertly she marked her place in the book and set it down. Smiling warmly, she stood to offer a brief embrace. "Mallory, darling," she said in a husky, drawling tone. "How nice of you to come by and visit us." Always one to remember the amenities, she acted as if it was a social call.

"Hello, Elissa." Mallory returned the hug. "I've come to see how Brad's doing. Is he up to having company yet?"

"Yes, but a nurse is tending to him right now. We'll have to wait until she's finished." She motioned for Mallory to take a seat. "These last four years have certainly been good for you. I think you've actually blossomed out on your own. You look so . . . confident."

"Thank you. You look well yourself. Please tell me about the accident. How serious was it this time?" Mallory sat on the edge of her seat, no stranger to the fact that her brother had suffered many injuries in his line of work.

"Any trauma is serious, of course, but the doctors have assured me that it's not nearly as grave as first suspected." Taking out a handkerchief, Elissa daintily plied it between nervous fingers. "I was so shattered to hear the news that it nearly did me in. I still get weak in the knees when I think about it. Apparently it was some metal casing that collapsed on Brad. His right leg was broken, and some of the bruises are absolutely atrocious. There were no burns, surprisingly. The main concern of his doctors has been over the possibility of internal injuries."

"Did he have to undergo any surgery?"

"Thank heavens, no. But he is under observation and will be for a few more days. After that time he'll be released and can convalesce at home. I intend to spoil him with coddling every single minute!" Elissa was in her glory when she could talk about her favorite subject, Brad.

Mallory didn't intend for any chagrin to show, but Elissa's patronizing attitude toward Brad made it surface. "We may not have been on the best of terms these past few years, but I thought someone would have the courtesy to call me about the accident. I happened to be watching television and learned it from a news broadcast. My brother could've died, and I wouldn't have known until it was too late."

Elissa angled her sable head and said softly, "What with your wheeling and dealing, no one ever knows exactly where you'll be at a given time, do they? Not even you. Perhaps if you'd kept in touch, you would've learned about it sooner."

"I have an answering service." Mallory had carefully cultivated a speech that was clipped and concise, a style ingrained while attending European schools and hobnobbing with other girls from upper-class families. But when angered, she often forgot herself and spoke with a colloquial Southern drawl. She resented Elissa's lame excuse, and her next words were spoken in the deceptively soft rhythms of her childhood. "That road runs two ways, so I could've easily been found."

"Well—" Elissa expected a stalemate, but not this early in the conversation. "Regardless of the breakdown in communication, I don't think it's wise to carry this petty gripe into Brad's sickroom. He isn't to have any upsets."

That was Elissa, nice and tidy, slightly disapproving of anything Mallory said or did, but too gracious to come right out and say it. It would do no good to argue, so Mallory didn't. Instead she said in a droll tone, "I wouldn't be so calloused as that. The important thing is that I'm here now and I'll do what I can to help."

She had grown up enough not to let Elissa's little digs

bother her anymore. At least, that's what she had kept telling herself during the plane ride to Baton Rouge.

With the preliminaries aside, they sat and contemplated each other, realizing that time had done little to change what was between them. Breaking the strained silence, Elissa picked up the threads of her earlier appraisal. "I like the way your hair is styled. It looks chic, like a mane curling to your shoulders. Does it require much upkeep?"

"Very little, actually. I'm on the go most of the time, and I needed something easy and light. That's why I keep it like this." Mallory shook her head and distractedly ran her fingers through the silky white-blond tresses. Her hair contrasted strikingly with the tweed outfit.

Elissa smoothed her carefully styled hair. "I've often thought of trying a new do, anything for a change. But you know how partial Brad is to chignons. I've worn it this way for so long that nothing else would be comfortable."

Mallory sat back and crossed her legs. "Whatever suits you. I've always liked it that way too." That was the end of the subject. She wondered how long they would have to keep up the pretense before the nurse finished with Brad.

A moment passed before Elissa said, "Brad keeps a picture of you on his desk at the office. It was snapped quite a while back. Although I think it's becoming, I'd say your new look suits you better. I rather imagined you'd wind up modeling, what with your perfect bone structure and that hourglass figure. I'd be willing to bet that the men are literally beating down your door in Houston."

Putting an elbow on her knee and cupping a hand against the flawless texture of her cheek, Mallory disregarded the ill-disguised prying. She was more intrigued with the comment about Brad. "You mean my brother actually left my picture in plain sight? That's a surprise. After our last falling out I would've thought he had everything belonging to me carried away and burned."

Elissa smiled. "He was very angry and roared a great deal, but New Orleans is still standing. Don't be too hard on him. Everything he's ever done was for your own good, even when it hurt him to do it." Impulsively Elissa reached out and patted her hand in a motherly gesture. "What does it really matter now? It should stay in the past for all of us."

Mallory gave her a level stare and decided to accept the words at face value. "I'm willing to let the past go if you are."

Elissa sat back and clasped her finely manicured hands. Outwardly she appeared calm, but Mallory plainly saw the spark of pleading in her eyes. "Brad has needed you for some time, but couldn't bring himself to be the first to call. When he was injured, he thought about contacting you personally. He forbade anyone else to make the call."

"Why?" Mallory sat up straight.

"Because your brother is a very proud, stubborn man." Elissa shrugged. "Most people won't readily cross him."

"How well I know." Mallory sighed.

Elissa continued in a confidential tone. "You may have been apart all this time, but Brad has followed your career through articles in the papers and talks with mutual friends who work along with your brokerage. Deep down I know he's very proud of you. I think this visit will do more good than any medicine. I'm sorry about my earlier behavior. Thank you for coming."

Feeling both foolish for the show of aggravation and touched by the admission, Mallory nodded. "It's all right. I wouldn't be here if I didn't want to be."

When the nurse finished and gave permission for visitors, Mallory went in alone. Her stride was light and easy, a statement of a graceful, matured confidence. There was no way to tell exactly how Brad would react to seeing her again, and she was determined not to allow any feelings of uncertainty to show.

She looked regal as she stood in the doorway, with her head held high as she studied Brad. At one time she might have shied from such an encounter, but now she faced him squarely.

His leg was in a cast suspended from a traction bar, and there were a few bruises on his shirtless torso. Aside from that he appeared to be the picture of tanned good health.

He pushed a stray wisp of chestnut hair from his forehead. A flicker of surprise crossed his green eyes—eyes dark and unfathomable like his sister's. For seconds their emerald gazes locked; there was no way to read the expression in either stare as the years melted away. The sickroom could easily become an arena with just one word. Mallory held her breath and waited.

Slowly her brother's face split into a slight uncertain smile as he welcomed her. That in itself was a generous gesture for the formidable Brad Steiner. "I told Elissa to give you time and you'd find your way here."

She took a tentative step forward and chided back, "It took you this long to think up a reason to get me here. I don't think it was a very smart one, though." It was a relief to see that his condition wasn't too serious after all.

"See what a guy has to put himself through to get your attention?" He joked amiably, successfully hiding the fact that he was as uncertain about the meeting as she.

"Next time just pick up the phone." She tilted her head and laughed deeply. "It would probably be less painful."

"I wouldn't know about that." His gaze turned opaque as a long silence suspended heavily between them. He had made a wrong move and tried to cover his embarrassment. "So, did anyone call you?"

"No. I came on my own."

Another silence.

"How've you been doing, Mal?" He leaned back on a pillow and stared her up and down. "Fancy clothes, a new hairdo. Looks like you've been eating pretty good."

"Thanks for nothing! I've dieted down to a size six, and that's the biggest compliment I get from a brute like you. I guess that's more than I can actually say in return. Those bruises look like hell." She wondered how long he would continue the banter before the real issues came to light. "I heard the well blew and you were the lucky one standing in the line of fire, right?"

He sighed, suddenly serious. "Better me than someone else. I thought a grappling hook was secure as it lowered the control head, but it wasn't. The head was sitting on the stunned well and the fire was out, ready to be capped. Before I had a chance to tighten the bolts, the whole business toppled over and I was pinned down. I was lucky that my people were close enough to pull me out before the flames shot up again."

She wasn't familiar with the terminology but pretended to understand.

"Well, you can't say you haven't had your share of ups and downs in this business," she remarked quietly.

"That's why I've made it a policy never to allow women anywhere around the fires. It's best if none of you know what's going on."

This wasn't the way she wanted to see the reunion handled. She said, "It's really immaterial now, isn't it? I mean, the damage has been done."

"In this case it was worth it. First time I've ever had to fight a fire on my own leases." He chuckled.

Her expression was thoughtful. "You mean you own property around Denham Springs?"

"All through the Tuscaloosa Trend, especially along the eastern end. Back in the seventies when they suspected hidden oil, I was lucky enough to help them bring in a well. I bought up as much of the land as I could and turned around and sold it for development of housing tracts. My company retained all options on the mineral rights. The rest is history."

"Then I'd say you made a very shrewd investment."

"I can't say this is all mine Mallory. Some of it was yours too." He looked toward the window. "Thirty percent of those producing wells are pumping for us, including the new one that blew in the Judson field."

"I guess now I know why you went out to this particular field. You really had a vested interest."

"Yeah, some consolation." He tapped his cast. After a minute went by, he embraced another subject. "I hear you're really setting world records with your oil business in Houston."

She laughed. "I wouldn't say that. It's a good living, and I've enjoyed it tremendously."

He studied her through pensive eyes. "You've got that satisfied look about you, so I'm inclined to believe what you say. I guess we all have to go after what we think is right."

"That we do."

"I've had a great deal of time to think during these last few days, Mal." He sighed deeply. "You know, I'm almost forty-four years old and can't afford too many more accidents."

She couldn't believe what she was hearing. "You mean you're finally admitting that it's just too dangerous?"

"Maybe just this once, and only to you, yes. But I don't ask any more of others than I do of myself. That includes family." For an instant his eyes hardened. She knew he was referring to the past. They softened again. "Are you in Baton Rouge on business?"

"No."

"Would I be assuming too much to ask if you've decided to finally come home?"

"Maybe." Her gaze was mysterious as she did little to expound upon her answer. "Then again, maybe not."

The moment had come, and they contemplated each other again. Mallory knew Brad was doing his best to give what he could, and there would be no more. The rest was up to her. When she could stand it no longer, she reached out at the same time he did.

His voice was soft as he beckoned, "Welcome home, Mallory. I've missed the hell out of you."

"I've missed you too!" she answered, and hugged him tightly. "Oh Brad, why does it seem like we've spent our lives patching up one misunderstanding after another?"

"Shhhh. I was wrong in trying to force your hand and make you come back," he admitted weakly.

"No, you made me stand on my own two feet and see what it's like to face the world with just my wits. I've grown up. I'm a better person for it," she insisted.

"Let's not bring up the past. Let it lay and we'll start fresh from today, eh? You're my baby sister and I love you. Neither of us should waste our time going back."

Mallory was more than willing to agree, not relishing the thought of dredging up fragments of their last and most serious disagreement. Regardless of the reasons for Brad's display of tender feelings, Mallory was thankful that her return was accepted so unconditionally on his part. Perhaps they could put the dissention to rest and finally get on with the business of once again becoming a family.

The visit was brief. Although Mallory wanted to stay longer, she knew that Brad had to have his rest. With a promise to return the following day, she left him.

As she stood at one end of the hospital corridor and thought about finding a hotel room, she froze on the spot with cold dread when a familiar figure stepped out of the elevator at the opposite end.

It felt like someone had poured a bucket of ice water on Mallory. She watched Quinn Chennault, the other half of Wild Wells Limited, saunter toward Brad's suite.

Darkly handsome and wearing his virility in the form of a powerful aura, he went through the fluid motions of walking like a dancer. There was only the barest hint of a proud arrogance in his carriage; his measured stride was almost sexual, daring. There was something feral in the way the action was executed. Although Quinn had always had an effect on Mallory, her senses hadn't felt it so acutely before.

In his late thirties and with an insatiable lust for adventure, Quinn Chennault and everything about him bespoke a careless affluence. He was dressed entirely in black. His silk shirt was tailored to accent the line of his wide shoulders, tapering to a lean waist and narrow hips. Handmade boots of soft kid leather hugged his thick calves. Mallory stood there mesmerized, unable to turn away as he came closer and closer.

Quinn was intense and masterful, as quietly commanding as Brad was aggressive, and the two represented an odd complement. Quinn was more than a match for anyone who tried to defy his iron will; he was the one man who had dared stand up to Brad Steiner and win. And he was the only person Mallory's brother entrusted his life to. This made Quinn Chennault one of a kind, and made the team of Steiner and Chennault a legend.

Temporarily thrown off balance by the ill-timed encounter, Mallory was forced to battle a fresh, uninvited onslaught of memories as she watched his intentional, unhurried approach. She hadn't counted on having to see Quinn so soon, and it was understandably upsetting.

Compared with the conflicting feelings that Quinn

suddenly evoked, the anxious anticipation about the reunion with Brad now seemed like little more than a mild case of the jitters. Mallory held the nervousness tightly in check as she faced him with an expression of cool, seeming indifference.

But although they were better left buried, old remembrances were too vivid to combat as they painfully reminded her that Quinn had played the most crucial part in her decision to leave four years ago.

Chapter Two

She had first met Quinn fifteen years before. Shortly after selling a family business in Shreveport and relocating to the oil fields near New Orleans, Brad had brought home a new friend one evening. He introduced Quinn Chennault as "the Cajun." Mallory was very young, barely in her teens. Even then Quinn's striking looks had made her stand and stare, painfully shy and speechless.

Tall and deeply tanned, his body was muscular and trim beneath a form-hugging tee shirt and jeans. His hair, a blue-black curly mass streaked with silver highlights from hours spent beneath the hot Louisiana sun, was the perfect frame for his handsome, rugged face. But what drew her attention most was the beautiful color of his eyes, an indigo that lightened and darkened with the intensity of feeling he chose to show. When he smiled they were almost blue; they turned dark when he looked at Brad with the respect that was to form the basis of their friendship.

The primary attraction for Mallory was his cocky, youthful assurance, coupled with a certain air of gracefulness. When it came to knowing his job, Quinn was seasoned; he had been around, and maintained a reputation as one of the toughest roughnecks to work the Gulf shores. He knew the ropes and was a respected man around the docks.

Given time, Mallory's brother intended to take Quinn under his wing and hone down the rough edges, making a polished gentleman out of the delta wildcatter. With such an obvious contrast between the two men, she thought it rather ironic that Brad should disregard his own preachings about mingling only with the upper crust.

That night Mallory was all ears as she listened to Quinn's story. In a soft-spoken way he related that he hailed from the Louisiana town of Morgan City. Its only great claim to fame was a fortress, Fort Brashear, that had housed Union soldiers during the Civil War. Until the 1930s the city had carried the fort's name.

Quinn grew up hunting and trapping with his father along the bayous of the Atchafalaya Basin; the only other kin was a brother still in school. But as much as he loved the irresponsible freedom of running the bayous in pirogues, Quinn realized early that he nurtured a spark of ambition and wanted to get ahead. For starters, that meant lying about his age and working the oil fields with roustabouts.

Watching him speak, Mallory thought that in spite of the stigma that most roughnecking carried, Quinn was of a definitely different sort. Self-taught, he was highly educated, his sense of practicality was finely developed, and his aspirations were loftier than most. Class showed in every facet of his character. He spoke eloquently, like a Southern gentleman, with only the faintest French accent beneath a Louisiana drawl. But beneath the polish, he still exuded an undercurrent of danger. He was always referred to as "the Cajun."

Cajuns were a unique, congenial minority, and he was proud to be one. Thanks to Brad, the Steiner influence soon gave him carte blanche entry into many worlds. But the handle would serve as a reminder of who and what he would always be.

Unlike other rig workers who risked their lives and then squandered fabulous earnings from offshore drilling, Quinn had a dream to someday build an empire, to be somebody, to be different. Together he and Brad spent a few years roughnecking on offshore derricks before making the decision to go into business together and forming Wild Wells Limited.

Fire-fighting work was more treacherous than anything they had ever done before, but with it came the power to command any salary they named. It was an exclusive, one-of-a-kind livelihood that gained worldwide attention. Following an inborn sense for adventure, a man could become rich very quickly. But he could forfeit his life just as quickly if those he trusted were careless.

Quinn and Brad formed a pact on the day the contract was drawn up, swearing an oath to always protect the other's life when it came to capping oil fires together. The promise had endured for over fifteen years.

From the time of that very first meeting, Mallory had thought Quinn to be extraordinarily attractive, more compelling than any man she had met before. There was a side of him that could be lethal, ruthless if a situation called for it. Those tiny glints of relentlessness only served to heighten the powerful appeal he held for any female who chanced a look into those arresting eyes.

As Mallory stood in the hallway by Brad's room, she had no way of explaining why the reaction to Quinn's good looks should still be so extreme, as it was that very first time. After what happened between them four years ago, she had every right to hate him.

Quinn's sexual impact was more potent than she recalled, and time hadn't erased that masculine glow of dauntless sophistication. There was only the slightest evidence of an old challenge in his gaze, a type of icy anger that had always seemed inexplicably inviting and forbidding at the same time.

Mallory sensed that a volcano was slowly bubbling beneath Quinn's indifferent surface. She felt her own spirit begin to slowly simmer in reaction to it. When he walked up to her and they stood face to face, Mallory's stare was at first uncertain and then blatantly defiant as she raised her chin and concentrated her emerald gaze directly at him. She looked sultry, provocative.

His indigo eyes came alive with a light she had never seen before. Was it expectancy? Or perhaps a well-disguised impudence? She couldn't tell, and was in no frame of mind to start analyzing.

His only greeting was a slight nod and a soft familiar accent as he said, "Mallory."

In a formal tone she answered, "Hello, Quinn."

The moment was tentative and strained. Mallory adjusted her purse and got ready to leave without further word. As far as she was concerned, there was nothing to say. But Quinn wouldn't allow a departure just yet. She tried to brush by, but his hand gently grasped the roundness of her shoulder. His touch was like a flash of static electricity as it made contact. Her first impulse was to pull away, but instead she stood perfectly still. She stared at him.

He said, "There's a solarium on the tenth floor. I have something important that we must discuss privately."

There was no trace of emotion in his expression, and Mallory felt a worrisome shiver inside. Was there something about Brad that no one had told her? She acquiesced with a nod and followed him to the elevator.

With no further conversation, they entered and Quinn keyed in the floor number. Staring at her reflection in the stainless-steel doors of the elevator, Mallory's thoughts flew back four years to a time when her world had consisted of little more than partying and defying all rules . . .

It was only a few months after graduation from college when Mallory returned to New Orleans. Against her better judgment, she gave in to Brad's wishes that she reside in the elegant, roomy town house he and Elissa called home. They were supposed to be one big, happy family, all together under one roof and obeying the word of the master, Brad.

Only it didn't work out as everyone expected. After attending school in Europe, Mallory was accustomed to coming and going as she pleased. With an infinite source of wealth to rely on, she had indulged in expensive cars, the finest clothes, everything her heart desired.

Still, it never seemed to be enough. There was always something just beyond arm's reach, an intangible prize around an emotional bend ahead that promised to satisfy. If only she could discover what it was and how to get to it.

At the time of her return, Quinn's younger brother, Cam Chennault, also lived in New Orleans. He held a key position on the fire-fighting team at Wild Wells Limited.

Cam and Quinn didn't look alike, but Cam was handsome in a boyish, almost mischievous way. The brothers also had totally different temperaments. Quinn was quiet, controlled; Cam was a hellraiser who loved to kick up his heels and have a good time, any time. He enthusiastically lived the carefree life of a typical Cajun, watching today skip by like one big celebration and letting tomorrow take care of itself. Cam was wild and sported his recklessness with laughing abandon. He excited the daredevil in Mallory, and they began dating steadily.

Brad didn't like the match, however casual, and let his feelings show. His thunderous objections only served to heighten Mallory's obstinacy. She knew she'd get away with doing as she pleased because Cam was indispensable when it came to Wild Wells Limited. But the situation started to get serious when Mallory and Cam became involved in a torrid affair and fancied themselves madly in love.

Wearing her rebellion like a sleek designer outfit, Mallory strolled into Brad's office one morning, intent on making an announcement.

Brad was on the phone, but cut the call short when he saw her. He placed the receiver on the cradle and reached for a cigar before leaning back and lighting it.

"Elissa and I waited up until almost three this morning. When did you get home?" He didn't say it in a kindly way.

Sulkily Mallory answered, "I'm twenty-four years old, Brad, and I can tell time. When are you going to stop trying to control my life as if I were a teenager?"

"When you start acting like a sensible adult!" he snapped.

"Then let me grow up!" she threw back.

"I'm trying."

"You want me to be responsible. That means living by your rules, right?"

"Right!" He puffed vehemently on the cigar.

"It's a little late, Brad. I've been on my own for quite a while now, and I don't like orders." She put a finger-tip to her lips and pretended to ponder the situation. "Maybe I have the answer to all your problems."

When she began to grin mysteriously, he squinted at her questioningly. "You didn't come here this morning to nitpick about my rules. What's on your mind?"

She saw her opening and answered silkily, "I just wanted to let you in on the latest news. Cam Chennault and I are planning to be married."

Brad's face turned crimson as he snapped stiffly to

attention and ground out the cigar. "Like hell you will!"

"Like hell I *will!*" she shouted back. "I want him and I intend to have him!"

"This sounds like the time you wanted a collie puppy and I bought it for you. Men aren't pets, to be bought and sold," Brad said evenly. "Listen, Mal, a union with Cam Chennault would be ridiculous for reasons too numerous to name. My main concern has always been that you'll make the mistake of marrying beneath you. We can't have that. Remember, we have an inherited responsibility to uphold our good family name."

"Then why haven't you had your own children to see that it's done exactly the way you expect, instead of putting it all on me?" she demanded.

He paled for a second. "Elissa and I haven't been able so far to start a family. You know that. And it's not the issue between us now. As a husband Cam just isn't suitable."

"You and your damn blue-blood talk! You think that having millions in the bank and rubbing elbows with snobs makes us better than everyone else." Mallory hissed as she stood to go. "What about feelings? Don't they count for anything?"

Brad sat back and studied her. She was beautiful, feisty, and unusually self-possessed for one so young. Still, he felt that he knew what was best for his sister. "I don't doubt that your feelings for Cam are probably very strong. But let's examine exactly what kind of feelings they are. Cam is in the money now, making hundreds of thousands of dollars as my foreman. It could be quite a stake, don't you think, for the future? What does Cam have to show for it, Mallory? I'll tell you. Good times, women, and fast cars. He has absolutely *nothing* to show for it. His behavior indicates that he doesn't care about his own family heritage, so he would be bringing very little into a marriage with you."

"As far as I'm concerned, he doesn't have to meet

any specific thoroughbred standards. He's everything I want and I'm everything he wants. That's enough for me."

Brad shook his head and said in a tone of finality, "I disagree. It will never work between you."

Still smoldering, Mallory shot back, "We can make it work! I have a life of my own to live and I'm free to make my own choices. That includes whether or not I'll stay in a gilded cage, or exercise the prerogative of consorting with a man you consider to be a low life. I choose Cam Chennault for my husband and he chooses me for his wife. It's time to let go, Brad. All you're supposed to do is wish us well and then step aside."

"And let you make the most serious mistake of your life? Never! You're nothing but a spoiled, overgrown child! You aren't ready for marriage or commitments, and Cam is even less prepared. I just won't hear of any marriage between the two of you. That's my final word."

Gracefully Mallory walked toward the door. She opened it, halted, and turned to face her brother again. "I'm going to marry Cam. Nothing you say or do will make me change my mind. I don't give a damn whether I have your blessing or not!" She walked out and slammed the door with a resounding thud.

By hook or crook, this was one argument Mallory intended to win. Every time she and Brad encountered each other, the roaring and screaming began again. Brad threatened to cut her off without a cent. The Steiner household became a battleground as the two willful siblings refused to give any quarter.

In desperation, Mallory decided to turn to Quinn for support. Through the entire ordeal he hadn't voiced an opinion one way or the other. Cool and quiet, he had merely stood outside the fringes and watched the fireworks. That was his way.

If she could convince Quinn of her feelings for Cam, perhaps he would be the one to intercede and talk some sense into Brad. After all, he had more influence over her brother than anyone. Quinn was her last, desperate hope. She couldn't and wouldn't back down from the impasse with Brad. Her pride was at stake.

One evening Mallory had time on her hands. Cam had called that afternoon, saying he had some supplies to mark and would be tied up until the early morning hours. She slipped into a stunning outfit of white silk slacks and a matching blouse. It was in her mind to try to find Quinn if she could.

She was lucky. After driving past several of his hangouts, she spotted his car parked near a popular supper club. She went inside to find him.

He was dining alone, a rarity as he normally indulged in the company of beautiful women. She took a deep breath and approached his table. He stood when he saw her coming.

"I'm sorry to interrupt your dinner, but can we talk?" She took the seat he offered.

"We both know damn well that you don't care whether you interrupt me or not." He smiled amusedly and looked her up and down in a slow, insolent way. It was obvious that he approved. "Would you like something to drink?"

"No thanks, I . . ." She looked around and realized there wasn't much privacy. "I wonder if you'd mind coming for a drive with me. That is, unless you have other plans."

Quinn shook his head and finished the last bite of food. "As a matter of fact, I was wondering what to do with the evening. A drive with you sure beats the hell out of turning in early."

Immediately she knew his mood was amiable. This was the perfect time to convince him to help her. They were friends, and tonight she intended to count heavily upon that friendship. She and Quinn had always played it straight with each other, even though she could never totally figure out what thoughts passed behind those penetrating indigo eyes. He, on the other hand, could read her like an open book.

Behind the wheel of her expensive sports car, Mallory threw all caution to the winds and roared through the New Orleans traffic. She wasn't wearing a scarf and her blond hair tumbled and danced wildly in the night wind.

She found a spot overlooking Lake Pontchartrain. After turning off the ignition, she looked expectantly at Quinn.

Fully aware of her intentions, he began the conversation. "I'd have to be a fool not to guess why you want to talk to me, Mallory."

"I think it's time. After all, Cam is your brother, and what goes on is all in the family."

"Yes, and I know him better than anyone, even you. Just because I haven't added a voice to this fracas doesn't mean I don't have some thoughts about your future, both positive and negative. They're mostly negative, I'm afraid."

"Brad is wrong to keep trying to dominate my life. He's also wrong in passing judgment over other people, especially Cam," Mallory said passionately. "Why won't he leave me alone?"

Quinn stared out at the lake, his profile straight and proud. "Maybe it's because you won't leave him alone. You seem to be playing this situation for all it's worth, and that's a very destructive thing to do. It's like you're calling his dare. Don't you realize that?"

"I'm fighting for my life!" she blazed. "I have a right to half of everything Brad owns. I also have the right to do as I please. He just won't let me have one without the other. It all has to be his way."

"Uh-huh." Quinn took out a cigarette. Striking a match, he cupped a hand and lit it. The glow of the fire reflected on his chiseled features. "And what goes on between you and Brad should stay there. What I say or do has no bearing on any of it."

She sat back and played with the steering wheel. "No, you're wrong. He's attacking your brother and you're letting him do it."

"I've known Brad for a long time. He doesn't mean anything personal against Cam or my family," came the reply. "He's just looking out for his interests, that's all. I'd do the same thing if I thought mine were threatened."

"I could agree with you if they were strictly his interests. But he's imposing his sense of values on me. It's getting a bit stale."

"What exactly is it that you want of me?"

"I think it's time that Brad Steiner is made to realize that his reasons for holding me back went out with chastity belts and dinosaurs. He's trying his best to hang on to what's left of a lopsided notion that we're royalty. The world is made up of many kinds of people, and I'm not going to wait around for some relic that he sanctions as a suitable partner. You have some clout where Brad is concerned. You're a man, you talk his language, and you're his best friend. You can reason and he'll listen to you, Quinn. I desperately need your help and support right now."

"You're asking a great deal. And you're putting me in a damn precarious position, little girl. I don't think I like it." He took another puff.

"Take another good look at me, Quinn, as you did in the restaurant. I'm not a little girl, I'm a woman," she said stiffly.

"Sorry. I've known you since you were a kid, so I guess it just keeps sticking in my mind that you're still so very young." His tone was soft, but his eyes darkened as they roamed over her body. "There's so much ahead of you . . ."

"I'm old enough to know what I'm doing. Why won't anyone believe me?" she said softly.

"I do believe you, Mallory. I do. And I also believe that you care about Cam, in your own way. Before I commit myself to your cause, I intend to put in my two cents' worth. Are you ready to hear it?"

She smiled. "I've sat still for everybody else. Why not you?"

Quinn turned slightly in the seat and stretched out his long legs to make himself more comfortable. "Just like Brad and you, I've watched over Cam since he was a kid. While growing up he trapped around the Atchafalaya, but I saw to it that he was given the advantage of having more than I did. I sent him to the finest schools, gave him the finest clothes. I even found the best jobs when he showed an interest in my line of work. I set him up in the oil fields so he could learn roughnecking before joining Wild Wells. And he did learn. Only it wasn't the right things."

"I don't understand. He's a valued employee, isn't he?"

"Of course. He's one hell of a fine worker, and he knows it. Somewhere along the line, though, he failed to pick up the basics of all this, the underlying reasons for living in the first place. Bear in mind, honey, that Cam Chennault is the type of man who doesn't like big doses of responsibility. He's almost twenty-six years old. It's time he worked at building some security in his life."

"But that's just it," Mallory interjected. "I can be his security."

"You're offering him a free ride, huh? Do you think for one minute that Brad would stand still and let Cam have what he's worked for all these years? He'd be a fool. Cam is a typical roughneck, living for today and getting his kicks hanging out in barrooms. He'd waste a fortune in no time. Your respect for him would dwindle quickly, believe me."

"You're coming down awfully hard on him, aren't you?"

"No, I'm not coming down hard enough. I made my mistake in indulging him, just as Brad indulged you.

You've at least benefited from your education and plan to do something with your life. Cam is a big disappointment to me because no matter how hard I've tried, I can't impress the importance of using his smarts and putting some money in the bank." There was a note of bitterness in his voice. "Most of the time he acts little better than the rigrats who trash up the coastal towns and live strictly for the drunken moment after quitting time. Don't you see that?"

"No, I don't. I see the promise of a man who can work his way to the top just as my brother did." She had to defend him. No one else cared enough to.

"Cam doesn't have the ambition, the drive to push that hard. All he has is good looks, an athletic body, and a line that would make the Queen drop her drawers. He'll always be content to work for someone else and then forget the hours of life-risking toil it took to earn those dollars. Cam isn't ready to settle down and work seriously at a marriage."

It was painful to hear this coming from Quinn, but Mallory pretended otherwise. "It's just your opinion, like everyone else's."

"I wish I were wrong, Mallory. More than anything I want to see you happy, content with your life. Tell me, what is it you really know about my brother? What do you see in him?"

She stared out at the black water of Lake Pontchartrain. A fat white moon reflected in the choppy waves as the wind gently whipped against the surface. "I see . . . a man who makes me feel like a woman. I know he's not going to set the world on fire with his ambition, but it's unfair to judge him by the standards that you and Brad have set for yourselves. Not all men can be supermen, you know. Cam is generous, almost to a fault. He calls every man friend, and he desires me above all other women."

Quinn shook his head and muttered under his breath, "Sex." In a louder voice he said, "What happens when the passions cool, Mallory? I have to agree with Brad about what little Cam has to offer in the way of supporting a wife. After you were born, you were carried home wearing purple, and you've worn it ever since. No man, especially my brother, will be able to keep you in the style to which you're accustomed."

"That remains to be seen," she said adamantly.

"Mallory, why don't you give it some more time? Cam isn't going anywhere and neither are you. Why the big rush to the altar?"

"Because I want him now."

"You're hot for him now is what you mean." His voice became gruff. "Try thinking with your brain, Mallory."

Her eyes glittered dangerously as anger sparked in them. Quinn's words had stung. They had also made her uneasy, but she refused to admit it, "I rather expected more from you than that."

"I've given it to you straight, baby." He took out another cigarette and lit it. "I have never talked to a more obstinate, hardheaded . . ."

"Now you sound like Brad," she said flatly. "We're all just going around in circles."

"Yep," he drawled. "But I have about a half penny's worth more to add and then I'll forever hold my peace. I'm standing on the outside and looking in at this little charade. Frankly, I think it's a big waste of time for all of us. You don't want anyone's opinion unless it agrees with what you've convinced yourself the truth should be. All you want is a pat on the back and the go-ahead to keep doing as you damn well please."

"Isn't that what growing up is all about? Adults are supposed to have the privilege of choice."

He turned the words back on her. "With you it never has been a problem of being denied any choices. You're enough of a spoiled brat to bulldoze your way to whatever it is you want. I have to give you credit for persistence, but that kind of behavior has nothing to do with being an adult."

"This is different!" she insisted.

"Is it? You're using Cam. He's just a small fish in a big ocean. When you get tired of him, you'll throw him back."

"I would never hurt him like that," she said resolutely.

"Maybe not deliberately, but I know you well enough to spot all the signs," he said. "You see a chance to openly defy Brad, and you intend to have your way no matter what the cost. You're also bent on disregarding the logic everyone puts before you, going so far as to cut off your own pretty little nose. You came to me and I've given you the truth about yourself as I see it. Now you'll ignore my words as well as Brad's. What's the game this time, Mallory?"

"There is no game. I'm deadly serious about everything I feel for Cam," she said stiffly. "I'm sorry to learn that you have such a low opinion of my character."

Quinn flicked the cigarette away. "Mallory, I've known you were a brat since the first time I met you. It hasn't put me off before, and it doesn't put me off now. In fact, sometimes I admire your spunk when you apply it wisely. That's why you and I get along so well, sweetheart. I just think it's a bit ironic that you've come to me to whine. It doesn't suit you."

"Well, regardless, I see that I have one more enemy to contend with. If you don't want to wish me well, then I'll turn my back on you too."

"It won't be necessary to switch to dramatics, Mallory. I said I was going to put my two cents' worth in, and I did. But it doesn't necessarily make me any more right or you any less wrong about the situation with you and Cam and Brad."

"It sounded more like a quarter's worth to me." The

conversation hadn't gone the way she would've liked, and she was sorry now for asking Quinn to help her.

"Maybe so." He chuckled. "Maybe so. I told Brad that I'd speak my piece, and I have. But don't you be so quick to forget that I said I also have a couple of good feelings about this. In spite of the fact that you're spoiled and impossible sometimes, I meant it when I said that your happiness is the most important thing to me. If marrying Cam will make that happiness brighter, then I have no choice except to give my heartiest congratulations and wish you every good thing."

She gazed at him in the moonlight. A moment ago he was giving her a thorough tongue-lashing. Now he was wishing her well. The soft glow of moonbeams haloed against the shiny blackness of his hair as his expression mirrored sincerity.

"You're congratulating me, but do you really mean it?" Her voice was small and uncertain.

"As much as a man like me can mean it, yes. Cam asked me to be best man at the wedding. Tomorrow I'll tell him to order my tuxedo."

"Even though you won't talk to Brad for me, you will show him that you're going along with it? You won't back out?"

"Cross my heart. I just don't ever want to see you hurt," he whispered.

"Oh, Quinn!" She leaned over and hugged him, resting her head against his chest. She was filled with a secure feeling as his arms held her. "It's been an uphill battle for Cam and me since the beginning. You're the only person who's at least tried to understand."

Biting his lip, he placed a warm hand against the bareness of her neck and fondled the soft silkiness of her long hair. "I'm trying my best, *mon cher.*"

She looked up at him, her skin shining like porcelain and her smile grateful. She was agonizingly beautiful as she said, "Thank you. And I forgive you for calling me a brat."

He cupped her cheeks and placed a fatherly kiss on her forehead. "Now if you'll let me take over the wheel, I have a surprise for you."

"What kind of surprise?" She sat up, suddenly eager.

"Call it a wedding present."

He opened the car door, unfolded his six-foot height, and stood upright. Mallory slid across to the passenger side as he eased in the driver's seat.

During the trip back to New Orleans, Mallory chattered gaily, talking about everything and nothing. It no longer mattered about Brad's disapproval. As long as she had Quinn's sanction, however reluctant, she felt strangely jubilant.

Impulsively, she moved closer to Quinn and looped her arm through his, feeling warm and enjoying the strength of his solid frame against her shoulder. She depended entirely on the fact that Quinn's acceptance would take care of everything.

"Please tell me where we're going," she begged.

"No way. You'll have to wait."

As they turned down a familiar boulevard, she smiled. "Aha! We're going to your house. The wedding present must really be something special."

"It is." He kept his eyes on the road as his hands tightly gripped the steering wheel.

After they pulled into the driveway, Quinn got out and offered a hand to Mallory. She continued to hold it after exiting the car.

The house Quinn owned was very old, a Tudor-style brick mansion in the garden district of New Orleans. Cam shared it with him. They went inside, with Mallory intrigued by his mysterious demeanor. Quinn turned to her. "Remember, *mon cher,* your happiness means everything to me."

They walked through the darkened rooms to the back of the house. Once there, Quinn flicked on a bedroom light. Mallory's sense of anticipation was suddenly turned to horror.

Cam was in bed with another woman. The entrance had caught the couple at a most inopportune time. Instantly Cam flipped over, cursing and covering himself with a sheet, while his partner dove beneath a blanket.

Quinn stood in the doorway, pale and cold as a statue, biting his lip in embarrassment and staring at Mallory.

Shocked and humiliated, Mallory was beyond response as she stared first at Cam and then Quinn. She had secretly suspected that Cam was a rounder. But she didn't want to believe that he'd have so little respect for her or himself. She had thought there was no reason to doubt when he told her he'd be working late.

"H-How could you?" she whispered to both of them. "Do I mean so very little?" Then she turned on her heel and bolted out the door.

Cam sprang from the bed and said savagely to his brother, "You bastard! I'll take care of you later!"

"I'll be waiting," Quinn answered with a deadly calm.

Mallory could hear Cam chasing her as she ran through the house, calling out her name and begging her to stop and listen. The front door wouldn't open to her rough jerking. Before she could get out, Cam came up behind her and roughly leaned a hand against it. "Honey, what you saw was . . ."

"I know what I saw!" she said icily. "Get out of my way!"

"But she doesn't mean anything to me. I'm in love with you!" Cam pleaded unconvincingly as he held the bed sheet around him. "Baby, you know how it is with men like me . . ."

Mallory looked at him. Her gaze was furious and dead-level. "Take your hand off the door."

He immediately did as she ordered. She opened it, and moonlight flowed into the spacious room. There was nothing more to say. Her eyes said it all, looking like shards of emerald ice as they filled with a sudden hatred for the man she had professed to want forever not more than an hour ago.

Cam knew better than to stop her as she ran from the house and jumped into her car. Flooring the accelerator, she drove wildly into the delta night. The headlights from nighttime traffic became a blur as she tearfully drove with angry abandon; her only thought was to get as far from Cam as she could. In fact, she wanted to put an entire continent between herself and every man she had ever known.

She drove up to Brad's town house and slammed on the brakes. Not bothering to kill the engine, she put the gearshift in park. She intended to stay only long enough to pack.

Elissa and Brad had gone out with friends, so the house was mercifully quiet. Mallory hurried up the stairs to her bedroom. Savagely she crammed her suitcases full. Without a note or a backward glance she headed for the lights of Houston.

She had no plans, no course of action. All Mallory knew was that she had to escape the crushing hurt of betrayal. It seemed that everyone she loved was intent on seeing her suffer. The only way to avoid heartache was to go away and assume a separate identity. Brad could have it all and do everything his way. She no longer needed to be a part of any family.

Chapter Three

As the whir of the elevator filled the air, Mallory continued to stare at her reflection. Four years was time enough to come to grips with the old disappointments and find a way to make her life content. Until now she thought she had. But after seeing Quinn again, she wasn't so certain anymore.

She wouldn't look at him, intent on first gathering the strange feelings he sparked and putting them in perspective before the upcoming conversation. This was no time to think of herself or dwell on the past. Quinn probably had something to relate about Brad's condition. She worried that it was bad news.

As the double doors opened, they stepped out. Across a hallway was a huge solarium. Quinn held the door as Mallory walked ahead. Airy and spacious, the solarium was quite a contrast to the fluorescent terrazzo decor of the hospital. Glassed on all sides and the roof, it afforded an expansive view of the capital city. Brick planters were placed at random, serving as dividers for gaily striped patio tables and matching metal chairs. Plants grew everywhere, some of them gigantic in the pseudo-greenhouse atmosphere, others trailing gracefully as they hung suspended from metal beams.

In a corner was a soft-drink machine. As Quinn offered a chair, he asked, "How about a cold drink?"

"I could use one, thank you." Mallory sat down as he strode to the machine and dropped in some coins.

Mallory's eyes followed his every move, drinking in the unexplainable charisma of his strong masculine appeal. The effect was unsettling, but she did her best to ignore it. Instead she sat back and tried to take an objective pleasure in watching him.

As he reached for the cold drinks, she studied his hands. His fingers were long, slender, not at all the type of hands one would think an oil fighter should have. The veins snaked through the muscles of his forearms, affirming the possession of great physical strength. One needed it for his type of vigorous work.

"I'm glad you decided to come to Baton Rouge, Mallory." He handed her a drink, and took a long swill of his. "We didn't have a chance to talk after the night you left for Houston."

She sipped daintily. "I doubt there would've been anything more to say." There was no bitterness in her tone, but her eyes were bright with wariness.

"Oh, but there was. Plenty. There are some things I've since realized, in retrospect, that I should've explained about people like Cam and me. For what it's worth, hindsight seems to be a hell of a lot more valuable than foresight. Trouble is, it comes too late."

Mallory could have stopped him, but decided instead to let him talk. She intended to openly pardon Quinn, in her own way and time. But it wouldn't hurt to put him on the spot and make him squirm a little first. It would give her a chance to see just how much the mistakes of the past really mattered to him.

"Until the time you left, your life was fairly sheltered

when it came to understanding our work and the way most fire fighters live. I'm sorry I showed you such a blatant truth in such a vulgar way, but at the time I didn't know what else to do to make you realize the mistake you were walking into with Cam. Oil fighters live fast and we live hard. We aren't guaranteed anything, especially tomorrows. Each fire brings its own set of circumstances, its own set of problems, and because we never know what's in store for us, we take whatever we can when we can."

A slight tilt of her head and the rise of a finely arched brow were followed with, "So you decided to play God for me and Cam? You had no right to pull such a dirty trick on me, Quinn."

"No, I didn't. But you have to put yourself in my place for just a minute in order to see why I did. My brother is a shining example of many men's attitude, including mine at one time. I hope I've managed to outgrow that wildness as I've gotten older, because I've decided to tempt the fates and live through all of it. I want a future, roots. Cam still hasn't come to this realization for himself."

"As I've gotten older, I've changed too," she said dryly. "I wasn't blind to the situation. The wildness was what I liked most about Cam, and we all knew it. Why couldn't you have explained it like this before?"

"I tried in every way I could think of, but you weren't listening to what I had to say. You don't know how many times I've regretted taking you back to my house. I wasn't even sure Cam would be there, but I had a sneaking suspicion. That afternoon when he called and lied to you about having to work late, I was standing nearby and knew otherwise. I didn't say anything to him; I just kept my mouth shut. It really wasn't any of my business. But then you sought me out because you needed my help." Quinn paused. "Until the very second we walked into my house, I didn't know exactly what I was going to do."

"Did Brad know anything about it?"

"Nope. He still doesn't. I was aware of his feelings from the beginning, though. Every day he came into the office and raised cain about one thing or another where you were concerned. He cared, and that's the point with me, Mallory. Do you recall the very last words I said to you?"

"Yes. You told me to always remember that my happiness means everything to you." She eyed him coolly. "It was the sorriest excuse for caring that I've ever seen. Why bother telling me this now?"

"Because I feel a need to explain why I did what I did."

"It's a little late to start rationalizing motives."

"Not if a person is sincere about being sorry," he said patiently.

"Your sincerity has a habit of ebbing away right before you knock someone flat on their face." Her eyes were narrowed, hard.

"I did what I had to do, Mallory. You left me no choice. I don't blame you if you hate me for everything that happened. It was a rotten setup."

She took a long drink, set the can down, and looked back at Quinn. "What do you think?"

"I think this bears further illustration if I'm to make any headway with this conversation. If memory serves, you've gone through quite a few phases since I've known you." Quinn finished his drink.

Mallory gave him a sloe-eyed look. "I suppose I have."

He stroked his chin thoughtfully and said, "Do you remember the night of your eighteenth-birthday party?"

Her lips puckered into an embarrassed smile as she flushed. "Yes."

She looked into the indigo depths of his amused eyes

and it suddenly came back to her with a surprising clarity . . .

On the night Mallory turned eighteen, Brad gave permission for her graduating class to throw a party on his yacht. It was moored in a marina on the shores of Lake Pontchartrain, and the kids were given carte blanche permission to enjoy it for the evening. Champagne and food flowed freely, a live band entertained, and multicolored lights lent atmosphere to the noisy celebration.

Brad surprised Mallory with a new Ferrari sports car, fire engine red, sleek and shiny. Half of the credit, and the price tag, were Quinn's contribution.

Thrilled, Mallory hugged her brother repeatedly. The only dampening moment came when she realized that Quinn wasn't there and hadn't extended excuses. He was the one person she had wanted most to see, hoping to display her newfound independence and gain his approval.

While the party was in full swing, Mallory went belowdecks to change. If Quinn wouldn't come to the celebration, she'd take it to him instead.

On the way out she finished a glass of champagne and grabbed a full bottle to take along. This was going to be her night, the time when she'd show Quinn she had become a woman. And nothing was going to spoil it.

She drove across town to Quinn's house. A single light burned in the living room window. After going up the porch steps, she rang the doorbell repeatedly. He wouldn't dare *not* be home.

A minute later Quinn opened the door, and the light spilled out on Mallory. She wore a gray trench coat and held up the bottle of champagne. "Happy birthday to me!"

Quinn raised a brow. "I didn't forget what night this was."

"Then why aren't you at the marina?" she threw back sassily.

"It's been a very long day and I just wasn't up to a party, that's all," he said quietly.

"Maybe this'll help." She continued to hold up the bottle and pushed her way inside. "Got any glasses?"

"Yes, but from the way you're glowing, I'd say you've had your quota of bubbly for one night, young lady." He took the bottle from her and placed it unopened on a coffee table.

"Spoilsport," Mallory returned.

When he turned back to her, he said, "And to what do I owe the honor of this visit? Shouldn't you be hostessing a party on the yacht tonight?"

"Oh, that." She waved a hand in front of her as if bored with the whole thing. "There's so much going on that they won't even miss me. No one even saw me leave."

"How'd you like your birthday present?" His eyes twinkled.

"It's beautiful and I love it, Quinn. I was so surprised." She moved closer to him as if she wanted an embrace.

"You really should be with your friends, Mallory." He smiled slightly, but took a step back.

"But what about my birthday kiss? I get one every year, you know." She was suddenly shy.

As he bent down to kiss her forehead, she stood on tiptoe and kissed him on the lips instead, slipping her arms around his neck and clinging to him.

Quinn grasped her shoulders firmly and pushed her out at arm's length. "Now I know you've had too much to drink."

She giggled deeply, swinging her head to the side and letting her hair fly freely. "I've only had two and I'm perfectly sober." His stare was cool as she stepped back and added, "Now it's my turn to give you a present."

"It's not my birthday." It was no longer a game, and his tone was serious.

Before he could say any more, she opened the trench coat to reveal an outfit of flimsy baby-doll pajamas that did little to hide what was beneath.

Although Quinn's expression never changed, he looked her up and down very slowly, his eyes stopping briefly on the supple swell of her breasts and pink nipples as they strained against the material. The outfit left nothing to the imagination, and every pretty curve was in evidence.

He shook his head and sighed. "It's not the right time, Mallory, and I'm not the right guy. Close the coat."

She ignored him and worked the covering from her shoulders in a deft motion. It fell to the floor behind her in a heap. "I say you are. Don't you like what I'm offering?"

Very patiently he explained, "It's not a question of whether I do or don't like anything."

"Don't you think I'm pretty?" Her eyes were luminous with a mounting excitement. She intended to have Quinn, someway, somehow.

"I think you're very beautiful, but pretty is as pretty does."

"Then why don't you want me?" She blinked innocently.

"Because you're nothing but an eighteen-year-old child," came the gruff reply. "I'm not in the habit of sleeping with immature young girls."

"I'm of legal age now. I can drink, I can vote, I can gamble. I can do what I want. It's all legal."

"No matter how old you get, there are going to be some things that will stay illegal where you and I are concerned. This is one of them."

Her bottom lip puckered prettily as she took a step closer and played with the buttonhole on his shirt. The move was purposeful and calculated. "Oh, Quinn. I'm old enough to know what I want."

He rolled his eyes heavenward. "But you're not old enough to know what you need. Would you really like to see how this is affecting me?"

She adopted a provocative expression, closed her eyes, and waited for the expected kiss. Instead, he reached down and snatched her coat off the floor. Then he grabbed her roughly by the upper arms and forced her back into it. He buttoned the top under her chin. The gesture was anything but tender.

Livid, she faced him. Tears sprang to her eyes. She rubbed her arms where his fingers had dug in painfully. She felt the tears slide down her cheeks. "Why did you do that?" she spat at him.

"To teach you that it's bad manners to play with a man. And because you asked for it. Now get out of here," he ordered.

She stood there and gritted her teeth, unwilling to obey. Quinn turned her around to face the door. In a deceptively soft voice he said, "I'm going to forget this ever happened. I suggest you do the same. Get in your car and go back to your party. And start acting your age, Mallory."

Deeply embarrassed, she marched out of the room and did as he said.

For months afterward she stayed angry at Quinn, avoiding him at all costs. But then somewhere along the way her thinking cleared when she realized that the anger was one-sided. Quinn didn't share in it. He had simply treated the episode as a lesson she had to learn about men and her power over them.

And it was a valuable lesson she would never forget. Quinn had certainly been the wrong man. And her timing, as usual, was lousy. He wasn't the kind of man a woman could approach and seduce. He liked to do the chasing. Mallory had tried to exercise her womanly wiles, but they just didn't work on Quinn. She vowed never again to attempt anything so stupid as a seduction, especially since he was obviously unaffected by her.

Without a word, the matter was laid to rest between them. A better, more solid relationship formed as time progressed, and Mallory learned that Quinn could be a true friend, one of the few men she felt could be trusted. That is, until the episode with Cam . . .

As she drew her emerald stare from Quinn's handsome face, she was able to look back on the time with a certain amount of objectivity. "Yes, I certainly do remember my eighteenth birthday. I thought I knew it all."

"Four years ago you thought you knew it all too. You were still immature and defiant when we talked that night at the lake. You had a vendetta to settle against Brad. All you did was raise the stakes by holding the threat of an unwanted marriage over his head."

"Which still didn't give you the power of assuming the part of judge and jury with regard to my future. You turned me down once, remember? It looked as if you didn't want me to have Cam either." Her tone remained level.

"Dammit, Mallory!" His patience started wearing thin. She wouldn't give him an inch. "That wasn't it. I really cared about what happened to you. I was doing it for your own good, as well as my brother's."

Mallory sighed. "Spare me the clichés, please? I've heard that particular one too many times. You made your point four years ago, and it's over and done with. So what now?"

He sat back and drummed his fingers on the table, taking a moment to weigh his words. "So now that time has passed and we both claim to have changed, I think we should see just how much of a change has been rendered."

"Why?"

"Because now that you're back, it'll be you and me and Brad again. It always has been the three of us. If you can find it in your heart to forgive your brother, why can't you let bygones be bygones where we're concerned?"

She considered his statement. "Why is it really so important to you, Quinn? Do you think I've come back to cause trouble?"

"That never entered my mind. It's important because I hurt you deeply and it's been an open sore ever since it happened."

"Oh, so now you're admitting that you actually have a conscience?" she said sarcastically. "Tell me, has it kept you awake nights?"

"Don't look at me through such caustic eyes, Mallory. I'm not an ogre and I'm not one to beg. I'm just a man who made a very serious mistake and wants to rectify it if he can."

"And if he can't?" she urged softly.

"Then he'll know he at least tried. That's all any man can do, isn't it?" He opened his hands in supplication and shrugged.

She studied him gravely for a few moments. Then her face softened. "It's about time you started admitting that you don't know everything there is to know, Quinn Chennault! I think you've been hanging around Brad Steiner for too long." A slight twitch of her mouth hinted that she knew she had gotten the better of him. Quinn Chennault had apologized.

He grinned slowly and nodded in genuine appreciation. "Excellent! You've gotten very good, Mallory, very, very good. The shoe is on the other foot and I deserve it. You made damn sure that this wasn't easy for me."

She lowered her guard. "This meeting was your idea, not mine. I'm ready to lay my cards on the table. What do you really want from me?"

"Just forgiveness."

Graciously she acquiesced and gave up the game. "I think I forgave you a long time ago, but refused to let go of the resentment until just now. I know how much it took to admit your mistake, Quinn."

"Do you?"

"Yes, because now it's my turn. My wishes of getting even with Brad, a foolish pride that nearly pushed me into a marriage I really didn't want . . . those things were childish and so dangerous. It was a no-win situation all the way around. Neither you nor I was all right or all wrong, just misguided. We followed feelings that were already pushed to the limit because of the contention with my brother."

"You've been mercilessly toying with me. I'm supposed to believe that you finally mean what you're saying?" he asked.

"Do you think for one minute if I hadn't recognized the truth for what it was, I'd be sitting here across from you now? You *better* believe it!" Her stare was guileless. There was no doubt that she meant every word.

He regarded her in a relaxed, measured way that was both familiar and unnerving at the same time. "Then you do understand?"

"Definitely."

"And you don't hate me?"

"No, I don't hate you. I've long since seen the kind of collision course I was on. I was too self-involved. I wanted to spite Brad and I just didn't care who I hurt doing it, including myself. It would never have worked with Cam, never."

Quinn wondered if she truly meant all that she said. Her words and expression gave credence to a new, mature Mallory, but the habits of a lifetime couldn't easily be broken, not even in four years. He once knew her better than she knew herself. But did he know her now?

She sensed his dubiousness and added, "It took

making it on my own to realize that it was wrong to play games with people's feelings. Believe me when I say I've grown up since then."

"In what ways?" he challenged.

Mallory's stare was opaque. "I don't feel it's necessary to prove myself to people any more. I know who I am."

"I guess I'll just have to give it time and take your word for it, won't I?" Her response satisfied him and he relaxed further. "How'd you find Houston?"

She shook her head. "Very lonely, very big. For a while I thought I'd starve. Brad cut off all my accounts and credit, and I wound up having little more than a nickel to my name. One day when I was at my wit's end, I seriously contemplated crawling back to New Orleans and begging to Brad. Something made me angry enough to sit up and take stock of my life. You talked about overindulging Cam and Brad overindulging me. That was the problem in a nutshell. I didn't know what it was to feel anything except what Mallory wanted to feel about Mallory. For so long I had lived my life strictly for myself, expecting to always have my way. When I didn't get it I stamped my feet, screamed loud, and did everything that poor little rich girls are supposed to do." She took another sip of her drink and gave him time to digest the words.

"That cleansing, desperate anger was what I needed to clear my head. If Brad could make a go of his life, then why couldn't I? After all, my name is Steiner too. That's when I found a phone book and started looking up the names of oil companies. I went to a pay phone and called every one in Houston, cajoling, badgering, pleading my way into their offices for an appointment. When I got my foot in the door, I talked them into letting me represent them without a contract until I could come through with a deal to prove myself. Once I showed them what I could do, my title became formal as an independent representative. It took a little while but I threw myself into working fourteen and sixteen hours a day. I made a go of it."

"Hmmm. That's impressive, but not a total wonder to me," was his only remark.

"The old Mallory couldn't have done it. As paradoxical as this sounds, I owe it all to you for being candid enough to show me the truth."

"But look at the cost," he said sadly. "I forfeited your trust in the bargain."

"And now you want it back again?"

"Yes."

She sighed. "Maybe we can work on a new relationship, but I wouldn't expect miracles right away if I were you. I have confidence in very few women and no men at all." Could she bring herself to ever trust Quinn again? Right now the answer was a dubious maybe. "As far as I'm concerned, all that happened between you and me and Cam is old news, history. Let's not let it cloud today, okay?"

A flicker of fascination turned his eyes a dark crystal. "I'm inclined to believe that you mean it. Am I to be given another chance?"

"A reprieve . . . I think we both could use it, Quinn," she said slowly. "When I first encountered you in the hallway, I had mixed feelings about seeing you again so soon. Now that we've cleared the air, I do feel better."

"Then we'll wipe the slate clean and start from square one again." A slight smile played along the sensuous line of his mouth. "I'd like to make it up to you somehow."

"I told you there's nothing to make up for."

"I'll be the judge of that," he answered solemnly. "I expected a cold turndown, a vicious viper attack, maybe. But your graciousness has baffled me in more ways than one. I want us to be friends again."

"We'll see . . ." Mallory answered with a smile. "You know, I thought we were coming up here to discuss Brad, and I was very worried. Will you tell me everything about the accident?"

Crushing the empty cold-drink can, Quinn got up to find a wastebasket. It was clearly a subject he didn't want to pursue at that time.

Mallory wasn't easily deterred and followed him. "I was right. There is something you aren't telling me."

He looked down at her. "No, *mon cher,* there isn't." The old endearing term was warming to hear after so long. A slight tingle inside made her aware of it. "I just don't like to think of how close Brad came to cashing it in. We've had problems during this last fire, bad problems."

"Then talk to me. I want to know."

He read the concern on her face. "We were called out to the Judson Field because a static leak formed somewhere in the well housing and blew the entire lid off the operation. We surveyed the damage. Brad was quick to say he didn't think it would be as complicated as we had first decided. I argued with him and wanted more of the scaffolding and twisted metal cleared off, but he didn't want to waste the time. He was in a big hurry to quell the blaze and get on with other things, so we did it his way. The fire was smothered and the control head was lowered for bolting into position when the accident happened."

"Exactly what is a control head?" she interrupted.

"It's a huge gauge that cuts off the pressure belowground with the turn of a wheel. When we cap fires, we have them built to our specifications, depending on the size of the casing where the fire shoots from. Our control heads have a special lip that fits over the casing and we bolt it down good and strong. You won't hear of a well blowing with one of our heads on it."

"I see." She cupped a palm beneath her chin, her face all interest. "Go on with the story, please."

"Well, we lowered the lip and lined it up over the casing, but it just didn't catch right away. As we tried to tighten it, pieces of nearby junk shifted on a dozer and knocked the head off balance. Brad was pushed off his feet and the control head fell on his leg. Lucky for him I had just grabbed a huge crescent wrench. I jammed it beneath the head as it fell. Otherwise his leg would've been crushed. I used the wrench as a lever to hold the weight while Cam pulled him out. We were clear for about three seconds when the well ignited even worse than the first time."

Mallory finished the story for him. "That Steiner pride made my brother careless. It was his well that blew, and he was probably intolerant of what he considered to be incompetence on the part of the drillers."

Quinn nodded gravely. "You've got it. He never was a patient man. The site is torn up pretty bad and it's a wayward blaze now."

"You don't have much hope of stopping it, do you?"

"I have to. Working one man short isn't going to make it any easier, but I have to do it."

"Are you sure you're telling me everything? You and Brad aren't at odds because of what happened?"

"I've told you the whole story and, no, we worked it out between us on the way to the hospital. He just wasn't objective about this one job. I doubt any of us will make that mistake again."

"From the looks of it, you can't afford to," she said ruefully.

"I didn't bring you up here to talk about the fire," Quinn reiterated. "But I'm glad we did. And you're certain that things are ironed out between the two of us?"

"We're on our way, aren't we?" Mallory's laugh was musical, soft. "Consider yourself practically forgiven."

"You'll forgive, but I highly doubt that either of us will forget, will we?"

"Forgetfulness is a bit much to ask of me so soon. Let's just bury the hatchet and give the rest time."

She offered a slender hand and he took it. Instead of a handshake, he pulled her close and wrapped her in a gentle hug. She returned the affectionate gesture, inhaling the delicious fragrance of his after-shave and feeling very strange being so close to him.

He looked down at her and said softly, "Welcome home, Mallory. I'll take my hello kiss now."

She tilted her face upward and waited for a brotherly kiss on the forehead. It came as a shock when Quinn lifted her chin with a finger and pressed his lips tenderly against hers.

It wasn't a passionate kiss, but it lasted a half second longer than was necessary. Mallory's head swam, and it took great willpower to keep from swaying against the solid length of Quinn as her balance threatened to leave her.

Confusion permeated the corners of her mind as the kiss stroked an erotic chord that had lain silent inside until now. The response was purely physical, a reaction to his unwitting attempt to sweep her off her feet. The only time she had experienced such feelings was on the night of her eighteenth birthday. Quinn was the man in her arms then, too, however briefly.

Mallory had thought herself too experienced to be drawn in by the superficial temptations of pure sensuality. Now she wasn't so confident. She fought an urge to kiss Quinn again and find out. As a protection against her own conflicting feelings, she chalked up the heady sensations to fatigue from the trip. She wouldn't allow room for any other explanation.

Casually Quinn broke the kiss, but he didn't let her go. He acted impassive, his demeanor as nonchalant as ever. "Are you going back down to see Brad?"

"No, I have to find a hotel room. Tell him I'll be back early tomorrow morning." She said the words in a breathless voice. Her heart raced and she trembled inside, still feeling his masculine warmth through her clothing. He kept a possessive arm around her waist as they walked together to the door. "I . . . think I'll take the stairs down this time. I need some exercise after the long plane ride."

Mallory was distracted, aloof, a total opposite of what she was mere moments ago when she played cat-and-mouse with Quinn. She knew without a doubt that it would be impossible to step into the closet atmosphere of the elevator and not expose her newly surfaced emotions. Quinn would immediately sense something, and she didn't want him to misread her behavior. She needed time to put old feelings back where they belonged. "I'll see you tomorrow."

"I'll give Brad your message," he said as he watched her walk away through intrigued, calculating eyes. Quinn hadn't missed a thing, not even a heartbeat, and absently pondered the true reasons for Mallory's hasty departure. Slowly he ran the tip of his tongue across his lips and tasted the lingering sweetness of her mouth.

Quinn entered Brad's hospital room and was greeted with a big smile of welcome. "It's about time you got here. Did you happen to see Mal on her way out?"

"As a matter of fact, I did," Quinn answered guardedly.

"That kid sister of mine really looks great." Pride tinged his words.

"She sure does."

"I figured she'd be coming back sooner or later," he boasted mildly. "After all, I want her here where she belongs."

Quinn's eyes narrowed slightly. "Mallory didn't come back because you want it. She's done a great deal of growing up and came because she wanted to."

Brad shrugged, his mood too elated to let Quinn's words affect him.

Quinn ambled up to the bed and rested an arm alongside the traction bar. "How's it going with you today? Been pinching any more nurses?"

Brad chuckled. "Not with Elissa watching. She gets jealous, you know. I'm doing as well as can be expected for being in prison, I guess." He pointed toward the window. "I don't have to ask what kind of luck you've been having at the Judson Field."

Quinn's answer was a pained expression. "The contractor is boosting up the water supply for the next try. The new control head I designed should be delivered sometime tomorrow, so we'll go after the fire on Monday."

"Sounds good." Brad put an arm behind his head and said thoughtfully, "You really did notice a marked difference in Mallory? I mean, aside from her appearance?"

"I told you I did. She's not the person she was before. At least, she claims not to be." Quinn pulled up a chair.

"No one knows how much it means to have her home again, pal. You really think she's on the level about staying this time?" Brad's expression was curious; he needed reassuring.

"Maybe. After I met her outside your door, we went up to the solarium to straighten a few things out. I talked, she listened. She did a turnaround on me, though, and I have to say I'm impressed with the new woman I met."

"I'm glad to hear it. You always did have a way with her. It'll make her much easier to handle." Brad missed the quick arch of Quinn's brow. No one handled Mallory Steiner, least of all Brad. "I hope you reminded her of what a wonderful person her brother is," he continued to joke.

"You do that enough for everybody," Quinn gave it back. "But I think I should tell you what we discussed. It's important."

There was no smile behind the words as Brad became serious. "Go on."

"I never made mention of it before, but on the night

Mallory left for Houston I was the last person she spoke with."

Brad tried to straighten in bed, but the clumsy cast kept him pinned down. "What are you trying to say?"

"On that last day you and she had scrapped badly about Cam, remember? You were also angry with me because I hadn't said anything to further your cause. Well, old buddy, the Cajun took the bull by the horns . . ."

"This is a hell of a fine time to tell me! Exactly what went on between you and my sister?" Brad interrupted excitedly, chagrin starting to color his features.

"Calm down a little bit, man. This won't do either of us a bit of good. It happened four years ago, not yesterday."

"I suppose you're right," Brad growled, trying to curb a volatile temper. "So tell me and get it over with."

"I didn't say one thing that you hadn't said first, Brad. What I did was show her the truth. It wasn't difficult, because Cam had a couple of women on the string along with Mallory. She saw it in the flesh at my house."

Brad contemplated the statement. "No wonder she blazed off like something wild. How come you didn't tell me before now?"

"Because it was none of your damn business. It was between Mallory and me. It still is." Quinn's expression was staunch and Brad knew better than to cross-examine him.

"There's nothing like zeroing in on the heart of the matter, is there?" was Brad's only comment.

"I shoot straight from the hip with everybody, but I was a little bit too close to the target when I pulled the trigger that time."

"Ah, hell"—Brad sighed, quick to forgive his best friend—"what difference does it make now? The end justified the means, and we kept her from making a mistake. You presented the facts to her in the best way there was. I'm not blaming you for that."

"Neither does Mallory. We straightened it out, but I still feel as though I owe her. She knows how sorry I am. Given time, I hope we'll be friends again, good friends."

For a fleeting second he recalled how breathtakingly beautiful she was as he approached her in the hallway. The effect on his senses was nothing short of delectable, and he wanted to explore the reasons why.

"Then I've got your means for making peace. And you'll be doing me a big favor at the same time." Brad's smile was filled with irony.

"That favor being . . . ?"

"If you say my sister finally has it all together, great. But I think she'll need a little help, some understanding while she copes with coming back into the fold. How about keeping a close eye on her while I'm in the hospital? Keep her occupied? I'd appreciate it."

Quinn raised a brow and returned the ironic expression. That was exactly what he had planned to do. Brad's sanction gave him the checkered flag. "No sweat."

Chapter Four

It was evening before Mallory finished the weary task of settling in at a local motel near the hospital. All afternoon she was unable to shake the picture of Quinn from her mind. The most simple, routine things became complicated because of her preoccupation.

She had thought her exaggerated reactions to his kiss were ridiculous, but there was still no explanation as to why they cropped up in the first place. It was best to attribute the reasons to fatigue, and let the matter drop before it aggravated her any further. So why was this so difficult to do?

If Quinn was truly sorry for hurting her and honestly wanted to be friends again, that was fine. But if he hadn't approached her, she had already decided that it wouldn't have mattered one way or the other. She was in Baton Rouge only long enough to see that Brad wasn't seriously hurt.

That night at bedtime she was still keyed up from the

trip and sipped at a snifter of brandy to help her relax. After stretching out beneath the crispness of fresh sheets, she stared up at the silver-blue ceiling of the motel room and emptied her mind for sleep. It wasn't long in coming.

At first she slept deeply and dreamlessly, snug beneath the covers. But as the night wore on she began to toss and turn. Tensions and unresolved feelings from the day began to fuzzily invade that tranquil bliss. Images formed and focused, and she saw herself within a breezy filigree of an illusion.

In slow motion, Mallory was once again walking down the hallway of the hospital. But there was no feeling of hesitancy this time, or apprehension. She knew she would be greeted with genuine affection, and couldn't wait to get to her destination.

Going directly into Brad's sickroom, she stopped short from surprise at what awaited her. Her brother was nowhere to be found. Instead, Quinn was the patient lying in traction and wearing a cast. Naked from the waist up, he looked dark and virile, reclining comfortably against the fuzzy luster of white sheets. His chest was broad, muscular, and thickly matted with blue-black hair.

It was as if her arrival was expected. He gazed through heavy-lidded eyes that undressed her and stared into her very soul. With open arms he smiled and said in a husky, tempting tone, "So you do care, mon cher, *but you've kept me waiting much too long. Come to me. I want you."*

Mallory was a jumble of discordant emotions as her head began to swim again. She was relieved to see that Quinn's injuries were minimal. At the same time, she felt a sense of panic and tried to flee. She didn't want to go to Quinn. He wasn't what she had expected to find.

She tried to turn away, but was trapped against the shimmering blankness of a wall that no longer had a doorway. The wall surrounded her and Quinn in a luminescent circle of light, isolating them from everything except each other.

Quinn beckoned again, this time more forcefully as the dark indigo of his eyes wrapped her in an invisible, hypnotic web. The pull was strong, relentless. "Come to me." The words echoed relentlessly through the hollows of her unconscious mind. There was no recourse except to obey his command.

Mallory felt herself floating to the side of the bed. Quinn was too powerful to resist, and her curiosity was piqued. For a long moment she stood there and looked down at him, wondering what he intended to do with her.

Slowly his hands grasped her shoulders and gently drew her to him, nestling her in the warmth of his inescapable embrace. The contact was like a ripple, breaking a dam of constraint that had taken four years to painstakingly build.

Reluctance was quickly replaced with an overflowing longing to hold him and weld herself to the nakedness of his hard chest. She hungered for the feel of him, drawn in by his musky male scent and his superior will.

She ignored a voice inside, a warning that she shouldn't feel these things, that she shouldn't give in. This was all wrong, distorted, out of place with her new life. Weak with wanting, she meekly tried to tell Quinn no. He appeared not to listen.

"Can't you understand that this isn't what I've come for?" she said softly. "Why are you doing this to me?"

"Because we both know that you couldn't stay away from me forever. I want you as much as you want me."

His eyes burned into hers as he slowly found her lips and kissed her passionately. During the kiss she eased on top of him. She no longer wore the tweed traveling suit, but was dressed in flimsy baby-doll pajamas.

Was she eighteen again? No, she couldn't be. This was now and they were in a hospital in Baton Rouge.

But she was outfitted as on the night of her birthday party. The only difference was that the seduction was turned around; Quinn pursued her.

His mouth covered hers possessively, trying to drown out all thought, all efforts at refusal. She heard herself crying out inside against the tender but determined resurrection of the very hungers that Quinn had squelched years ago. It had been his will that they never have a chance to know true appeasement. Why couldn't he leave it at that?

How dare he now assume the right to tamper with emotions that she had thought were long dead, gone!

That was the way Mallory awoke, crying and trembling from the force of the gossamer dream. She sat up in the darkness with a start, panting raggedly and trying to ascertain the fact that it was, indeed, only a dream.

Pushing back stray strands of hair with a hand, she glanced at a traveling clock that ticked away on a bedside table. The illuminated dial said it was four-thirty in the morning. Too late to go back to sleep, but too early to rise.

Covered with a sheet, she drew her knees to her chin and wrapped her arms around them. She reached over to the nightstand for a cigarette. It was an occasional habit she hadn't been able to break. Every action, every sensation, every word from the fantasy was still vivid in her mind, as if it had actually happened only a few moments before. It made her tremble, but she didn't know why.

Very carefully she sorted out her thoughts. She had renounced all claims to family and heritage by abruptly leaving four years ago, and would have been happy to leave things as they were had it not been for the accident. Genuine concern was what had prompted her to ignore the lengthy silence and come back to Louisiana. The reason she had returned was that she feared Brad might die before she had a chance to tell him that she still cared.

So why had Quinn suddenly intruded into her subconscious in Brad's place? She knew sooner or later that their paths would have to cross. But maybe her reaction at seeing him went deeper than she first realized because it was so unexpected.

Yes, that had to be it. Emotionally she had been put through a wringer the day before. That, coupled with Quinn's pointed reminders about their past, could have easily infiltrated her mind and caused such an unlikely dream.

There was a thin barrier between love and hate, and for four years she had teetered on that line where Quinn's unscrupulous trick was concerned. Forgiveness and the attempt to reestablish some form of good will between them had simply become confused with the ridiculousness of an old one-sided temptation. Hence, the dream.

In a couple of days Brad would go home to New Orleans and she'd be on a jet headed back to her life in Houston. All concerns about Quinn Chennault should and would remain inconsequential. At least, those were her plans.

Satisfied that the dream was nothing more than an overblown reflection that had mysteriously threaded its way from an adolescent wellspring, she relaxed and waited for the sun to rise.

Although it was Sunday, the job of lining up crude oil couldn't wait another twenty-four hours. For once Mallory was glad to have something to keep her occupied after such a disturbing night. The advantage of an independent oil brokerage was that she could conduct business from anywhere in the world, at any time. All she needed was a briefcase and a telephone.

Her clients' work week began on Monday and concluded on Wednesday. Hence she would need a weekend contact if she was to succeed with a sale before time ran out. The last four days of the week would be spent watching international price indexes on petroleum stabilize, and overseeing deliveries before the following week's rates applied. Synchronicity was the key to staying on top of the oil game.

It was unusual to find oil men in their offices during the weekend, but Mallory had made prior arrangements with a Louisiana company. Her call was expected. As she held the receiver between her neck and shoulder and let the number ring, she thumbed through folders randomly laid out on the bed and picked up the one she needed.

When the client came on the line, she said, "Mr. Parker, this is Mallory Steiner calling from Baton Rouge. I'm sorry I couldn't get back to you right away, but there was an accident in my family. I had to take care of some personal matters."

The voice on the other end was amiable and deep. "I readily understand, Miss Steiner."

"As I told you the other day, my buyers in Houston are looking for 150,000 barrels of Louisiana Sweet and Colonial oil. I've been authorized to purchase them at the going rate. I would like to do business with your firm if you happen to have enough to fill my need."

They talked prices for a few moments. As a matter of course she explained the procedure for delivery, transactions, and pickup.

Having been allowed representation by the Houston base, Mallory had the power to guarantee the amount of money it would take. Working as their buyer, she made arrangements to meet Mr. Parker in Baytown, Texas after receiving written confirmation that he'd supply the type of oil specified. In return, he had confirmation of her bank draft and agreed to have the oil waiting for transfer at the Baytown docks.

In the middle of the conversation there was a knock at the door. Mallory excused herself and answered it. There stood Quinn, leaning lazily against the outside frame and smiling in an arrogantly charming way.

He had always had a habit of popping up at the most

unexpected moments, but there wasn't time to think about it as she invited him inside. Briefly she explained that a call was in progress, and gestured toward an easy chair. He took it, fluidly wasting no motion as he sat back and stretched out his tall frame.

Patiently he watched a very businesslike Mallory wheel and deal like a pro. Every inch of her bespoke confidence, and a definite respect began to grow as he looked beyond the transaction and at the woman. She was poised and commanding at the same time, a trait picked up from Brad, no doubt. Damn, but she was beautiful!

She wore a shorts outfit of soft blue. The contrast against her white-blond hair and pale complexion was very soft, feminine.

Instinctively aware of the scrutiny, Mallory automatically struck a very female pose by crossing her long legs and half-lying on a corner of the bed. The delicate rise of rounded hips and the firm flatness of her belly were emphasized by the snug fit of the shorts.

Quinn openly admired the picture. She leaned on an elbow and read aloud from a file. The most innocent gesture seemed provocative as she slowly pulled back a curtain of blond hair that cascaded to one side and partially hid her face. Quinn fought the urge to help her. Instead, he took out a cigarette and lit it, having to find something to do with his hands.

Mallory concluded the call and pretended to be so intent on making notes that she forgot about her guest. It was a ploy to buy time before starting a conversation with Quinn. The click of his lighter brought her to attention.

Still reclining, she smiled at him, never once letting on that she was nervous. "Thank you for waiting."

"It was my pleasure." She'd never know just how much he meant that. "Your business sounds pretty impressive."

"Right now I don't look at it that way." She sighed

tiredly and sat up. "Sometimes it gets a little harrowing trying to line up schedules and making certain that one set of consignments doesn't get mixed up with another. Add that to the fact that it's very hard trying to find the types of oil I need."

"Tell me exactly what you're looking for." He was genuinely interested.

"I've currently lined up a sizeable quota of Louisiana Sweet and Colonial, but tomorrow I'll have to find a million barrels of Pipeline or Grade Seventy-six or Seventy-seven for a California-based operation."

He whistled softly. "You like to play the big numbers, don't you? I didn't think there was that much spot oil around at one time."

"There is, but I have to track it down and beat my competitors to the punch. When there's a demand I intend to be the first to fill it. That's my business."

A hint of the old obstinate Mallory flickered in her eyes, and Quinn openly appreciated it for the first time. One needed the tenacity of a bulldog to climb in the ring and scrap against other buyers for a deal. In that respect, Mallory's upbringing and temperament had certainly prepared her for any battle that might arise.

Quinn flicked some ashes into a nearby ashtray. "This is nothing more than an off-the-cuff suggestion, but why don't you think about purchasing oil from the Middle East?"

She shook her head. "I tired long ago of chasing foreign crude. It's too hard to make the connection when the time comes to buy. I can't always depend on international trade. It's safer to bargain with American dealers I know."

"It seems that Evergreen contracts would make it doubly hard for you to work stateside."

Quinn's knowledge of dealing impressed her. In the business there was an unwritten law that refined oil was automatically spoken for a month in advance to a current consignee. It was known as an Evergreen contract, and was the guideline by which refineries based their output.

During the rare times that Evergreen oil wasn't claimed, brokers like Mallory were given the opportunity to fill a sudden demand that opened in other companies. Everyone profited, refineries were delighted with uninterrupted shipments, and business continued as usual. It was known in the trade as lagniappe.

"You really have your work cut out for you." He smiled obligingly, knowing she'd find oil where there was none. "I have some friends in the business. I'll see if I can get my hands on some Pipeline for you."

"Even the smallest tip will be appreciated," she said as she gathered files and replaced them in a briefcase. With business talk aside, the conversation turned personal. "To what do I owe the honor of this visit?"

He put out the cigarette and drawled slowly, "Well, Brad mentioned that you might need a little company while he's in the hospital. . . ."

"And maybe you should keep an eye on me while I'm here? You're troubleshooting for him?" She raised a brow and smiled, reading Brad's intentions very clearly. She couldn't resist the urge to playfully taunt Quinn. "What surprises me is that you're doing as he orders."

"You didn't let me finish. . . ."

She laughed and answered in a very slow drawl, "What Brad does or doesn't want has nothing to do with you and me, so let's get that straight right now. I don't listen to him any more than you do. Now, why are you really here?"

The statement let him know that she was in Baton Rouge more for herself than for Brad, and he appreciated her candor. He chuckled. "Okay, fair enough. You and I agreed that we should work on a new relationship. I thought today would be as good as any to give it a shot."

"Why now?"

"You fascinated me yesterday. I think I'd like to get to know the new Mallory Steiner."

Vague recollections of last night's dream filtered through her mind, making her stomach flip. Had it been more than just a fantasy? Maybe even a premonition? Throatily she answered, "Perhaps it would be better if the mystique remains as it is."

"Better for who, you or me?" He gave her an inviting look.

"Both of us." Her laugh was unhurried.

Quinn pressed on. "I'm game if you are."

Pushing aside nagging twinges of skepticism, she gave in. "Since there's no one else to spend today with, and I had planned to take it easy anyway . . ."

"It's nice to know I'll do in a pinch." He fiddled with the ashtray. "A beautiful woman should never be stuck in a motel room on Sunday."

"As long as you're sure that's all there is to this, and it is your idea," she chided further. "You're under no obligation to entertain me."

"If you doubt my sincerity in coming here for myself, then consider this my way of collecting in advance on helping you with your next oil deal."

"Okay, I'll take you at your word. Now that that's settled, what do you have in mind?"

"There are places to visit. A nice long drive will clear my head of the worries of fire-fighting. I really welcome your company. Why, I may even turn it into a personal tour of my homeland."

"You're making offers that I simply can't refuse," she said easily. "I've never seriously taken the time to visit the old South, so this is going to be a treat."

Since she had already seen Brad earlier that morning and didn't intend to visit the hospital again that day, there was no reason not to go sightseeing. It took only a minute to find a matching wraparound skirt to cover her shorts, and she was ready to go.

"Where to first?" She settled into Quinn's convertible. As long as the mood stayed light, she could handle a visit with him.

"Around," was all he'd say. There was no definite course. It would be a lazy, casual drive.

They sped through the Baton Rouge traffic and enjoyed the quietness of the city. It was easy to spot the imposing structure of the capitol building against the city skyline. As the tallest skyscraper, it looked like a gigantic gray rocket protruding heavenward above the other buildings.

Mallory tied a blue scarf around her head and laughed when the wind threatened to whip the long tendrils out of the chiffon prison. Her mood was gay, carefree.

"Do you remember the times Brad and I took you along when we drove to Baton Rouge?" Quinn asked thoughtfully.

She smiled at the memories. "How can I forget? Let's see . . . you used to put a quarter on the dash, betting everyone you'd be the first to see the outline of the capitol."

"And you always won," he reminded her. "It was a diversion to pass the time when we traveled."

She looked over at him. "I think you and Brad let me win, but it was fun anyway. The big treat for me was riding the elevator all those floors to the top of the capitol building. It was dizzying to stand at the top and look down for miles and miles. I can still remember the thrill."

He met her gaze and said in a deliberate voice, "There's no need to outgrow that sense of wonder. As we get older, we find there are other things equally exciting. Maybe more."

Sitting next to Quinn and considering the pointed innuendo, it was difficult not to believe that the attraction was mutual. She all but forgot how hard she had fought against him in the dream. "Yes, there are."

She wasn't dreaming now, and somehow it felt right

to indulge. From the corner of her eye she studied his svelte form. Quinn wore jeans and a simple plaid shirt that did nothing to take away from the devastating handsomeness that had rocked Mallory upon their previous meeting. His hair was brushed back in a casual style. The wind gently played with the soft raven locks, and the sun glinted against the rich color.

Mallory hoped that she wasn't the only one who had changed over four years. At one time Quinn was a typically strong, silent type who stayed mostly on the sidelines. Was he still basically that way today? Would there now be an openness to his character that hadn't been there before? Mallory knew Quinn as the type of man who had a reason for everything he did. He had told her that he wanted to be friends again. But was that all he was really after? She couldn't help but question the true basis for his interest.

Perhaps now Quinn would allow her a small glimpse of what was inside the man. He would have to trust first if he wanted to make the treaty work. She, in turn, would patiently sit back and get to know him all over again. Silence was one way of finding out the answers to questions that she had no intention of asking.

Mallory's eyes returned to the road and she thought of making the day a kind of contest. Situations involving opposition were her forte; now was no exception. She viewed Quinn as a challenge, and his invitation had afforded her the option to accept or decline a match. This could become more of an adventure than either of them had counted on.

They drove in a southwesterly direction, quitting the main highway and going along the small back roads that cut through the Atchafalaya Basin. Flood levees protected the outer perimeters of the natural bowl, separating it from the rest of the world.

For Mallory it was like traveling from modern times to primeval ones with the blink of an eye. Gray-black waters, brackish and mysterious, surrounded ghost forests of cypress. The angular stumps looked like charred volcanoes long dead, their massive trunks having once towered hundreds of feet before the loggers came. The newer trees were heavily bearded with masses of light gray Spanish moss. They added the only fullness to a barren area that was cut off from the main streams of the Atchafalaya.

As they drove farther in, the land became greener and swamp turned to healthy bayou. The nourishing water was unencumbered as it meandered southward, turning the landscape lush.

As if to complete the scene of wild delta beauty, a single oarsman in a pirogue glided along with the lazy summertime current. He stood in its center and formed a living mast as he gracefully maneuvered the small craft.

Mallory pointed his way. "You used one of those when you were a boy, didn't you?"

Quinn gave her an amused look. "I didn't think you listened when I told those old stories."

"Of course I did. Is there anything else I should know about your adventures in the bayous?" She was eager to hear.

"No, not much." He slowed the car and gave her a chance to watch the man. "The pirogue looks primitive compared to what I'm now accustomed to, but it's still the way to travel for many of the bayou people. It's not as easy as it looks to paddle a pirogue through a swamp laced with roots, but Cajuns think nothing of it. Some folks live so deep in the marsh that it's their only means of transportation."

"I wonder what that kind of life would've been like," she said wistfully, "for someone like me."

"Not the ideal you're probably entertaining in that pretty head," he answered truthfully. "In contrast to the raw beauty, it's a tough way to go, filled with endless work and sacrifice. It's the only way my people know, but it suits them."

"Are you saying I wouldn't have what it takes?"

"Maybe, maybe not. It depends on how you'd use it." He looked over at her. "A foreigner like you would last about ten minutes before giving up and going back to the city."

Mallory laughed. "You're probably right." In a more thoughtful tone she asked, "Have you ever missed it?"

He paused for a moment. "I suppose I have at one time or another. In its own way it was an idyllic life, the pace slow. There were no pressures except filling my belly and keeping the roof from leaking when it rained. What I do now isn't so different, except for a bit more excitement and the chance to travel farther. Basically they both involve living one day at a time. I'm cut out for either, taking what today has to offer and not worrying about tomorrow until it gets to my doorstep." As an afterthought Quinn added, "It's because of hardship that we Cajuns are intent on having a good time when it comes around. *Laissez les bons temps rouler.*"

"Let the good times roll." She translated the words readily, not having forgotten the creed of the Cajun.

They drove on. Deep within remote swamplands, tiny cabins dotted the countryside. The tranquility was slightly marred when silver drilling derricks wedged into the serene picture. Mounted on beds of clustered pilings, the mechanical trees clinked and pumped rhythmically as life continued undisturbed around them. This was home to the Lousiana French, and no amount of modern technology would completely take away the old rustic charm.

In time, they came upon a country church. Quinn stopped the car. A white wood facade contrasted with moss-blanketed oaks that shaded long tables laden with an abundance of food.

It was the celebration of a Cajun wedding. Laughter carried over the air as gaily dressed people clustered and partied merrily. Little ones skittered the perimeter of the crowd, playing games of tag around gigantic trees. It was a pleasant, old-fashioned picture.

Music for the festivities was provided by some of the elders who played French mouth harps and aged fiddles. The bride and groom began the first dance, beaming at each other as the guests clapped and sang along to the French tune. From time to time one of the young men in the crowd would boldly cut into the waltz, pinning dollar bills on the bride's veil for the privilege.

One of the guests noticed Mallory and Quinn watching from the car. Stocky and dark, he looked typically Cajun. Without a second's hesitation he walked toward them, smiling broadly and holding a can of beer in one hand. "Ya'll come dance the wedding dance with us, *mon cher!* Everyone's welcome today!" His voice boomed out loud and exuberant.

"This is what's meant when it's said that a Cajun never meets a stranger." Quinn turned to Mallory. "How about it?"

She nodded, and they followed the man back to the group.

Mallory was handed a cup of punch. One of the ladies made conversation in broken English. "They's a nice wedding, huh?"

"Very nice," she agreed amicably. "The lucky couple looks so happy."

She watched as Quinn approached the beaming bride and pinned a hundred-dollar bill on her veil. Everyone voiced hearty approval as he assumed the honor of a dance in return.

Gracefully he waltzed with her, the movements languid and practiced, his form tall and well muscled. For a brief second Mallory saw him through the pulsating gauziness of her dream, and felt drawn to his male beauty. Something inside made her envious of the dance. *She* wanted to be the one in his arms, smiling up at him and waltzing beneath the viridescent umbrella of live oaks. The jealousy died quickly, but a strange emptiness remained.

"I'm pretty good with a step, me," a friendly older man boasted mildly as he broke into her thoughts. "*Mais,* I never did dance before with such a pretty Northern lady. You want to spin a li'l bit, ma'am?"

Delighted with the compliment, Mallory smiled graciously and curtsied. "I'd like that very much, kind sir."

She walked across the carpet of thick grass and waltzed with her new partner. It had been a long time since she'd spent a Sunday afternoon such as this, and she was enjoying every bit of it.

Quite unexpectedly, Quinn changed partners and took Mallory in his arms. Her wish to waltz with him had come true. She gave him her most fetching smile as the light pressure of his hand spanned half of her waist.

"You know, this is the first time I can recall that we've danced together," Mallory said sweetly.

Sweeping her around and around in a loose embrace, Quinn gave her a knowing look. "Yes, there seem to be many things we've never done together. I'm beginning to wonder just how much I've missed."

Gratified beyond words, Mallory felt the wind lift her hair as she laughed gaily. After all this time Quinn was still a charmer. She laughed at herself for giving him the satisfaction of knowing it worked. The moment was perfect and she didn't want to see it end.

When the dance was over, Quinn led her to the sidelines. They clapped in rhythm as some of the elders demonstrated the folk dances of the Acadian coast.

"Are you having a good time?" Quinn took a sip of his beer.

"Wonderful." Mallory smiled at him, her eyes shining. "It's very special, isn't it?"

"It couldn't have turned out better if I had planned it. I'm glad you approve."

"If I didn't know better, I'd think that my approval is very important to you."

"It is. If you want to really know me, the best place to start is at my roots. What you see around you is what I am inside. If you accept them, you accept me."

Mallory looked up at him. "Then consider it so. I've never met a more hospitable group. They don't even know us, and yet here we are in their midst, drinking and acting as if we've been friends for years."

"That's our way." He shrugged before concentrating on his beer again.

One of the elders approached Quinn and vigorously voiced recognition of their unexpected guest. After much backslapping and laughing, Mallory was fascinated as the duo talked half in English and half in French about oil fires and the men who fought them. Their hands gesticulated wildly during the exchange, and she tried to follow every movement with her eyes. Listening intently, she was able to pick up the gist of the conversation and even laugh along with their homespun jokes.

Too soon it was time to say farewell and get on with the day's sojourn. As Quinn helped Mallory into the car, he said, "I appreciate your being a good sport and going along with our cutting up."

"I understood most of the conversation," she answered. "But why not all in English?"

"Sometimes it's easier to say a word in French than to translate. The language is very beautiful, but it loses something in the translation. It also hinders an exchange when we have to stop and hunt for the proper English expression."

"I wish I had paid enough attention to learn the language." There was true regret in her voice. "It's so romantic, so graceful."

"I can remember hearing you say a few French words," he teased.

"They were swear words I learned from you and

Brad." She flushed slightly. "Nothing that really counted."

"Then I'll have to see about educating you properly, won't I?" He stepped on the gas and they drove away.

In due time they crossed the east protection levee of the basin and arrived at a quaint French settlement called Pierre Part. It was time for lunch, and the area boasted the tastiest Cajun cuisine.

The restaurant Quinn chose had been erected on the shores of Lake Verret and extended partially over the placid water. Built of weathered cypress and roofed with slate, it looked like a part of the landscape. A huge porch surrounded the structure. Inside, large windows provided all the light that was needed.

After they settled in and ordered lunch, Mallory stared out of a picture window and absorbed the peaceful view. On one side of the lake a fisherman tried his best to procure lunch, while young water-skiers utilized the other side.

"You seem far away. Care to tell me what's going through your head?" Quinn's voice was soft.

"There's nothing like this in Houston. I was just thinking about how charming today has been," she said quietly. "Your origins are so simple, so peaceful. And yet you're like Brad, needing fire and excitement in order to be happy."

"For a little while, yes. But this will all be here waiting for the time when I come back."

She picked up a glass of wine and said, "Will you ever go back, Quinn?"

It was his turn to stare at the lake, his eyes shining silver as they reflected the shimmer off the water. "One day I'll decide to put it away and return here. As time passes, I seem to be getting a bit more superstitious about fighting fires. Especially on Sundays. You think it might have something to do with another place that has fire and brimstone?" They laughed together. "Seriously, no one can keep up the pace indefinitely. I've been around the world a few times, and I've just about seen everything there is to see. That takes care of the wanderlust in me. The only excitement now is the fire itself."

"What happens when that ceases?"

"It won't." His tone was final. "I'll just get tired and quit."

"Or maybe trade it for another kind of fulfillment?" she probed innocently.

His answer was a deep, unnerving stare. The unmistakable warmth of a telltale flush crept up Mallory's neck, along with a strong awareness that an invisible net of sensuality was slowly reaching out to cloak her. It was a helpless sensation and she fought it, for it identified too closely with the unconscious familiarity that had filled her dreams the night before.

Only after Quinn broke the stare and concentrated on his wine did her thinking clear. He had meant nothing by the look. His intentions were figments of her imagination, she knew, and her reactions to them were ridiculously exaggerated. She had to forget about that damn, disturbing dream. It had nothing to do with reality.

Lunch was served and they ate heartily of crawfish etouffées, a spicy dish of thick gravy brimming with plump crawfish. Next came the Southern standard of red beans and rice piled high on a plate with corn bread and butter.

"I don't know where I'm going to put all this." Mallory eyed the mountain of food uncertainly.

"You'll find room. You look like you could use it," was Quinn's only remark as he scooped a forkful and ate.

"Brad said just the opposite. Who am I supposed to believe?" she teased.

"Me. I like my women full and rounded. Gives a man more to hold on to. Eat."

"So much for dieting. It's nice to know I'm liked for

myself." Mallory obeyed and attacked the food with genuine enthusiasm. She felt warmed by Quinn's playful words.

Quinn began to speak of his early years in the delta. His demeanor reflected the pleasure he felt in talking of old times. Unlike the man Mallory remembered as a girl, the Quinn who sat across from her seemed content, peacefully weathered, as the old, unexplainable angers lay temporarily assuaged. For now the volcano was still.

Quinn's immediate family was small. Remembrances of his mother were vague, but he hadn't felt cheated after she died. There were aunts, uncles, cousins all like the generous country folk they had danced with that morning, who were more than glad to show affection to a growing boy.

Home consisted of a converted barge moored in one of the channels of Lake Palourde near Morgan City. Belowdecks were sleeping quarters and a small galley, both of which were rarely used by the adventurous Quinn. He liked the out-of-doors, slipping into his pirogue and living in the waterways and swamps for days at a time. For food he trapped wild game, camped out, and cooked over open fires. There were long, lazy days of fishing, and hot steamy nights beneath the stars as he read by kerosene lantern.

When Cam was old enough, summers were spent taking turns speeding around the lake in an old boat, skiing with careless abandon, and laughing at life. The brothers were close then and had shared every secret.

On Saturdays Quinn went to Morgan City, rain or shine. He visited the library, intent on reading every book he could carry home. Those visits were the basis of his education. Quinn attended school, but lessons were sporadic because he was needed to help his father with a winter harvest of nutra pelts. Money was short most of the time, and he often found himself without shoes or decent clothes.

It was during a particularly sparse winter when he decided that there had to be more to life than trapping. He wanted to see how the other half lived. Well-developed for his age, he gathered his meager savings and bought a one-way bus ticket to Dulac, a tiny town on the southernmost tip of the Louisiana boot. It was easy to sign on with a drilling crew, and soon he made a life on the giant rigs that dotted the rich waters of the Gulf of Mexico.

Quick to learn and as physically agile as a cat, Quinn worked his way to head driller on one roughnecking team. It was a treacherous livelihood, dependent as much on wit as skill. It was there he met and befriended Brad.

Quinn knew the newcomer was observing everyone closely, but he didn't know why at first. During the trial period the two became fast, though competitive, friends. Intuitively guessing Brad's motives, Quinn did his best to show how worthy he could be as a worker, and it paid off. It took a while, but Brad approached with an offer of going into business together.

Quinn hadn't once doubted the decision to incorporate Wild Wells Limited, and enthusiastically he began the dangerous task of snuffing out oil fires.

When Mallory pressed for the reasons why he chose such hazardous work, he couldn't explain. He only knew that he lived and breathed the danger of the fires; a person would have to be there to know what he meant. It was something he had to do, a peril he readily faced time after time.

With the meal finished, they relaxed and gazed languidly at each other across the table. Café noir, a thick black Cajun coffee, was the last perfect accent to the fare.

Mallory played with her cup. "You said earlier in jest that I'm a foreigner. It's true that I've been gone for a while and my accent is different from what you're accustomed to hearing. But is that how you really see me? As a foreigner?"

Quinn chewed on a toothpick and quietly studied her. "I like what I see more than I ever did before, and I'm having a hell of a time trying to decipher the reasons why. You're capable of handling business better than a man, and can cut your way through a world that doesn't always give women the credit they rightly deserve. I also see a courage that wasn't there before, an attitude that certainly brings out the best in you. Most of all you're a girl who has finally learned what it is to be a woman."

"At twenty-nine I can hardly hide behind the reckless naiveté that kept me in hot water so many years ago, can I?" she returned. "Yes, I feel like I finally have grown up."

"It's about time," he growled softly. "For both of us."

Chapter Five

By late afternoon the sightseeing neared a conclusion. It was a magical day, an unforgettable journey into a world that Mallory had forgotten since childhood. It also marked the discovery of a sensitivity and depth she hadn't known Quinn capable of. They talked easily about every imaginable subject and considered themselves thoroughly reacquainted.

Cruising slowly on the way home, Quinn finally asked the question that was uppermost in his mind since early that day. "How do you feel now about Brad?"

"The same as I've always felt, I guess. He's the best," she answered matter-of-factly.

"That reply might've sufficed when you were a schoolgirl, but I'm asking it of the new Mallory. You wouldn't have stayed away four years if something hadn't changed between you. And you wouldn't have come back if you weren't strong enough to show him exactly who and what you are."

She bit her lip, reluctant to pursue the subject, but she knew some things had to be said. "Maybe if I start at the beginning, I can sort it out for you like I did for myself. I don't remember our parents at all. I just know we were left well off after they died. From the time I was little, Brad was all I had to hang on to. I can remember every night at bedtime he'd tell me stories about swashbuckling pirates and adventurous explorers. I'd pretend that he was the leader and I went along as his accomplice." Her expression was pensive with the tender memories. "I think in his own way he was trying to tell me that he had to get out, had to do something more with his life. My rebellion didn't begin until we moved to New Orleans and he married Elissa."

Quinn's brows knitted together. "I always thought the three of you got along very well."

"Only because I gave in most of the time and kept my mouth shut. It really wasn't Elissa that I resented, although in my young mind I thought at first she was the lure that made him leave our home and friends for New Orleans. That move was a turning point in my life, and in the relationship with my brother. Suddenly I wasn't the center of Brad's world anymore. She was. They needed time together and I needed to get away, so I went abroad to school."

"Do you want to return to Shreveport someday?" he asked gently. "To find what you may have left behind?"

"No, not anymore. There's nothing left to return to. We're the last of our line, the last of a staunch old Southern family with a haughty pride as our calling card. I don't know exactly what it is about our name, but Brad used to tell me that I was more Steiner than he. Maybe they left something out of us or put too much of something in. Whatever it is, Brad did a good job on me when it came to expectations from life. I paid hell for it when I went off to school. No matter what I did, it was never enough; no matter what I had, I wanted more. It's taken all I have to curb a compulsion inside to search for excitement anywhere I can find it. What does that sound like to you?"

"It sounds like much of what I've felt for most of my life," he said flatly. "It spoils us for regular living."

She laughed ruefully. "Aren't we all spoiled in one way or another anyhow?"

He nodded. "I suppose so."

They were both silent for a moment. Then Mallory picked up the threads of the earlier conversation. "I've always loved Brad. When I was a child I would've done anything he wanted, with little or no objection. But not anymore. I'm responsible only for myself and I live strictly for myself."

"And now the relationship with your brother has taken a markedly different slant. It's no longer just a daredevil defiance to get him to notice you?"

"That's right. I came simply to tell him that I love him. I can get along fine with or without his approval. Only I don't think he sees it yet. He and Elissa have a tendency to blow the whole family scene out of proportion, especially Brad."

Quinn's answer was the rise of a brow.

"It's not fair for people to assume the right of deciding what's best for another person. We have free wills and should use them. Brad has tried to play God one time too many." She noticed a thoughtful expression in his dark eyes. "Quinn, tell me how you see my brother. How have you managed to get along with him all these years and not feel the lash?"

"Brad is a very special kind of man. When he believes in you, you have a friend for life. When he loves you, he'll fight the fires of hell to prove it."

"But . . ." she prodded.

"But he doesn't always know when he's wrong. He and I were both wrong when it came to making decisions for you. I'll be the first to admit it."

"You'll probably be the only one to admit it. Brad is too obstinate for his own good."

"Yes, but that doesn't concern me. And about the lash . . . I have a scar or two, but I give as good as I get." He chuckled. "Even with the recent brush with death, Brad hasn't softened that much. It'll take some doing to set things straight between you two, Mallory."

"I've tried not to think about it, but I imagine I'll have to. As long as Brad remains receptive and attentive to my feelings, it'll be an easy transition. I think you know what will happen if he does otherwise."

"I thought you said you've grown up?"

"I have, and that includes calling my own shots. Brad may be king to everyone else in the dynasty, but he's still just my brother."

Quinn laughed aloud, the tone deep and resonant. It was infectious, and Mallory laughed along with him as he explained, "We're quite a pair, you and me. I never thought we'd ally on anything that concerns Brad, but here we are discussing him very candidly and agreeing that he's pigheaded."

"Now that we've talked about my family, I think it's time we discussed yours. What happened between Cam and you after I left for Houston?"

Quinn shrugged. "Nothing that wasn't straightened out with time. Cam was pretty hot at me for the dirty trick, and our argument turned into a free-for-all. He had been itching for it for some time and needed a reminder as to who was a man and who was still a boy. I had to tell him a few home truths, and he didn't appreciate it."

"He didn't run away like I did?" she asked.

"Nope. He moved out of the house, though, and found his own place. It was good for him to be on his own and take care of himself. After a while the bruises healed between us, and he managed to straighten up. We talked it out over a couple of beers and things have been fine ever since."

"Then he bears no grudges?"

"None. I still haven't broken him of two-timing, though. Not that I care to anymore. You're the only person whose feelings mattered anyway."

The words made Mallory feel protected, wanted.

"Brothers." She sighed. "Are we really supposed to be their keepers?"

"That's what I've always heard." He chuckled. "Although you'll never convince Brad that he doesn't have to take it literally where you're concerned."

"I intend to try," she said soberly. "He doesn't have the first bit of influence over me, Quinn. No man does. I'm glad you and I were able to pick up the pieces and mend our friendship."

"Me too," was all he'd say.

There was another pause and Quinn pointed to a thick stand of oak trees. "I have one more thing to show you and then we head for home." He stopped the car. "Follow me, *mon cher.*"

They walked down a narrow country lane shaded by beautiful oaks as he related a story that had become legend in the bayou country.

"In the 1800s there was a rich plantation owner named Charles Durand. He was a very headstrong man, very materialistic. His home was the grandest plantation, built on the shores of Bayou Teche in a place called Petit Paris. Ah, what a merry life he led. And such a partying spirit!

"Monsieur Durand had two beautiful daughters, both of whom were courted by neighboring gentlemen. When the young men approached their future father-in-law and declared their feelings, he gave approval for a double marriage to take place.

"Because it was the custom for the father of the bride to take care of arrangements, and because Monsieur Durand was a wealthy flamboyant type, he wanted to make the wedding something that would be talked about for years. He was also a showman, somewhat arrogant, but brilliant.

"One day he walked outside and studied the beauty of nature, marveling at the tender way the oaks on either side of the lane entwined their branches as if embracing."

Mallory stopped and looked up. It was as Quinn had described; golden shafts of sunlight filtered through the branches, dappling the path ahead. The air was softly shrouded in a golden light, lending credence to the enchanting story.

"An idea suddenly hit Monsieur Durand like a bolt out of the blue. He set about laying plans. He wrote to Cathy and imported spiders for the basis of a natural ornamentation.

"Shortly before the wedding day, he instructed slaves to release thousands of spiders in the trees. For days and days the little creatures wove lacey webs from one tree to another, making a gauzy covering over the branches.

"On the morning of the wedding, Monsieur Durand had slaves sprinkle gold and silver dust on the dew-covered webs. As the sun glittered through the gossamer screen, the brides and grooms proudly walked beneath the natural canopy and were married at an altar set at one end. It was breathtaking, memorable, and the story has endured until this day."

In her mind Mallory pictured such a setting. She walked ahead of Quinn and reached out to touch an old scarred tree trunk. The soft light of sunset shone on her hair. It was easy to lose herself in time as a gentle breeze ruffled the foliage overhead.

Completely spellbound, she asked, "Didn't Monsieur Durand worry about rain?"

"Of course he didn't," Quinn scoffed. "He was a headstrong man and wouldn't have allowed the weather to interfere with the spectacle."

"How very romantic." She smiled at the story and the man who told it. She didn't know Quinn had a tender leaning, and it put him in a very appealing light. "You know, Monsieur Durand reminds me of you and Brad."

He settled next to her and leaned against the cool bark of the tree. "How's that?"

"It's like both of you consider yourselves a deity and have to rule no matter what. Brad is blustery and often overbearing, while you're subtle and straightforward. Yet each of you seems to hone in on the same goals and get them accomplished."

Quinn laughed good-naturedly. "I have to agree that we do like to give all the orders if we can. It comes from doing the most exciting work in the world. We command entire governments in countries where there's an oil fire. They bend over backward to do whatever we say. That's power, Mallory, and it tastes sweeter than anything ever could."

"I daresay you and Brad would control heaven and earth if the means were set before you, wouldn't you?" she challenged.

"Damn straight we would. Somebody's got to do it."

"You see? I was right." She laughed.

He turned the conversation around. "So you think Brad and I are two of a kind, huh? What about you women? I've known my fair share of females who are damn dictatorial when the mood suits them."

"Of course there are pushy women. But you haven't been looking very hard at us, Quinn." She blinked innocently. "Most of us are still the weaker, gentler sex."

"Weaker, maybe. But gentler?" He raised a brow, and his grin was invitingly crooked. "You can look at a man with those angelic green eyes and cut his heart out at the same time. He won't even know it until you get through with him and cast him aside for someone else."

The statement left her a trifle intrigued. He thought

he still knew her, but he didn't. Beneath the veneer of polished sophistication, Mallory had a certain vulnerability and was capable of great empathy. Her strength of character projected the haughty, false facade as a protection. Quinn would have to take a good hard look in order to realize it. It pleased her to think that it was he who now had something to learn.

She glanced his way and whispered. "Twice today we've seen weddings. You've been glib about it, but I'm wondering why you've never taken a wife."

"I haven't dated much," he said noncommittally.

"Come off it. This is Mallory, remember? I've seen quite a few beautiful women on your arm, but you've never been serious about any of them. Why not?"

"I thought I had explained that before. A man like me doesn't have the right to expect a woman to just stand by. I never know where I'm going to be at any given time or what I'll be doing. That's not any kind of life for people to live. I just can't promise anything."

"I see." She studied his profile as he leaned against the tree and stared out at the lush landscape.

Quinn turned his head to meet her gaze. "I would imagine a beauty like yourself has quite a few men waiting around."

"Of course." She smiled mysteriously. "I always keep at least two or three prospects on a string. But I haven't made up my mind about what I want. I probably won't for a good long time. The idea of settling down doesn't appeal right now."

He knew her exaggerations were lightly made. "You're a young woman and should make a home soon. What's really stopping you?"

Her expression changed to seriousness. "These last four years have seen me working for everything. That hasn't left much time for socializing. I've met a few nice men and it's been lovely, but my work always comes first."

"Aha! So it's been all work and no play, right?"

She lowered her gaze to her lap. "You didn't ask that. You just wanted to know if there was anyone serious in my life. I'm footloose and fancy-free." She looked back up at him and their eyes locked. For minutes an unexplainable glitter illuminated their gazes. Quinn pushed himself away from the tree and put some space between them.

"We don't have the right to pry into each other's private lives," he said briskly. "I'm sorry I asked."

"Don't be. Friends are supposed to confide in each other," she reminded him. "I didn't consider your questions prying."

"Friends." He repeated the word softly. "Is that all we're destined to be? Friends again, as we once were?"

"Are you offering more?" She threw back carelessly.

"Do I have the right? After all, exactly who and what have we become over the last four years?"

The question made her take a good hard look at Quinn. It came as no surprise when overpowering feelings of attraction filled her every sense. Quinn had a charisma that was undeniable, and Mallory was enthralled with what she saw. He was alluring and menacing at the same time, the forbidden fruit that she had more than once dreamed of tasting, but never dared. Except in her dreams.

It had taken a long time to realize that he was dangerous, but the secret conflicts, old and new, were pushed aside when he questioned her in such an intimate tone.

Quinn had spent the entire day subtly challenging the old defiance, testing her temperament in a most unorthodox way, and she had responded every time. It was too late for a rebuff. Her eyes became flickering emerald orbs, matching the unwavering indigo illumination that emanated from his. There was no more hiding it, even if they wanted to.

"Nothing stands between me and the world," she

said slowly, reluctant to admit that Brad wasn't the only reason for her return. "I make my own choices, as do you." For the first time in a long time Mallory felt the twinges of a deep desire, a feeling that had surfaced for no other man except Quinn. Her mouth went dry and she was unable to say more.

Long ago she had gone to Quinn and he'd made it known that anything more than a friendship between them was taboo. Now there seemed to be an open invitation in his expression, an eagerness in his manner. Or was there?

No, there was no mistaking his intentions in this case. He knew exactly what he was doing. So did she.

The peace of the ancient glade did little to cool the sudden charge of desire that enveloped them in an invisible prison of awareness. They weren't timeless like the giant oaks or the story of the Durand wedding. They were a man and a woman standing across from each other as a multitude of memories tried to hold them at bay. But nothing mattered to Mallory except the present. All she wanted to think about was the feel of Quinn's arms around her. As she stood there looking small and indecisive, he made the first gesture and held out his arms.

She floated into them, reliving the beauty of last night's dream as the strength of his embrace locked solidly around her. How reassuring it was to have him hold her close and gently stroke her hair.

The vulnerability inside surfaced as Mallory looked up in wonder at his handsome face. He smiled, his teeth startlingly white against the tanness of skin. Silently he mouthed her name, "Mallory."

Her lips parted slightly as his mouth slowly descended toward hers. The agony of waiting and the excitement of expectation played havoc inside Mallory as their lips tenderly made contact. Soft and tentative, it was like the kiss she had received the day before.

Quinn broke it for only a second before claiming her once more. This time she read the stark truth of his passion as the pressure increased and he eased a warm, wet tongue inside her mouth.

The embrace tightened. Mallory pressed her body against the length of him her breasts flattening with the pressure of his chest, her hips fitting against him as she leaned into the pronounced ridge of his sudden arousal.

Her tongue glided across the even span of his teeth, tasting the unique flavor of his mouth. The exchange was an exciting sensation, and the elation she felt was intoxicating. Like ripples on a placid pond, the exquisite contact with his mouth coaxed her sexuality to life, making her doubly aware of the ardor that grew between them.

Arching her back, Mallory felt his animal heat pulsate through her blouse, scorching her sensitive nipples and making them stand at attention. With one hand between her shoulders, he pressed her even closer; with the other he braced her bottom and tightened her thighs securely against his.

She had to touch him, and she ran her palms against the thick muscles of his shoulders and back. She wished there was no clothing between them so she could know the texture of his skin.

He wished the same thing as he followed the line of her hips with his hands, first upward to the sides of her breasts and then downward to her thighs and shapely buttocks.

Mallory was breathless when his lips left hers and made a wayward trail down her cheek and along the side of her sensitive neck. Every nerve in her skin was alive from the contact. She had never felt such rapture from a mere kiss, making her alive and vibrant, as if his very life's blood flowed into her. His hands were touching everywhere, searching, probing, learning, and she felt him tremble as passion threatened to take control of him.

The battle lasted for only a second before he abruptly broke away. He leaned a hand against a strong tree trunk for support, then forced his eyes to meet hers again. They were fevered with torture.

She stood there looking as if she were on fire, her skin alive with a flush of erotic desire that he had given life to. She didn't know what to do.

They were both too shaken from the intensity of the moment to speak or to understand how it had happened. They knew instinctively that it had to stop then and there or they would both be consumed by a force that had yet to be reckoned with.

With a supreme effort they kept their distance and gave each other time to come to grips with the powerful feelings. When some semblance of control was evident, Quinn motioned that it was time to leave.

They walked back to the car as the last traces of sunset left the sky. The drive home was made in total silence.

Elissa stared out of the hospital window and watched as night descended. It had been a long Sunday afternoon, broken occasionally by calls and visits from well-wishing friends.

Brad was presently on the phone. She waited patiently and listened as he gave Cam last-minute instructions.

"Okay, be sure you get it straight for tomorrow. And have all our equipment double-checked. Stay behind those people about an early delivery on the control head too," he said intently. "When you see Quinn, have him give me a call at once."

She turned and studied her husband, the man she adored. Even in a hospital bed he looked every inch a formidable businessman. Knowing him as well as she did, she also noticed the small worry lines beneath his eyes, and the almost imperceptible droop of his head as fatigue settled in. Brad was one who acted as if he didn't know his limits, or didn't care. He would push until there was no energy left.

"Remember what I said," he reminded Cam. "I want to hear from Quinn first thing."

He pressed the buttons on the phone and began to make another call when Elissa gently placed a hand over his. "You've been on that thing for hours, darling," she drawled softly. "I think you should rest a bit now, don't you?"

He glanced her way, at first annoyed and then softening. "They're going to cap the well tomorrow, Elissa. I have to see that everything is in order."

She shook her head. "You know it's not necessary. Quinn has everything under control and will take care of it for you. Come now, relax a bit and talk to me. I'm lonesome."

"That's just it," he explained gruffly. "I haven't seen hide nor hair of Quinn Chennault since yesterday. No one knows where he's gone to or what he's doing."

"We all have our private lives, Brad," she said softly. "Is it fair for Quinn to have to report to you every day?"

"When it concerns a project, yes. I'm lying here practically helpless and it looks like no one cares to stay on top of it. Add to that an ungrateful sister who came by for about five minutes this morning and then flew the coop. I've been trying to reach her all day too with no luck." His temper was frayed around the edges.

Elissa decided to let him finish the tirade before trying to cajole him into a good mood.

"I didn't get to the top by sitting on my haunches and waiting for things to take care of themselves," he continued. "People are so damned inconsiderate!"

"There, there." It was time for a little tender loving care. She had to make him see how unreasonable he sounded. She touched his forehead with a gentle hand. "Need I remind you about doctor's orders? You need rest, peace, and quiet so that leg will mend and those bruises will heal. If you keep yourself in a state of excitement, you'll never leave this place and go home with me."

He looked up at Elissa's classic face and read concern in the soft features. She was so protective of him, so understanding, and he felt foolish for the outburst. "I'm sorry, honey. I get so damned tired of just lying here all the time, staring at the same four walls . . ."

"I know. But I've stayed here with you since the beginning, haven't I? You're not going through this alone," she crooned to him. As usual, it had a very positive effect on his nerves.

Elissa could encounter the harshest situation and make it seem not nearly so bad, a talent she had picked up from generations of gentle breeding. It was a woman's place to take the hurts from a man, to be his pillow whenever he needed her. Brad seemed to need her now more than ever, and the knowledge made her all the more intent on showering him with affection and understanding.

Brad looked up at his wife. When he had first met Elissa, he had been taken with her classy looks and high-bred ideals. She was everything he thought a Southern belle should be. She turned out to be even more than he had expected, having nineteenth-century values that dictated total devotion to a man. No matter what the issue, he knew he'd have her full support with very little objection in return.

That was the type of man he was. He liked being able to tell people what to do. Elissa always gave in, intent on pleasing him in any way she could. It was very easy to love Elissa, to spoil her as he had once spoiled Mallory.

Noticing a faraway look in his eyes, Elissa asked, "Care to tell me what's on your mind?"

His emerald stare was opaque as he considered

opening up to her. "I was just thinking about Mallory and wondering about her future."

"I'm glad, because I think we should discuss her. It took a great deal for her to put everything down and come to your side, Brad. She's as strong as you are, do you realize that?"

He lifted a brow. "I would've done no less if the tables were turned."

His answer came as a surprise and she wondered if it was sincere. "That's not the case now. She hurt you terribly in the very beginning, but I honestly don't think she intended to embarrass us. She knew of no other way to declare her independence and make us realize that she was hurting just as much."

"She was rebellious," he drawled tiredly. "Every teenager gets into one kind of mischief or another."

"I'm glad we agree about that." She sighed. "I think sending her abroad was very good at the time, but it made the later years more complicated. Do you remember how much she had changed when she came home after graduation from college?"

"I could've understood, had it just been on the outside. But inside she was more willful than ever. I should've cracked down harder when she was growing up."

"It's too late to dwell on it, Brad. I think she did fairly well in the growing up department, most of the time."

"Have you forgotten about her behavior with Cam Chennault?" The memory made him flush angrily.

"It took two, Bradley. You can't entirely blame your sister for that."

"Well I sure as hell don't blame Cam. A man can only go as far as a woman lets him. Mallory shouldered the responsibility as far as I'm concerned." Brad wouldn't give an inch where that particular misbehavior was concerned.

"We see now that understanding was a key we failed to use. Perhaps she wouldn't have felt so threatened if we had stood back and allowed her some independence. She was trying to prove that she was no longer a child."

"In my mind Mallory will always be immature, a liability I have to look out for if I can," he said briskly.

"That's where you're wrong. She's a woman now. After talking with her yesterday, I'm convinced of it."

"What's the point of all this anyway? Why are we discussing my sister?"

"Because she'll need room if you two are going to have a future together. I can't interfere if there's a blowup this time, because you're adults and the issues may get too complicated."

"You know, you're the second person who's told me this," he said sharply. "Doesn't anyone think I have sense enough to realize the score for myself? What's wrong with wanting my sister to need me and wanting to be there to keep her on the right track if I can?"

"Nothing, Brad, nothing, but she's not on the wrong track." Elissa could see that the subject was upsetting him, and regretted admitting how she really felt. "Your intentions are good, and I think Mallory will see that. Just remember that she can't be treated like she was before."

"It won't be like it was in the past. We've all changed enough to accommodate any new problems."

But had they? Brad intended to give, but it would be in his own way and time. To his way of thinking, Mallory had taken four years to learn the error of her ways. Coming back was an admission to that effect. She needed Brad and he needed her. Wasn't that all that mattered?

"In the short amount of time I spent with Mallory, I felt as if we had finally worked out a way to meet on common ground. I noticed a tolerance that wasn't there before, and a sensitivity that's genuine." Elissa busied herself with getting him some ice water and a straw.

"Well," he mumbled, "that's fine and dandy for all of us, especially when it comes to me. It's nice to know that Mallory won't turn into a spitting witch any more. I don't see why you keep worrying about it."

"Everything will be fine if you'll remember to back off and let her be herself."

"I keep telling you that I don't have to, Elissa. She and I decided to let sleeping dogs lie and get on with today. We won't gain anything by going back and trying to rehash something that's dead and buried."

The statement bothered Elissa, but she knew better than to pursue it. She handed Brad the glass and watched as he sipped slowly. He was such a strong, gallant man, but sometimes he was so impossible that it took every bit of patience to understand and accept him. She knew that Brad was still the immovable object, the one who loved too fiercely and wanted to protect everything he held dear. There was no way he could face a future with Mallory unless they went back and settled old debts first.

"It's time to rest a while." Elissa put the glass on a bedside table and helped him settle down beneath a sheet. He obeyed without a word, his mind buried in his own thoughts.

After making sure he was comfortable, Elissa went back to the window and looked out at the darkened landscape. She knew in her heart that Brad would never be the one to give any quarter, although in his mind he thought he had. She also suspected that this was merely a visit from her sister-in-law, not the final homecoming that Brad had envisioned. The terms of the truce would be up to Mallory, and there was serious doubt that she'd be foolish enough to allow Brad a free rein to dominate again. And Elissa couldn't blame her.

A feeling of dread brought a sudden chill over Elissa as she foresaw a storm on the horizon. She knew she was helpless to prevent it.

Chapter Six

The next day Mallory sat before a vanity mirror in her hotel room and stared at the hollow, questioning expression in her jade eyes.

It bothered her that neither she nor Quinn had volunteered a single word during the long ride home after their encounter. Her last memory was of an uncertain glance in his direction before getting out of the car and watching as he drove away. His expression was totally unreadable, but there was no mistaking a surfacing of the old discontentments behind his dark, almost sullen stare. With no communication between them, she was left feeling more perturbed than confused, wondering if he blamed her for anything.

She still couldn't figure how things had gotten out of hand so quickly. One minute they were talking about weddings and friendships. The next minute they were wrapped in a fevered embrace, devouring each other like hungry felines.

Perhaps the dream two days before was a premonition after all, but to what end? Just a single look from Quinn was all it took for every defense inside to melt. She didn't know if she liked the idea of being that vulnerable.

She had spent the previous night tossing and turning, her body alive with a hunger she had never known could be so intense. Even the sheet sliding across her nude breasts was arousing. She finally gave up the pursuit of a peaceful sleep and tried to make sense out of the barrage of feelings.

No matter which way she looked at it, the conclusion was always the same, although she did her best to deny it. It took hours of pacing before she admitted to herself that the hunger was solely for Quinn. So was most of the anger. All she had to do was picture him in her mind, and the heated remembrances continued on their own. Brief though it was, his touch was like a spark to gunpowder. Over and over she relived the waves of wild abandonment she'd felt as she had willingly allowed his hands to explore her body.

She was exasperated with Quinn because she had wanted to go further, to make love with him and know once and for all the mystery of his powerful masculinity. Another part of the chagrin was directed at herself. How could she have been so quick to relinquish control? Hadn't the years away taught her anything? She wasn't a girl anymore, and her immature, willful tendencies toward self-indulgence had been carefully curbed and brought to heel. Until Quinn.

If he had just tried to talk to her afterward, had said something, *anything,* it might have been easier to face what happened and view it objectively. Together they could've rationalized what had erupted between them.

Was it possible that the tone of the visit had led to the encounter at the day's end? There was the excitement of visiting the countryside, the beautiful, carefree Cajun wedding, and the romantic story of the Durand ceremony. The conversations were sprinkled with a great deal of innuendo, however kiddingly, on both their parts. All those elements could have easily worked to catch them unaware.

She was totally bewildered, not knowing his true feelings, and wondered if the episode had served to set them back to square one again. Maybe it had damaged things so badly that they could never be friends of any kind. Why should the thought upset her so?

Quinn shouldn't have clammed up and pushed it aside so abruptly. She shouldn't have allowed him to retreat into a cold silence. It should've been talked out right then and there.

Mallory finished dressing for a visit to the hospital. While there she hoped to run into Quinn again in the hallway. It would be her turn to lead the way to the solarium for another heart-to-heart talk. She had no idea what she'd say, but she knew things couldn't be left as they were.

By the time Mallory walked into Brad's hospital room, she knew Quinn wouldn't be anywhere around. She had been informed that he had visited earlier that morning.

She knocked lightly on the door. "Anyone home?"

Brad was looking over a construction journal and Elissa sat nearby doing needlepoint.

Brad smiled up at his sister. "Come on in. It's nice to see you looking so pretty this morning."

"You're mighty chipper yourself." She returned the compliment and hugged him. Looking down, she acknowledged her sister-in-law. "Elissa."

"Can you stand some good news?" Brad's face was aglow with excitement.

"Any time. What's going on?"

"They're letting me out of this prison at the end of the week." He beamed. "I'll be a free man again."

"That's wonderful!" Mallory's smile matched his.

"It's also a relief," Elissa interjected. "For all of us. Brad is starting to get too thin. I think he needs some of my down-home cooking to put him back on his feet."

Brad patted his trim stomach. "She's been working on menus all day long. I guess she figures if she fattens me up, I won't be able to waddle back to the job site."

"Elissa, after all these years don't you know the way to Brad's heart is through his hard hat, not his stomach?" They shared a laugh as Mallory sat at the foot of the bed.

"Y'all just keep poking fun and laughing. I like the sound of it. I haven't forgotten how you both adore my rice dressing and creole potato salad."

Brother and sister looked at each other and nodded. Among Elissa's many talents, cooking ranked the highest.

"Now we know what your wife's plans are. What's the first thing you're going to do when you get home?" Mallory asked.

"Find a pair of crutches so I can walk from room to room and kiss the walls," he said decidedly. "No more sterile conditions, no more nurses in white uniforms, no more bedpans and sponge baths. I'll have the welcome comfort of familiar surroundings."

While he talked, Mallory dug in her purse and found a package of cigarettes. Without thinking, she took one out and lit it.

Brad stopped talking and gave her a hard look. "When did you start smoking?"

"About three years ago. It's not a regular thing, though. You don't mind, do you?" She took another short puff.

"As a matter of fact, I do. I don't like the idea of your smoking. I want you to put it out."

Mallory looked at him with a baffled expression. "More than once you've lit up cigars in front of me. What's the difference now?"

"The difference is I'm a man and you're a woman," he said evenly. "Put the cigarette out."

Now that he knew he'd have the run of his little dynasty soon, Brad was back to being his old self again. That included telling Mallory what to do.

At first she had thought him kidding, but knew by the look on his face that he meant for her to obey without question. She was annoyed with the idea of taking his orders, but figured a cigarette was too inconsequential a thing to argue over.

"If you want it out, it's out," she said boredly, and pressed it into a nearby ashtray. "Who cares about a stupid cigarette anyway?"

It appeared to be forgotten as soon as it happened.

Later she and Elissa went downstairs together for lunch in the hospital cafeteria. It was cheerfully decorated, much like an indoor sidewalk café, and the patrons were obliged to serve themselves.

As the women walked together in line near the cashier's stand, Elissa rolled her eyes. "I've eaten here so much that everything tastes the same to me."

"That tends to happen to me too," Mallory answered. "At times I seem to live on the road. One restaurant starts to look the same as another."

They found a table near a corner of the cafeteria and sat down. Elissa took a bite. "Just as I thought. This stuff tastes like cardboard."

"I haven't seen a hospital yet that offers more." Mallory sweetened her iced tea. "Four more days and you won't have this bother."

"Yes, and that's all I'm living for." Elissa sparkled as she made plans for the homecoming. "I've called ahead to our staff in New Orleans. They'll have the town house open and ready for when Brad comes home. Please don't tell him, but I'm seriously considering hiring a private nurse to look after him for the first few days."

"What for? They won't let him leave here without a clean bill of health. Is a nurse really necessary?"

"I thought maybe we could use the extra help. I've

done what I can, but he's too much for me to handle alone." She sipped her coffee and stared thoughtfully into space. "I have a grand idea, Mallory. Why don't you consider moving back to New Orleans with us? You'd be such a tremendous help with Brad. Then I wouldn't need a nurse."

"I'm flattered with the invitation, but I haven't looked that far ahead. I have my own responsibilities in Houston to tend to." Mallory took a bite of food and thought about the proposal.

"Oh, come on now. It's just for a little while. We could be one big happy family again. It'd tickle Brad pink, and the two of you could be together like you want. It would be good for all of us." Her sincerity was apparent.

Because she hadn't intended to stay in Louisiana for more than a couple of days, Mallory was reluctant to commit herself to the plan. Right now Quinn was the dominant figure in her considerations, and she'd need time to think.

There were other things to weigh, like the little disruption over the cigarette. The incident was still disturbingly fresh on her mind. She wondered if it might be a prelude to more complex disagreements later on.

She put Elissa off with, "I'll give it some thought and let you know."

Elissa was correct about the food tasting drab, and Mallory found that she had little appetite for it. She lit a cigarette and finished her tea, wondering if her sister-in-law would say anything about her lighting up again. In the old days a mere disapproving look conveyed her feelings, but today she seemed to accept without reaction.

"I hope Brad didn't hurt your feelings upstairs." Elissa referred to the earlier cigarette.

"No." Mallory looked at the fire as it burned the tobacco at the tip. "It came as a small surprise that he'd pull an old trick so soon, though. I thought he had changed his monocratic habits."

"He has, but it's just not evident right now because he has cabin fever. Give him time." Elissa dabbed at the corners of her mouth with a napkin.

Mallory tilted her head and studied her sister-in-law. "You've been very good to my brother. Up to now I hadn't realized just how good."

Elissa smiled slightly. "What you're saying is that you wouldn't put up with half the things I do."

"I guess so." Mallory stubbed out the cigarette. It tasted as flat as the food. "How do you feel about his going back to work when the cast comes off?"

Elissa took a deep breath. "I've never told this to anyone, but each time that phone rings and he's called away, I go through hell. My insides turn to lead and stay that way until he's safely home again."

"Why don't you go with him? It might make you feel better."

"He wouldn't allow it. What I experience is a crippling fear for my husband's life, and it would show. I'd be a hindrance to his concentration, not a help." Her gaze was far away. "No one knows what it's like to sit home day after day when Brad is gone, wondering what's happening, if he's going to make it alive. It would be worse actually being there and seeing it for myself."

"You're that apprehensive?"

"Yes." She looked down at her hands. "I've always been that afraid."

Mallory rested her chin on a hand and thought about it. She didn't totally comprehend Elissa's logic. For her, danger was exciting. "Frankly, I don't see the difference in being home or being with him, especially since you live in fear anyway. How could accompanying Brad be any worse?"

"In more ways than I care to think about. Brad isn't

aware that I know he handles things like nitroglycerin and dynamite. He wouldn't want me around in case someone mishandles the explosives and they go off. Heavy bulldozers may be a help to his cause, but I see those big menacing machines as a threat. Just one wrong turn . . . The scariest thought is of the fire itself. If there's an equipment failure, or in this last case an accident, it could be over in seconds."

"For you, too much knowledge can be a dangerous thing." Mallory began to understand.

"That's right. I'm strong in some ways, but it's my nature to fall to pieces at the wrong times. In that respect I'm ill-suited for anything except the present type of arrangement. That's why I wait for Brad and we go off together after each of the fires."

"No wonder you're always honeymooning." Everything started to fall into place. "You live in constant fear, and yet Brad doesn't know how you really feel about his work."

"He can't know. I'm supposed to be his better half, the softness in his life, the solace. He's my entire existence, Mallory. Brad isn't alive unless he's fighting a fire. I'm not alive unless he is. The anxieties I feel are for him, not for myself, but this is the price I gladly pay. All I live for are the times we can be together after the fires. That's when he needs me the most."

"That just doesn't seem fair, Elissa. It's like a half-life for you, always teetering on a fence and never knowing when it's going to come out from under you. Still, it's a choice you've made, and you obviously haven't wavered all these years." Mallory's voice softened. "I think I owe you a long overdue apology."

"Whatever for?"

"All this time I've thought your possessiveness of Brad was because you didn't want to share him with me. It never occurred to me just how much it meant for you to protect what you have. You've been right in doing it. You love him very much, and he's lucky to have you."

"Thank you, Mallory." Elissa smiled slowly. The moment had lightened with the accepted apology. "So now Brad is preparing to leave for home and Quinn has the responsibility of taking over the entire operation single-handedly. I personally think this is one fire they should walk away from and not look back."

"So do I." Mallory said offhandedly, not knowing why she was in agreement. "Do you know what's going on right now?"

Elissa nodded. "I heard Brad talking to Cam last night. A new control head has been built and it's expected today. With Quinn leading the team, they'll try to smother the blaze sometime this afternoon. It's going to be very rough and more dangerous than the first time, but Quinn is a good fighter. He keeps a cooler head than Brad and is more methodical."

"You certainly do know more than you're supposed to."

Mallory had a disturbing feeling about Quinn's attacking the fire, but didn't give voice to it. She desperately wanted to speak with him about the night before, but the opportunity would have to wait until after the work was completed. Quinn couldn't afford any distractions, and she knew better than to try seeing him now. That meant waiting out the day for his call and trying to decide what she'd say to him when the time came.

Elissa pointed to the package of cigarettes lying on the table. "May I have one of those?" Without waiting for an answer, she took one and lit it, inhaling deeply and expertly blowing a cloud of smoke toward the ceiling.

The action took Mallory completely by surprise. "You smoke?"

"When I feel the need for it, yes. Brad has his little

secrets and I have mine." She grinned impishly and winked. For the first time Mallory actually liked her.

It was the longest day of Mallory's life as she waited tensely to hear from Quinn. He could have called, even for a minute, but she sat alone in her hotel room and knew the phone wouldn't ring. When she could stand it no longer, she decided to take matters into her own hands and be the first to make contact.

It was evening by the time she arrived at the site. For miles around, traffic was backed up to the highway as eager spectators stopped to watch the still-wayward blaze. The closer Mallory got to the security gates, the more chaos she encountered. Television people and radio announcers swarmed through the crowds with trucks, camera crews, and microphones. It was like a three-ring circus, noisy and disquieting. Mallory harbored little hope of getting to Quinn through the confusion.

When a guard approached her for identification, she talked her way through the gate, telling him that she was Brad Steiner's sister, a VIP, and was personally invited by Quinn Chennault. The guard obliged and pointed out the crew of fire fighters dressed in yellow coveralls. They were all at the ready, standing at the perimeter of the blaze.

With a purposeful gait Mallory went to the edge of a makeshift fence that held all personnel at bay except the team of fire fighters. Even at that distance the heat was almost unbearable. She wondered how Quinn could stand it.

In talking with a field superintendent, she learned that they had worked the entire afternoon with little success. Although equipment and water levels were in ample supply, it was next to impossible to synchronize conditions and make them favorable for lowering the control head.

Following this narrative above the roar of the inferno, she watched the scene through fascinated eyes. Three bulldozers, modified with long cranes and giant grappling hooks, formed a semicircle and were backed around the fire, blocking one's view of the activity going on at the core.

Some of the crew stood nearby and held metal shields with special windows for use in approaching the blaze. Still others manned hoses and continually sprayed down the flames and well head in order to cool the old casing for a possible approach.

The bulldozers were designed to pull double duty, first clearing off debris and making a direct entry possible. Damaged metal from the explosion could remain hot and reignite the well head, as it had the first time, so the area was relatively clean.

Now the crew's most important function was close at hand. With the trash removed, a single column of fire burned bright and high, inviting the fighters to try quelling it if they could.

The bulldozer in the center held a fifty-five-gallon drum secured at the end of a long crane. After Quinn made preparations of nitroglycerin wrapped in thick packaging, the bundle would be placed in the drum and insulated with thick asbestos. With a continual hosing-down, the crane would slowly back the drum into the heart of the fire. At the precise time a detonator would trip a guide wire and blow up the nitroglycerin, eliminating oxygen and stunning the fire with the blast.

Simultaneous with the preparation of the drum, another crane crew was readying the new control head on a long arm, intending to set it over the dead site. It had to be done quickly, because any spark could easily blow up the site again.

A third set of workers kept spraying down Quinn and Cam, who were dressed in silver asbestos suits and heavy-duty helmets for protection. They would be the two responsible for going into the danger zone and securing the new control head before the blaze had a chance to rear up again and possibly explode.

From time to time Mallory saw Quinn signaling to Cam as they tried to prepare and go in. It was decided that no further attempts would be made. The project was aborted when Quinn finally shook his head and gave a thumbs-down signal. Something wasn't right, and he wouldn't risk it again.

For the second time the fire had won, and it seemed to grow hotter and brighter in the triumph of staying alive against all efforts to control it. The equipment was moved a safe distance away and parked until needed again.

As the crew shut down the water supply, Quinn pulled off his helmet and gloves, tucking them beneath an arm. He wiped a gritty brow with the back of a sweaty hand and slowly walked toward the trailer that served as both headquarters and home.

Halfway there he spotted Mallory standing near the fence. She wore a sexy red dress with a single halter neck strap that held the bodice in place. He was glad to see such a beautiful, welcome sight after the tenseness of an unsuccessful day. At the same time misgivings filled him. She had no business anywhere around a fire.

His welcome to her smile was a maddening show of cool indifference, which she promptly ignored. "I waited as long as I could for your call. Would you like to take me to dinner?"

"You shouldn't be here," came the answer as he took her by the arm. "How the hell did you get in?"

"I told the guard that I was Brad Steiner's sister and that you invited me."

"It's too dangerous for you to be anywhere near here," he said slowly. "I'll walk you back to your car to make sure you leave the same way you came."

"Don't I have any say about this?" She could read nothing in his steady gaze. "Is it because you don't want me here?"

"Quit trying to confuse the issue. Brad and I made the rules years ago, and they still stand. It's not a matter of what anyone wants. It pertains to safety. Period."

"What about the fire? Why didn't you put it out?" She pointed a thumb over a shoulder as he led her away.

"It was too risky because of wind conditions. We'll give it another shot tomorrow. Now let's get you out of this area before I get into big trouble with the boss, okay?"

"But *you're* the boss."

He raised a brow and gave her a stern look. "You know what I mean. Now let's move it."

She knew he meant business and wouldn't be deterred from personally seeing her escorted away from the danger. Her timing was definitely off, and he was in no mood to talk to her right now. Not one to beg for attention, she decided to let it ride just this once. Stopping to say goodbye, she chanced a glance over his broad shoulder.

A picture of the blaze contrasted with the twilight behind him, turning his asbestos suit a golden brown. She stepped to one side, encountering the full impact of the spectacle, and came face-to-face for the first time with the orange monster that Quinn had spent his life battling.

It groaned and howled like a great dragon, boiling and billowing as if trying to escape the tight container that fed it. The colors were vivid, ever-changing, overwhelming as it raged greedily from side to side in the wind. It was hungry for anything that dared to come close enough to touch it.

The effect was devastating, making the hair on the back of Mallory's neck stand up. The blood drained from her face, and her pale body turned stiff as she stood rooted to the spot.

Quinn took her by the shoulders, fearing that she was

upset and frightened. As he looked deeply into her dilated pupils, he realized the truth. Mallory was ecstatic from the excitement of the danger. Her expression was nothing short of rapture.

"I'll be damned!" he swore quietly. "I think you're experiencing what it's like for Brad and me!"

She was barely breathing, her nostrils flaring slightly when she did. Quinn shook her, forcing her to pull her gaze away from the dramatic exhibition and look at him.

"Are you okay?" His brows were drawn together in consternation. She looked as if she had just made love with someone, and it cut through him like nothing ever had before.

"Y-Yes, I think so," she said softly. "I never realized . . ."

There was no way to explain the sudden exhilaration that filled her. It was like standing at the top of the world and being tempted to jump off and fly.

"Look, I have to go inside and get out of this suit before I fry. I'm going to take a shower and clean up. If you don't mind waiting, I'll take you to dinner after all."

"I'm not going anywhere," she said breathlessly, feeling herself starting to come down. "I'll stay out here."

She went as far as the porch and leaned weakly against a railing as he entered the trailer. It would take a little time to subdue the unexpected excitement from the fire, and she welcomed the few minutes to herself.

Long moments passed before she was once again back to normal. Not paying much attention, she didn't see Cam Chennault until he approached from out of the darkness. He stood at the bottom step and looked up at her. In those few seconds as the golden flames flickered across his face, Mallory saw a fleeting glimpse of a younger version of Quinn.

The illusion was shattered when he spoke. His dialect

wasn't as elegant as Quinn's, the accent more pronounced. "I saw you talking with my brother and I wondered if . . . I mean, I'm real sorry, Mallory. This is the first chance I've had to say it." The tone was apologetic in spite of his cocky demeanor.

It came as a surprise that she didn't feel uncomfortable with Cam so near. In fact, she didn't feel anything. The memories flooded back, but they were no longer upsetting. There was no pain in seeing him again. "Hello, Cam."

"You're more beautiful than I remembered. I was a stupid fool for letting you go. About that last night I saw you . . ."

"Save it. You don't have to explain anything to me now. I've had plenty of time to face the truth and handle it."

"Which truth is that?" His blue eyes sparkled devilishly as he tried to bait her. Always one to play games, he did his best to turn on the charm even now. At one time his stare had caused her to melt right down to her shoes. It no longer had any effect.

"The truth that what happened between us was for the best. We didn't really love each other. We were . . . in love with love, too hotheaded for our own good. It was fun while it lasted, but it's long dead."

"Yeah, I guess you're right. I killed it."

"Given time and other circumstances, I would be the one confessing to the murder right now instead of you. That and a few other things I won't mention. We were too different and didn't have the good sense to see it. You're you and I'm me. We would've destroyed each other, Cam. Nobody should fault anybody for what happened yesterday, okay?"

"I'm glad you feel that way. You don't know what a chump I've felt like each time you've crossed my mind. I had no intention of hurting you, ever. It just happened." He shuffled his feet as a silence filled the moment between them. "Somebody said you're in the oil game and doing well for yourself. I think that's great."

"Thank you. I hear you've been promoted on the team now that Brad is down. This looks like quite a proving ground for you."

He turned and looked at the fire, his expression sour. "You can say that again. Quinn isn't going to give up easily, and I'm not about to walk away if he doesn't. I'll hang in there as long as he does."

"Then I want you to know that you both have a friend rooting for you." She offered a hand for a shake.

His smile was dazzling as he accepted. "Thanks. You're really something, Mallory. I figured somehow we'd see each other again. I'm glad it turned out this way."

"So am I." There was nothing left to say as she smiled down at him.

He gave her a short salute before ambling away. She watched his retreating figure, and thought how easy it was to face the memories before tucking them away and forgetting they ever existed.

She wondered what had drawn them together in the first place. Was it a wildness, a surliness that Cam still wore like a badge? In Mallory's gullible, rebellious state, it hadn't taken much to encourage her to do the same. One defiance had fed the other, and for a time it was exciting. Now Cam wore it poorly, and it gave credence to an immaturity that should no longer be there. She saw it for what it was, along with Cam's faded appeal.

Quinn had hit the mark years ago when he quietly pointed out that the couple had nothing at all in common and would outgrow each other. How could he have known the truth better than she?

Chapter Seven

As Mallory waited patiently on the porch, the door to the trailer opened. Quinn stepped out showered and shaved, looking refreshed and somewhat rested. His hair was still damp from the water, and he carelessly brushed the wayward curls from his forehead.

"Thanks for hanging around." He finished tucking his shirt into his jeans. "It was nice to have someone waiting for me."

"I'll bet you say that to all the girls." She grinned, glad that he was finally at ease.

"It's good to see you're back to yourself again too." He smiled back. "Let's go."

They walked across the area without any further conversation, taking care to skirt the crowd and avoid the television cameras.

Mallory's keys were still in the ignition. Quinn automatically slipped into the driver's seat. She settled on the passenger side. As they headed toward the main highway, Quinn didn't have much to say. She could tell by his expression that he didn't want to talk. He seemed preoccupied, distant.

Instead of taking a left to go back to town, he went right and headed out toward open country. Giving her a lazy sideways glance, he drawled, "I hope you don't mind waiting a little while for dinner. It was one hell of a day, more hectic than I'd anticipated. I have to do some walking and thinking in order to unwind."

She didn't mind. They drove a couple of miles down the road and came to a glade that shielded a man-made reservoir. It fed the pumps at the drilling site. Deserted, the placid pond lay between them and the fire, reflecting a picture of the horizon.

Quinn turned off the ignition. Leisurely he took out a cigarette, lit it, and then motioned for her to get out of the car with him. Wordlessly they walked together, taking their time going along the hard bank of the reservoir.

Mallory tried not to look at Quinn, knowing he was bothered and needed solitude. When she just couldn't stand it any more, she said, "I don't think I've ever seen you quite this preoccupied."

"I have so much on my mind right now," came his noncommittal reply.

"Maybe if you talk about it you'll feel better. It's the fire that's eating you, isn't it?"

He looked out in the direction of the blaze. The landscape was flat and almost barren, affording a clear picture of the fire. She copied the gesture and answered for him. "Yes, I can see it's the fire."

She studied the flames swirling against the black of night, flames so bright that they dulled the white of the moon. On the horizon the panorama seemed to pyramid into the darkness, climbing repeatedly and falling short of its destiny. Mallory likened the scene to a competition between the elements, as orange-gold demons licked continuously at the black virginity of night. They rumbled and complained, curling tongues of heat and gray surges of thick smoke in constant enticement. The boiling was endless against the unyielding ebony flesh of the sky. The attempt was made against all odds, and would continue again and again until the fire was no more.

Mallory recalled how earthshaking it had been to initially encounter the flames. It made something snap inside, loosening the reins of conduct and making her feel wild and defiant, totally free. The gut-wrenching reaction also made it easier to comprehend Quinn's attitude. There was nothing like experiencing danger firsthand.

It took a special man to dare quieting those unruly calls and the ceaseless taunts against the sky. And Quinn was suddenly very special. Mallory was more than eager to share any insights he cared to give concerning his work as well as feelings.

She looked at him again. "Tell me what you see when you look out there."

He finished the cigarette and dropped it to the ground. Hooking his thumbs in the belt loops of his jeans, he said, "I see a woman. She's very beautiful, alluring, voluptuous, brazen. She's naked, and her skin is golden, glowing as she moves in front of me. She's an impossible woman doing a sensual dance of destruction, twisting and turning, bumping and grinding, doing everything imaginable to turn my blood hot for her. She wants me to want her, wants me to walk into the middle of that inferno and give myself up to her. I do want her, but I want to dominate and prove that she isn't the one who'll win. When I go in, I intend to be in control. She'll ultimately allow it. She has no choice."

The words were very passionate. Mallory was speechless, never having heard him talk that way before. His very tone was enough to make her insides quiver with excitement. She tried to push the emotions away.

"Is that why you keep going back again and again?" she asked shakily.

"Yes. I'm compelled to do it for my own reasons, not for Brad's or anyone else's. It's a struggle of wills, and my will is going to reign supreme." The words had a powerful intent and were not lightly spoken.

Staring at the fire, she couldn't help but think that she had been given more insight than she bargained for. "Now that you've related it in human terms, I can understand."

"Can you really?" His expression was wry.

"I . . . I think so. I didn't know before tonight exactly what it was, but now I do." She looked back at the horizon. "She's so dangerous, so exciting that you want to turn away and not look at her. But you can't."

"Something like that, yes."

"You know the fire might very well destroy you, but you keep going at it anyway. Above all else, you must experience it."

"That's right, Mallory. Above all else. Sometimes it's enough to distort a man's thinking." His voice was low and appreciative. "But I've been a fool for lesser things."

"Haven't we all?" She had assumed the truth, to a degree. He was impressed with her acceptance of his unexplainable thirst for peril. In fact, she seemed to share it. That much about Mallory hadn't changed.

As they talked about the fire, her expression mirrored the earlier rapture of that first encounter with the overwhelming picture of the flames. The look on her face did something to him as she allowed herself to become hypnotized again. The glow, even from that distance, reflected softly on her features and illuminated the things that went through her mind. Mallory was quite a woman, markedly different from any he had known.

Even though Quinn had opened up, there was still a

curtain of reserve between them. There was more on his mind, and Mallory waited patiently for him to continue the conversation.

Finally he decided to tell her the truth and be done with it. "It's not the fire that's bothering me, Mallory. Not this time."

She bit her lip, knowing what he was going to say. She had to allow him to say it.

"It's us. It's what happened yesterday and last night. I don't know what came over me. I was out of line to want you."

Her reaction was a defensive one. How dare he try to talk his way out of things that needed to be discussed, explained!

"Are you apologizing, or finding fault with your desires?" she asked icily.

"A little of both, I guess," he said sheepishly.

"It took two of us, in case you didn't notice. I wanted you just as much."

"The pull has been strong ever since I saw you at the hospital, and I had enough of a chip on my shoulder to think I could do as I damn well please with you. I can't. I should've kept a cooler head," he insisted. "It . . . was my intention to go after you, but it was wrong. It won't happen again." A muscle in his jaw clenched as he held himself with iron control.

"It won't happen again, or you won't let it happen?" she challenged.

He crossed his arms and looked back at the fire. She knew what he was saying, but didn't want to accept it. Not right now, anyway. Although every instinct ordered her to heed the words, a tiny glimmer of the old belligerence kept getting in the way. That, and the recollections of her dream. So it was a premonition after all.

Her gaze followed the line of his finely chiseled features, the brawny set of his shoulders and thick arms, his body strong and sturdy as the trees that grew around them. There would be no staying away from Quinn Chennault and trying to deny what he did to her. The hungers were alive inside and she could do nothing to control them.

"You think it's because we're so different, don't you?" she asked quietly.

"That, among other things."

"You've got it wrong, Quinn. We're more alike than either of us would care to believe. It's all right if you don't want to accept me, but I wouldn't have you any other way."

"You *shouldn't* have me any way at all, and I shouldn't have you. We'd be poison to each other. I can't make it any clearer than that."

"When I think of the way your hands felt as they touched me all over . . ." She closed her eyes and whispered. "I was as alive as that fire out there, and I would've done anything to keep you near me."

"I know it, but don't say any more, Mallory." He groaned. "It's tough enough . . ."

"Then you're admitting that you felt the same?" She studied his masculine profile through adoring eyes.

Slowly he turned and looked down at her, the torment and hunger swimming in his dark stare. "Yes, but look at the years between us, all the things that have passed from the first day we met. It's as if we're playing with a container of nitro, tossing it back and forth and waiting for the explosion. We can't let it happen no matter how much we think we might want it."

"I meant it when I said that nothing stands between me and the world," she reminded him. "Is it so wrong to go after what we want?"

"It is when it's this dangerous," he warned. "We're adults, and we're talking about adult needs. This isn't some little game of hide-and-seek."

"So you'll content yourself with window-shopping and admiring from a safe distance," she said angrily.

"The only thing I've ever seen you commit yourself to is that damned fire! You'll never spend anything on me because it's too risky. You're afraid that I'm not worth it!"

"You're not going to get anywhere by trying to taunt me." His eyes glinted. "I haven't been talking all this time about the fire. *You're* the golden-skinned woman who's tempting me. The only reason I've held out is that I'm not fool enough to fall prey to any of your feminine schemes."

"Then tell me what it is I have to do to convince you that my feelings are as genuine as yours? I've grown up, Quinn, and I don't play games with people's emotions any more, especially my own. I want you. That's all there is to it. Can you be that honest with yourself?"

The hunger grew in his eyes as he looked at Mallory. Her exposed shoulders were creamy and round against the scarlet color of a dress that ended just above the tops of her full breasts. He wanted to take their weight in each hand and press them together, burying his face in the soft cleavage. Her tiny waist curved into full, inviting hips. He imagined what it would be like to have her beneath him, her body a feminine pillow cradling his rigid male caress.

Mallory stood perfectly still, reading every thought as his eyes undressed her.

"I pushed you away years ago because you were nothing more than an impetuous little girl, spoiled and willful. Even then I caught a glimpse of the passion you could offer a man once you became a woman. The willfulness is still there, along with a new maturity. I have enough sense to know that it's not good for us." He caught his breath. "But with you so close, I can hardly stand not touching you. I don't have the right . . ."

It was torture staring at her pale blond beauty looking even paler against the black velvet of night.

The very air between them was charged as a sexual magnetism grew and danced upon the currents.

She came closer, whispering, "I'll grant you the right . . ."

Trembling visibly, they stood at the threshold of a tightly leashed sensuality. Once the die was cast, there would be no turning back. There was no thought for tomorrow. Only now.

Quinn felt a familiar tightening deep inside, and helplessly gave in to a tidal wave of ardor. In softly slurring French he muttered hoarsely, *"Je desire . . ."*

There was no need to go on. Mallory knew. Slowly she unbuttoned his shirt and slipped her hand beneath it to stroke his chest. All the while she never took her eyes from his, losing herself in the consuming indigo depths.

Eagerly he pulled her shapely softness into his arms and imprisoned her waiting lips with his. Her body was pliant, female, molding against his hard lines, returning as readily as he gave. Mallory knew without letting him finish the sentence that the invisible curtain between them had finally been lifted. It was time to taste the essence of each other.

Quinn's lips were at first savage, demanding. But as the kiss deepened, he lightened the pressure and began to thoroughly taste her with his tongue.

Mallory eased closer, welcoming the tightness of the embrace and straining to give him all she could. She didn't want to pull her mouth away, savoring the warmth of contact. When the kiss was broken she sought another and another until they were both weak from breathlessness.

Quinn's big hands opened against her bare back, following the natural contour of her spine. This time there was no hurry as he began a sensual exploration of her body. Curves, dips, hollows were lightly passed over with a promise of a more intimate search when her clothing no longer posed a barrier. Nothing mattered but the two of them, and Mallory gave herself to the total bliss of his caress.

Quinn unsnapped the single strap that held her dress. As the soft material fell to her belted waist, he caught her naked breasts in his warm hands and kissed each one tenderly. His earlier wish was granted as he squeezed them together and buried his face between them, inhaling the sweet fragrance that was uniquely Mallory.

She closed her eyes and leaned back slightly to accommodate him. His voice was deep, throaty, as he muttered erotic endearments in French. It mattered not that she didn't understand the words. His actions would ultimately make the intentions known. She would easily read them.

He slipped out of his shirt, and she marveled at the powerful lines of his well-developed torso. Her senses came alive as they absorbed the texture of his skin and the motion of knotted muscles moving beneath. Her touch outlined the hard curve of his shoulder, the sinewy ridges of his back and rib cage, the corded hardness of his flat belly. He was sleek and proportioned in a physical condition that was sublimely animal.

Mallory's hands were curious to know him in a more intimate way, but she waited until he stepped back and said, "I want to look at all of you."

Trembling from sheer arousal, she undressed. He did the same.

Nude, they stood apart as the soft glow of the fire threw shadows and light against their bodies.

Quinn looked like a magnificent savage, his skin like shimmering copper, his chest hair as black and rich as the thick mane that covered his head. With every inch ruggedly male, he stood primitive and arrogant. His dark eyes were alive, glowing like burning embers as he whispered in English, "This is maddening! Never in my wildest dreams did I envision how perfect you are without clothes."

"Only for you," she whispered back as she held out her arms in invitation.

The contact with his hot skin was like a brand that seared them together, as naked flesh touched naked flesh. Slowly they eased to their knees, kissing hungrily and pressing ever closer.

Quinn ran his tongue along the outside of her lips, making a trail down her throat and along the tops of her breasts. He slowly squeezed one and took a nipple between his lips. With tiny nibbles he made exquisite love to it, giving it life and commanding it to remain erect as he concentrated a similar ministration on the other.

As he suckled and tantalized, Mallory wet a finger with her tongue and traced the outline of his lips, making the act even more intimate.

There was no measure to compare to the delight she experienced in easing back and lying on the soft night grass with him. Quinn pressed his chest against hers, but left the bottom part of her body uncovered. Her skin was softer than he had imagined, and he played with the silky feel of her.

His hands made lazy, circular motions down her stomach, stopping at the pelvic rise and massaging slower, more deliberately. Her legs parted and his hand slipped between them, pressing the heated female flesh. With his mouth against her ear, a torrent of passionate French words tumbled out.

He stiffened slightly and sighed when she matched the caress, holding him in an intimate grasp. He wanted to take her then and there, but it was too soon, much too soon.

Quinn was a very experienced lover, making certain that no erotic stone lay unturned as he encouraged

Mallory's desires to develop as intensely as his. He would expect no less, since they were bound to perform a consummate act.

The loveplay went on for some time as they stroked and tickled, making the wanting between them grow to a tangible throb. Mallory had never experienced such an acute appreciation for a lover's intimate attentiveness. He tenderly fondled her as if she was a rare, valuable treasure. She came alive with his touch. For her, it was like the first time.

The man ardently charming her was much like the delta bayous he had sprung from, with secrets and promises dark and mysterious. Much of his fervency remained concealed beneath a placid facade, but inflamed he could no longer hide anything inside. Mallory read the seduction, coming to realize that his greatest secret was his hidden desire for her. The knowledge made her feel powerful.

The moment of union was nearing as Quinn positioned himself between Mallory's knees. He looked deeply into her eyes, as if asking one last time that she was certain she wanted him. The answer was clear when an emerald fire reached out and entrapped him in a silken, sensuous stare. Her expression matched the love-drugged look that the flames had evoked earlier.

He eased over her as she closed her eyes in anticipation of the thrill of finally knowing him. Still he seemed hesitant, with hips hovering above hers. She felt compelled to reach up and press him downward, guiding him into the ultimate pleasure as she arched lovingly against him.

They joined upon the silent grass, expanding the precious moment for as long as they could. Without warning, the loving burst into an inferno as his hot French blood raised hers to fever pitch. They came together and melded, following the rhythm of their hearts.

Apart and together, up and down, the sexual exchange continued. The sinuous movements of their silhouettes were outlined by the fire that continued to burn hotly in the distance. It was forgotten and could no longer claim Quinn's courtship.

As they gently rolled across the cool turf, Mallory felt as she had in her dream. She gave totally and received totally as Quinn unfolded her fantasies with his potent virility.

She knew she wasn't dreaming when the act hinted at fulfillment. Quinn's time was nearing too, because the wild play slowed, replaced by an ever-increasing tempo.

Propped on his elbows, Quinn looked down at her. "Open your eyes and watch me love you, Mallory."

As the first waves of satisfaction washed over her, she tried to focus on the inky black of his hypnotic stare. He moved above her, and his image wavered and fluttered before her eyes. She moaned in ecstasy when he urged her to pay the supreme compliment to his masculinity.

At the same time, he reached his climax. She felt him shudder inside her. He groaned, arching with the flow of the feeling.

Breathlessly he repeated, "*Mon cher,* my sweet, *mon cher,*" before collapsing limply in her arms.

They held each other for a long while. For Mallory, the intimacy represented a tangible step up to a new plateau in her womanhood. She sighed, knowing total contentment for the first time. Could Quinn be the elusive goal that had always stayed just out of arm's reach? She laughed as the good feelings overtook her. Quinn rolled on his side, his face a puzzle as he wondered what had brought it on.

"I'm sorry," she said between gulps of air. "I feel so marvelous right now! You make me happier than I've ever been, Quinn Chennault."

"That's one of the nicest things you've ever said to me." He chuckled too. "Never have I had a woman laugh after I've made love to her. Of course, I'm finding out that you're not like other women."

"Don't you think it's time?" The laughter was now a self-satisfied smile.

"You didn't mind laying with me on a bed of grass?" he teased while he played with one of her nipples.

"I'd lay with you anywhere," she whispered. "Any time." She reached out and stroked his face, feeling wonder that such a dauntless man could want her so much and hide it so well. "A penny for your thoughts."

"I'm starving," he said matter-of-factly. "We haven't had dinner yet."

"Shame on us." She sat up and stretched, looking out toward the fire one last time. "I guess I shouldn't have dragged you away like this."

He stood and helped her. "It took two of us, in case you didn't notice. I did my fair share of dragging too."

"Well it's time to take you back to town and feed you," she said crisply as she dressed.

"We're going back to your motel. I don't want to share you with anything or anyone else just yet," he said slowly.

"Then we better get some food, because I have the feeling this is going to be a long night. I want to be alone with you too."

They drove back to the motel, talking the entire time. On the way they picked up a jar of olives, a six-pack of beer, and two grilled steaks. Mallory cubed the food and skewered it with toothpicks while Quinn made a picnic area on the bed.

They sat cross-legged with the plates and beverages between them, enjoying the meal and the comfortable atmosphere.

When it was finished and the plates were neatly stacked on a nightstand, they stretched out side by side on the bed. Quinn was no longer the withdrawn stranger she had encountered earlier in the evening. He was open and amiable, as he had been the day before.

"I don't know when I've enjoyed an evening more." He sighed contentedly. "Good food, good beer, a good woman. Who could ask for more?"

She accepted the compliment with a slight nod. "I could."

He raised a brow. "You mean I'm going to have to show you again what it means to know a man like me?"

"Only after you tell me something."

"Anything you want to know." He lay back and put an arm around her shoulders, drawing her with him.

His shirt was open, and as she rested against his strong chest, she stroked the short, curly hairs. "Every time you spoke to me when we made love, you said the words in French. They sounded beautiful, and I want to know what you said."

He chuckled softly. "I think you already do."

"I mean it, Quinn. Tell me?"

"When I touched you, I said it was like stroking velvet. I've never seen breasts so white and perfect, or hair so blond before. You're quite a woman, Mallory."

"That's lovely," she whispered, reaching up to kiss his cheek. He turned and met her lips with his instead.

"When I was inside you, it was as if I ceased to be. I've never made that kind of love before to any woman," he whispered thickly against her mouth. The words had an arousing effect, and he kissed her deeply. "Do you need to know anything else?"

"Yes," she said. "Show me again?"

Chapter Eight

The next morning dawned bright as a shaft of sunlight awakened Mallory. Nude, she lay stretched beneath the sheets and leisurely turned to Quinn's side of the bed. Even in slumber her smile was content, her body satiated with the total satisfaction of having been loved and appeased beyond her wildest expectations.

She reached out and found the other half of the bed empty. It didn't matter. Although Quinn's physical presence was no longer there, his essence remained. She cuddled the pillow and smelled the alluring scent of him that still lingered.

Briefly she recalled the beauty of their glorious night together. Never had she felt so vibrant, so exhilarated as when Quinn showed her what it was to make passionate love to a man who appreciated everything she had to offer. Every shapely inch experienced the tenderness of his touch, the warmth of his lips.

Opening her eyes, Mallory turned on her side and

stretched again. She didn't know she could be so happy, and she thought about the sequence of events that had led to the intimacy with Quinn.

Over the last four years she had purposely stayed as far away as she could from New Orleans and Wild Wells Limited. Brad's accident was the perfect excuse to return to Louisiana. Hadn't she openly admitted to Quinn that she was there for herself, not exclusively for her brother? But had she also come back for Quinn as well?

Searching her mind, she recalled the reactions his appearance had evoked on the morning she encountered him in the hospital corridor. The physical attraction was overwhelming, but she hadn't once considered going to bed with him. Or had she?

Maybe she had wanted to make love with him all along, but after the episode on her eighteenth birthday, she knew it would do no good to pursue Quinn. He had let her know that the feeling wasn't mutual.

Had her secret desire for Quinn been the reason for Cam to enter the picture the first time? she wondered.

Although the brothers looked nothing alike physically, she recognized a subliminal similarity only the night before when the glow of the flames had cast a shadow on Cam's face. For a brief second he had looked like a younger version of Quinn.

Perhaps her infatuation four years ago had been really little more than a suppressed yearning for the older Chennault brother, not the younger one. Subconsciously Mallory had pushed in Quinn's direction all along, even in her dreams. Acknowledging such a truth took her breath away.

She decided it unwise to ponder the past, or the future for that matter. There was no reason to consider a serious involvement with Quinn. It was understood that he would be gone this morning because of an early call to cap the Judson well. He had also stressed more than once that he wasn't the type to settle into any kind of a lasting arrangement. Whatever went on between them must be strictly for the moment.

They agreed to follow the motto of fire fighters: live only for today and take what you will. It suited Mallory because the life she chose took her in a different direction from Quinn's. Where there were no ties, there could be no pain.

She sat up on the side of the bed and was satisfied with the realistic attitude. It was the easiest way for everyone involved. No repercussions or recriminations if things went sour, only the pure enjoyment of being alone together.

As Mallory finished brushing her teeth, an explosion rocked the motel. She knew without a doubt that it came from the Judson Field, and she rushed to her suitcase and pulled out some clothes.

Slipping into her jeans and a blouse, she ran outside and scanned the horizon. The crew had missed again, as evidenced by a roaring blaze that blackened a portion of the sky.

"Damn!" she swore softly. She hoped they'd be finished once and for all today, but from the looks of things Quinn was still having terrible luck.

She went back into the motel room and looked at her briefcase. There were calls and contacts to make, but she just wasn't in the mood. She couldn't concentrate on anything but Quinn and the fire. She had to return to the site and see if the men could quell the blaze once and for all. Calls to oil companies could wait until later.

She took her time getting to the site. As she walked toward the safety zone, she saw Quinn standing at its perimeter and shaking his head in defeat. He looked tired and exasperated. Dressed in silver asbestos suits, he and Cam put their heads together and tried to work out another strategy.

Mallory stayed a safe distance away but knew instinctively that they were arguing. She couldn't hear the words, but the tone was enough to convince her that it was serious.

When the brothers finished talking, Quinn turned to see Mallory waiting for him. She flashed a big smile and approached him.

"Nothing can be so bad that it has to wear you down like this, can it?" she said brightly.

He raised a brow. "You'd be surprised. I thought I told you last night that we have rules about women coming around sites?"

"You did. But in case you forgot, I'm not like other women. I'm not afraid. And this morning I feel strong enough to face anything." She was still riding on the euphoria of their stolen night together.

Quinn, on the other hand, seemed uncharacteristically irritable as he snapped, "You'd better damn well be scared, Mallory. Fear is what keeps us on our toes and makes us careful in most situations. When you stop fearing, you have serious accidents like Brad did."

"Touchy, touchy, Quinn," she said cajolingly. "Have you forgotten so soon that my name is Steiner? Surely that has to count for something."

"Yeah," he growled. "Stupidity."

Until that moment Mallory had accepted the flippant remarks, but her good humor suddenly wore thin. She didn't know the hows or whys of Quinn's moods, but he had no right or reason to talk to her that way.

"The stunts that Brad Steiner pulls are his business," she snapped back angrily. "You should never compare me to him. It's not fair."

"Isn't it?" he returned sharply. "Just because your name is Steiner doesn't mean you have carte blanche to traipse around any field you like. Especially this one. I'm at work with serious business, and I don't need any distractions."

"I'm not allowed to stand back as a spectator?" she

demanded. Extending an arm to encompass the area, she finished, "It's alright for every television camera and all the glory guys to swarm around. But not me. Put me back somewhere until you push a button, right? I'm not a groupie, Quinn. Somehow I thought maybe you'd welcome me this morning, not shun me."

During it all, Cam had stood aside and watched without comment. Quinn gave Mallory an apologetic glance. Before answering, he took her by the arm and led her away so they could talk privately.

When they were out of earshot he tried to explain, "Look, it's been a tough day, and I don't know how many more tries I'll have to give it before throwing in the towel and quitting this impossible site. Your brother is badgering me like crazy, Cam doesn't want to do as he's told, and I'm so damned tired I can't see straight."

"I'm only responsible for one aspect of your problem, not all three." She looked up at him defiantly. "There's something deflating about spending the night with a man and having him treat me like this the next day. I had hoped the good feelings would go with you when you left this morning, but I guess they didn't."

"I'm sorry, *mon cher.* I shouldn't be snapping at you. Of course I haven't forgotten last night and what happened between us." He took her hand and squeezed it. "You're the last person I should be griping at. It's just that I'm under a strain right now. I lose my temper every time we miss capping a fire."

"Then give it up," she urged. "Closing down this one well won't break Brad. It's not worth what you're going through."

"Can't do it." He grinned slightly. "I'm superstitious. I have a score to settle with fate. If I don't win this one, I'll worry about Brad on every future job."

She didn't understand his logic, but then she never could. "What do you intend to do?"

"I'm going to give it one more good try for today.

The nitro is packed and ready. Whether we win or not, I'll close down the whole operation until I can figure something out. In the meantime, there was some bad weather at the other end of the state last night and lightning cracked a well head. Sparks have been flying since early this morning and the owners are getting pretty itchy. I have to take a chopper out to check for the possibility of another fire."

"If you really want to make it up to me about a while ago, take me with you."

"I can't, Mallory. You know the rules—"

"Forget the rules. I want to go. I'll keep a discreet distance, and I promise not to open my mouth if you let me tag along. You won't even know I'm there."

"No," he said emphatically. "You've gotten your way too much already. As it is, you're lucky I'm letting you stay here. Now get behind the fence so I can go back to work." His words sounded harsh, but his expression had softened considerably.

"I'm not taking no for an answer, Chennault," she said over a shoulder, and smiled as she walked away.

"We'll see about that, Steiner!" he called back as he put on his helmet and returned to the danger zone.

One way or the other, Mallory intended to be on that chopper. She'd figure a way to talk Quinn into it. But for now he had to concentrate on taking care of this fire.

There was a difference in the influence of today's blaze as Mallory studied it from a safe distance. It was still just as threatening and wayward, but against the blueness of the morning sky it didn't appear as massive or as bold as it had in the darkness.

A tenacious enthusiasm still filled her inside. She looked at Quinn, and it intensified when she thought about the hot passions that had flowed between them only hours ago. Exactly what was Quinn's allure? she asked herself. Did he represent a supreme challenge?

Perhaps she was the current challenge for him? Why did they want each other? She desired him as she had no other; did he feel the same?

Mallory didn't contemplate the answers to the questions. It was enough to know that sweet desire pumped through her veins, making her more aware of her sexuality than ever before.

She watched as Quinn went through the ritual of fire fighting once again. As hoses sprayed him from all directions, he loaded the nitroglycerin into a large drum attached to a crane. With the thumbs-up signal, the driver slowly backed the drum into the heart of the blaze. All the workers took cover. When the drum was positioned just right, the driver hopped out of the bulldozer and ran behind another piece of machinery. Cam nodded and Quinn pushed down a detonator that was guide-wired to the nitroglycerin.

The explosion was deafening. Mallory winced and covered her ears.

For a long second there was total silence at the site. The team began backing the new control head into place as Cam and Quinn armed themselves with brass tools. Regular metal couldn't be used, because any spark could set the blaze off again.

Oil shot from the dead hole, gushing upward and spraying everything within a twenty-foot radius. Quinn guided a crane into lowering the control head as he and Cam fought the spewing liquid. Giant bolts were pushed into the special lip that covered the casing, and the two worked frantically to tighten the new well head.

During the procedure, the well continued to rumble and groan, protesting the fact that it had to once again submit to a rigid control. When the last bolt was tightened, Cam reached up and turned the huge steering wheel that shut off the flow completely. The well was capped and the fire was finally dead. The area was as silent as a tomb.

Crews and spectators filled the air with boisterous cheers. The Chennault brothers were the heroes of the day. This was one of the toughest fires they had ever encountered. There was tremendous relief in seeing it finally over.

Mallory filled with pride as she watched Quinn saunter away from the well. Some television people were nearby and stopped him long enough to ask a few questions.

He obliged, and as he looked out at the audience he spotted Mallory. His smile was slow, meaningful, meant only for her. It hinted at a secret knowledge they had discovered mutually only the night before. The look warmed her.

When asked about the reasons for his failure to kill the blaze during the previous tries, Quinn explained that he was working one man short. His timing was off because of it. A few words were spoken about Brad, and then he cheerfully concluded the interview and continued alone toward the trailer.

It appeared as if he was going to ignore Mallory. As she stood waiting by the fence, he turned and gave her a look that promised more than a congratulatory hug. It would have to wait until they were alone, but she didn't mind.

As he approached her, he took off the oil-slicked asbestos suit and dropped it to the ground. Beneath it he wore jeans and a tee shirt. With an arm around her shoulders, he led her to the trailer.

"What would you say if a hungry fellow asked you to cook some breakfast for him?"

"I'd say fine." She saw a twinkle in his eyes. "I was in such a hurry to get here that I completely forgot my own breakfast."

"Then let's go inside so you can see about taking care of me, shall we?"

The trailer was small and cramped, serving as both

an office and an on-site residence for Quinn. A desk filled up part of the living room. Graphs and paperwork were scattered all over the floor.

"There's something to be said for your housekeeping," Mallory remarked lightly as he made a point of locking the door behind them. "I just don't know what it is."

"This place definitely needs a woman's touch," he said. "So do I. Come here."

She went into his arms, and they kissed hungrily. Only a few hours had passed since their last intimacy, but it felt more like months.

Mallory sighed. "I hated waking up alone today. It made me think that maybe last night was just a lovely fantasy."

"Everything was real, believe me. It was all I could do to leave you this morning," he answered softly in her ear. "You're beautiful when you sleep, but I'm not the type of man who can afford to hang around for long. I told you that last night."

"I remember. And I'm not complaining. There's no law that says we can't want more of each other today, is there?"

"No." He smiled and kissed her again, molding her against him.

Mallory felt secure in Quinn's arms, as if she'd always had the sanctuary of his embrace. A tingle passed through her as she remembered the naked feel of him the night before, and the ecstasy of finally knowing what made him so masculine, so desirable.

"I have to take a shower." He nuzzled the words against her neck.

"And I have to fix breakfast," she answered as they kissed again. His hands slowly traveled her body, stopping at the rounded swell of her breasts before gliding lower to her waist and hips. "We'll never get anything accomplished at this rate."

Reluctantly he released her. "You're right. To be continued later?"

She nodded and turned toward the refrigerator in search of eggs, bacon, anything they could use for breakfast. Quinn went to the back of the trailer. She heard the water run as he turned on the shower.

Mallory searched the cabinets for pots and pans, but it proved fruitless. When she couldn't find anything, she called out to Quinn. He couldn't hear above the noise, so she went into the bathroom and called out again. "I said where do you keep your skillets?"

He opened the curtain slightly, his voice innocent. "In here."

She rolled her eyes in pretended exasperation. "I'm serious. How do you expect to have eggs and bacon if I don't have anything to cook them in?"

"Right now I don't. This isn't the time to think about food." He opened the curtain wider and showed her his reason for wanting company in the shower. "Come on in. The water's fine."

"Have you noticed that we can never have a meal before making love?" She tried to play hard to get.

"I don't see either of us starving because of it, do you? Come and wash me, woman."

The request bordered on a dare. Mallory kept her eyes on Quinn's face as she slowly unbuttoned her shirt. With painstaking movements she did a striptease, reading his arousal in his dark gaze. When she was totally undressed, she said, "Is this what you wanted?"

He opened the curtain wider, inviting her to share the warm spray of the shower. "Partly."

She climbed into the tub and stood behind him as he shielded her from the spray. Turning, he pulled her into his wet embrace, found her mouth, and kissed it. His touch was slippery against the dryness of her skin.

When the kiss was broken, Mallory picked up the soap and worked a rich lather in her hands. She began washing the thick column of Quinn's neck, working in circular motions and covering him with frothy bubbles. She reached up to do the tops of his shoulders, and noted how the muscles felt knotted and hard beneath her rubbing. His skin was darkly tanned against the whiteness of the soap, the hair shiny and black as it curled across his broad chest.

It was easy to lose herself in the pleasurable entertainment of fondling Quinn. She soaped farther down, following the corded sinew of his flat belly and the trail of hair that led even lower. He stood still and proud like a stallion, every inch of him unquestionably male. When she looked into his eyes, she saw them clouded with undisguised desire.

"Now for my own enjoyment." He took the soap and began similar ministrations. He started with her neck, going down slowly as he cupped the undersides of her breasts and thoroughly aroused the nipples with moist fingertips. Her stomach quivered slightly as his experienced touch traveled over it. He raised a brow in delight. She wasn't the only one who could tenderly torment.

With a generous motion, his soapy hands massaged her rounded hips and traveled up her spine. He edged closer, putting his arms around her. With hands gliding up and down her back, he kissed her softly, licking away the fine mist that covered her lips. His soapy quest eased to the blond triangle between her thighs, and she became slightly limp in his arms, accommodating him.

Quinn pulled her into the warm spray to rinse off. Mallory watched as the water traveled in small rivulets around him. He towered over her, his body magnificent, powerful, masculine. How had she existed so long without really knowing him?

When the spray from the shower started to cool, Mallory said, "I think we've managed to use up all the hot water. It's time to get out."

"Maybe so," he agreed, "but it's not time to stop."

He stepped out of the tub first and offered a hand to help her. When they both stood on a bath mat, Quinn bent down and licked the water from Mallory's breasts. She swayed slightly and clutched at his slick arms.

When he finished, she did the same, tasting the cool moisture that collected around his nipples. The play was simple, but so seductive that neither of them could wait much longer.

Quinn picked her up as she protested, "But we haven't dried off yet . . . !"

"Don't worry about it," he growled softly, and carried her to the bedroom.

Gently he settled her on the bed and lay next to her, fondling a soft breast as he nibbled on the sensitive column of her neck. She snuggled into his damp embrace, feeling the wetness of her body ply with his.

Passion settled in quickly, carrying them away from reality and bringing them into a secret world, a place where no one else could go. When Mallory was alone with Quinn, everything and everyone ceased to exist. It was only the two of them, and time lay suspended as she waited for the rapture that only he could initiate.

Following the line of her voluptuous figure, his hands eased across her flesh and stopped to rest at the base of her spine. Groaning, he rubbed tightly against her in slow, feline movements. The gesture served to heighten a flow of warmth between them. Mallory automatically matched his ardor with movements of her own.

"*Mon cher,*" he whispered hoarsely. "So willful, so wild and independent. I had expected the wine to turn to vinegar, but it's pure nectar, is it not?"

Opening her palms, she smoothed them across his broad back, feeling the muscles ripple. It made a thrill travel up her arms and throughout her body. "Only for the man I allow to taste it."

He kissed her again before rising up and kneeling over her. As Mallory lay beneath him, she kept moaning softly, drinking in the little pleasures and wanting more. "Please hold me close to you, Quinn?"

He stretched out next to her again as she became pliant beneath his curious fingers.

"I desire you more now than I did the first time," she admitted in a small voice.

"Then I've definitely done something right." His smile was soft, tender. "Our time together will be all the sweeter because I spent the morning thinking about the things I intended to do with you once I had you in my bed again." Quinn shifted, bridging his body over hers once more. He held her prisoner with his knees and enticingly followed her form with his lips.

His tongue moistened every curve, making a wet circle of her navel as he slowed perceptibly. When he dared to become even more intimate with her, she gasped, "You're going to make me crazy if you do that."

Burying his face against the softness of her thighs, he said, "Then you'll know what I've been going through."

She bent a knee and allowed him to complete the journey, dizzy and near fainting from the impact of his tender assault in so intimate a place. The soft wet strokes aroused her further, and she moved against them, gyrating in a flame that had burned steadily since the evening before.

He had called her a golden temptress who brazenly did everything she could to turn his blood hot for her. She saw him in the same way, realizing that she should have taken more care in treading the perimeter of his powerfully dangerous attraction.

Since their last time together, Quinn had come to know Mallory even better than she knew herself. He was putting that knowledge into maddening practice. Unabashedly she sought to mold herself closer to the tantalizing actions. The sweet desire that was satiated when Mallory awoke that morning was again growing into a tangible need. It was a need that was almost frightening in its intensity, like the conflagration Quinn had fought. Was that why he had seemed at first reluctant to give in to an intimacy with her?

"I don't know if I'll ever get enough of you," she panted softly.

"Then I'll see what I can do about it." He moved back up her body. His expression was amused as he looked down into her passion-glazed eyes.

"You're spoiling me with pleasure, and we both know it."

They kissed again, and she arched against him, nipping at his shoulders and kissing the fresh-scrubbed taste of his flesh. It became more than just a physical act for Mallory, but she didn't have the concentration to think about it yet. All she knew was that Quinn made her burn, made her aware of the fiery needs that lived inside.

Quinn eased his hips away and casually pushed a leg between hers. He fondled her for a time, knowing it served to make her want him all the more. That was when Mallory decided it fitting to let her deeds speak in return.

Guiding him backward and making him lie on the bed, she stretched on top of him and placed a soft kiss on his mouth. Slowly she rubbed against him, lowering her lips to his neck and outlining the protuberance of his jaw with fanning lashes.

"So now you're going to tease me, huh?" His voice reflected acceptance, but he couldn't pass up a chance to tease her as well.

"You've made it a point to show me just how much a man can do," she said throatily, "so it's about time you see for yourself that a woman can wield the same power when she puts her mind to it."

She practiced the wiles of womanhood, using her hands to graze the sleek lines of a body she was coming to know very well. With a feeling of superiority she stroked and taunted his manhood, thrilling him like the vamp she wanted to be. She wished to become everything beautiful to him, everything desirable. Unabashed, Mallory sought to unleash the wild, primitive libido that lay beneath the surface of Quinn's disciplined demeanor.

She had surmised that his true reason for ambivalence was that he had to constantly keep strong desires in check, desires that could totally overtake him if he allowed them to. She wanted to see if she had the power to override Quinn's will and call them herself.

He began to tremble beneath the feathery softness of her fingers. When she brazenly held him in her grasp, his sensuality jumped to full flame.

In seconds she was folded tightly into his arms and quickly flipped beneath him. She didn't succeed in replacing his will with her own, in spite of the merciless loveplay.

Breathless, he looked down at the glittering jade in her eyes. "Either I taught you too well last night, or I underestimated the effect you have on me. Let's see how well you hold up to the same torture."

"You already know I can't," she said thickly.

"Ah, but what I've demanded so far isn't enough to please me, *mon cher.*" With that he began to murmur in French. He gathered her close and buried his face in her neck. The words were beautiful, rhythmic, and the passionate tones caressed Mallory's ears.

As his lips raked a pleasurable path from her neck to her breast, his hand made another journey down the pale flatness of her stomach. It moved along the silkiness of her inside thigh, and parted her knees. She quivered with anticipation as his probing fingers gently opened her legs farther. He readied her to accept him.

For Mallory, making love with Quinn was no longer just play. She went far beyond mere arousal and satisfaction. It was a prelude to a joining that began to transcend the physical, with the depth of emotion working its way into her heart.

She arched slightly, responding as a deep reaction controlled her. Her breathing quickened as he relentlessly continued, sandwiching the outward side of her thigh between his.

"If only for the moment, you're completely mine, *mon cher,*" he whispered fiercely. "I intend to take everything that belongs to me."

Mallory couldn't answer; her breath became ragged, almost panting as she was only aware of responding to the male in Quinn. Reason ceased to exist when she gave in to the whirling heights of excitement.

Easing on top of her, Quinn clasped her buttocks with both hands, preparing her with further suggestive movements.

The second of ultimate union occurred like the explosion she had witnessed that morning, pulling them into a scorching void with something akin to a centrifugal force.

The lovemaking was now more expert, tailored to their physical needs as they moved together. Looping her arms inside his, she gripped his shoulders and gyrated rhythmically with him, feeding her flame with a vigor that matched his.

Mallory was the first to experience satisfaction, and as wave after wave of sexual elation gripped her, she felt Quinn's pace accommodate her movements.

Catching her breath, she relaxed slightly as he worked to achieve the same satisfaction. She could tell it wouldn't be long. As he loved her totally, she said, "Now it's your turn to belong only to me."

He shuddered with release. She worked her hips, coaxing a complete response from him. They clutched each other, trying to bring their bodies as close together as possible. Then their breathing slowed, and their caresses grew more relaxed and tender.

Quinn rolled on his side. As Mallory embraced him, he said, "What, no laughing this time?"

Her expression was tender. "Every part of me is smiling. Can't you see it?"

He nodded. "That and more, *mon cher*. I hadn't planned for it to happen between us this morning."

"That makes it better, don't you think?"

"Definitely." He glanced at a bedside clock. "It's still early. If you have no place else to go for the next couple of hours, I need to get a little shut-eye."

"My time is yours. Wouldn't you like something to eat before taking a nap?" She could tell he was tired because traces of dark smudging showed beneath his eyes.

"Later." He kissed her nose. "Just lie here with me and let's rest."

As he put an arm over his eyes and relaxed for slumber, Mallory said, "Quinn?"

"Hmmmm?"

"Take me with you this afternoon when you go to check out the new site?" She turned on her side and put her chin against his shoulder. Her eyes were imploring as she waited for him to look at her.

He raised his arm slightly and cocked an eye her way. "I already told you it's out of the question. This is business, and you have no place there."

"I wouldn't be going just for the fun of it. Look at it from a professional angle. It would be a chance to meet a new supplier of crude. You did say you were meeting the owners of the field, didn't you?"

He sighed. "That I did."

"Then you'd be doing me a favor by helping my brokerage business. If I don't go with you today, I'll have to find some other way to meet them on my own."

"Maybe that would be the best arrangement for both of us." He put his arm back over his eyes.

"But you've already collected on a favor you never even granted." She pouted. "I may have thought lots of things about you, but I never thought you'd renege on your word."

He swore very softly. "Dammit, woman, you were probably planning this . . . blackmail the whole time I made love to you." He looked at her with both eyes uncovered. Her expression was blank. "You're not going to let me rest until I say yes, are you?"

She smiled. "You've got the picture."

"Then by all means come with me, and I'll do my best to introduce you to all the right people. I wouldn't want to be thought of as a liar or an Indian giver."

Grateful, she kissed him hard on the lips. "You've just restored my faith in the promises of mankind."

"And you've just reinforced my suspicions about womankind," he muttered with a chuckle. "Now keep quiet and let me go to sleep?"

Mallory was thrilled to be sitting in the glass bubble of Quinn's helicopter as she accompanied him to the new site. He piloted the aircraft himself. She admired the smooth way he handled the mechanical bird, better than the professional pilot who had flown her into Baton Rouge.

As they flew toward the Texas border, Mallory made conversation. "Until now I wondered very little about the hows and whys of your job. Tell me how you go about setting up for new fires?"

"It's relatively simple." He adjusted his headphones with one hand and kept the other on the throttle. "Our New Orleans base is responsible for filtering calls worldwide, choosing those that we can accommodate the quickest."

"How is that accomplished?"

"First we get the name of the company in trouble. Then we find out if it's a gas, oil, or steam fire. After that we plot locations, whether it's within the continental United States or overseas. We maintain files on equipment manufactured all over the world and rely on maps to keep us in touch with the nearest base for supplying dozers."

"Why not supply your own?"

"Because it's too costly and time-consuming. The longer a fire burns, the more risky conditions become. We also have to take the water supply into consideration. It has to be checked and rechecked. Until all vital information is supplied, we don't make a move."

"What happens if you can't find a factory close enough, or the water isn't sufficient?"

"Then we can't do it. There's enough risk as it is with favorable conditions. A man would have to be a fool to go into it without all the plusses on his side."

"I see. And if it's a good site, you jet yourselves there, right?"

"That's right. Once we arrive, it's all ours. Brad and I take over completely. It's done our way or not at all." He reached for a cigarette but decided he didn't want it.

They knew that they were nearing the site when they saw a forbidding beacon of black smoke curled high into the air, marring the perfect blueness of the afternoon sky. From the aerial vantage point Mallory could tell that this fire was infinitely more vicious, somehow wilder than the one Quinn had recently quelled. The demon was greedier, reaching in every direction for something to slake its voracious appetite.

She studied Quinn's expression as he took a microphone in hand and announced, "Breaker five nine, this is the Cajun flying Wild Wells Three. Anyone down there?"

There was a click and a voice answered, "Yeah, we're here. She's starting to look bad. We're sure glad to know you could get here so soon."

"I'm going to take the chopper around and give her a good going-over before putting down. Come back." He clicked the mike.

"That sounds great. See you then." The radio clicked off.

As they slowly circled the fire, taking care to keep a safe distance from the treacherous smoke, Quinn surveyed the situation through the transparent bubble of the chopper. Mallory had no idea what he was thinking. His expression was guarded, cold, totally professional. It wasn't a time to ask questions.

Once on the ground, she followed him to an on-site shack where the owners waited. After introductions were made, the men answered Quinn's questions, discussing the difficult aspects of the blaze.

Mallory looked out at the fire. They were a good two hundred yards away, but the noise and heat were crippling. She knew this situation was definitely going to be different.

When the owners started to argue with Quinn, she turned and listened.

". . . and you'd do well to bring in a crew to cap it with a relief mold," Quinn was saying. "My men won't touch it."

"But you have to help us!" One of the men replied.

"I'm helping by giving sound, experienced advice. That fire has cratered. No one in his right mind would try to take it on." He was staunch in the refusal.

"We just spent sixteen million dollars on that hole, Cajun, and we aim to see it pumping again. Just name your figure."

"No amount of money will do. You'll have to find yourself another boy."

"If Steiner could get around, he'd take it on!"

A muscle twitched on the side of his jaw, a sure sign that Quinn was beginning to anger. "It's my ballgame this time, not his. I won't risk the lives of my crew for it."

He took Mallory by the arm and together they walked back toward the helicopter. The owners followed them, pleading with Quinn to reconsider.

Finally he turned and said flatly, "I told you no, and I meant it. Human lives are more important than a few million bucks' worth of oil. This hot little baby won't go down without taking a couple of men with her. Sorry I couldn't do more for you fellows. Good luck in finding a fool who'll take it on."

With that he opened the door to the cockpit and helped Mallory inside. She wasn't granted the opportunity to speak with the businessmen on her own behalf. But with the situation so tense, it would have been a futile attempt. There would be a more relaxed, opportune time in the future.

Once the blades were rotating and they were airborne again, she ventured a remark. "I understood what happened a few minutes ago, but I'd appreciate a further explanation."

Quinn shrugged away the shield of anger. "When that particular well blew, all of the casing and protective housing was either broken off at ground level or cracked so deeply that it burned away. It's called cratering. Our business is to cap wells and keep them pumping, not to play with trying to replace faulty casing. They can dynamite it from the air and put a relief mold over the hole to contain the pressure. Production from that well will be totally nil, and their money will go up in smoke, but that's not my problem."

"Even I noticed a marked difference between this fire and the last one, and I'm just a novice. They didn't like your advice one bit."

"No one does when they see us walk away from a fire. The reason my hide has lasted this long is that I have enough sense to know what I can and can't do." They circled the fire once more and he gestured toward it with a jerk of his head. "It would be suicide to go into something like that."

"Those men questioned your judgment. Would Brad have turned them down like you just did?" Her curiosity got the better of her.

He flicked a sharp look her way. "At this stage of the game I'm inclined to say no. He would've wanted to take a shot at it."

"But why?"

"Lately he seems to be courting danger, thinking he has something to prove, I suppose. The more treacherous the circumstances, the better he likes it. I like a challenge myself, but I'm not crazy. Walking away from a fire has been the source of more than one argument between us."

Mallory considered his words and remembered what Elissa had said about Quinn being the more levelheaded of the two.

At the same time she couldn't totally fault Brad. The trait of derring-do ran in the family. She couldn't blame Brad for trying to live every second to the fullest, because she found herself wanting that with Quinn.

All things considered, she couldn't help but admire the deliberate mind, the calculating restraint that Quinn displayed. He was much stronger than Brad in every way, and he was the only man who could control Brad when the occasion called for it. Her regard for him intensified. Unlike the childhood feelings of awe she once had for her brother's power, she felt appreciative of Quinn's strength and thought herself lucky to be the woman sitting by his side.

There was little more said as Quinn concentrated on flying. Mallory sensed the beginnings of another withdrawal, but it didn't immediately bother her. Quinn was a very complex man, and it would take a little time to figure him out.

Earlier, before the departure, Quinn had followed her to the motel so she could change and leave her car. Now that they were landed at the heliport, she fully expected him to take her back to the trailer for another night of love. She was slowly learning how to keep him open and responsive; all they needed was time alone.

Mallory didn't say anything until Quinn took a turn

toward the motel instead of heading for the old site. Her expectancy turned into a well-hidden chagrin.

When Quinn pulled up to her door, she gave him a seductive look. "I've enjoyed the day, especially our shower this morning." She moved closer and put her arms around his neck, seeking his lips.

He obliged and kissed her deeply. When it was finished he said softly, "I have some loose ends to wrap up, and you're proving to be a distraction again."

"I hope so." She smiled. "Is it going to be my place tonight or yours?"

He shook his head. "Neither. I have some late business to take care of. I'll have to say goodnight now, Mallory."

She stayed in his arms, trying to coax him into taking her home with him. "You know, you still haven't shown me where you keep your skillets."

His brow arched slightly as he unwound her arms from around his neck. Gently he pulled her out of the car with him. "You got your way twice today, first by staying and watching the fire, and secondly by accompanying me to the new site. I wouldn't want to spoil you by letting you have your head too much."

He wasn't going to budge, and she knew it. The question was, why didn't he want her?

She accepted his flimsy explanation and walked to her door alone, pretending it didn't matter. "I've neglected my own business today, too. I'll probably spend part of the night making calls anyway. I'll see you around."

As Quinn drove along the highway, he thought about the last few days. Lovemaking had been on his mind all afternoon, and it was time to do some serious thinking about what was happening between him and Mallory.

He had never desired a woman more intensely than her. But he was having second thoughts about giving in and sleeping with her. She was so beautiful, so alluring, that his feelings threatened to go rampant from wanting. It was getting too easy to expect her to come to his bed. And he liked the feel of her in his arms as they slept. She was making it damn hard for him to back off each time she offered.

He should have been stronger and insisted that they not get involved. Why? Because everything he was, everything he had, was suddenly at stake. He honestly didn't know if any woman was worth that kind of risk, especially Mallory. He knew her better than anyone, and she could be a firebrand when she put her mind to it.

The initial agreement was to indulge only for the moment. Because of their tempestuous natures, the relationship could turn into a contest of wills, veering them toward a more dangerous collision course than Mallory and Cam had ridden four years ago. The stakes were dangerously higher, too, and he had the most to lose.

The entanglement was gaining momentum faster than he liked, and it was time to thoroughly examine his feelings.

As he clenched the steering wheel, a realization of the situation hit him full force. He sternly reprimanded himself for such uncharacteristic naiveté. "What the hell am I doing? This is Brad's sister I'm fooling around with, not some little gal I can leave at a roadside bar. I've been holding a loaded gun to my head each time I touch her. I have to be crazy to even think it would work!"

There was only one clear alternative. Quinn was relieved to know that the decision to stop had taken care of itself when he dropped Mallory off at her motel.

Chapter Nine

It was the afternoon of the following day. Mallory was aboard a plane taking off from Baytown, Texas, where she had witnessed a connection and collected a hefty commission on her current deal.

The business arrangement for the Texas locale was made via telephone the night before, following Quinn's hasty departure and her sudden need to put some distance and time between them.

So much was happening so fast. Although Mallory reveled in the sensuous whirlwind with Quinn, his turndown was a favor in disguise. She needed time to take stock of the situation and analyze what she felt. The flight gave her that time.

On her way back to Louisiana, she came to quite a few interesting conclusions about Quinn. She should have verbalized more when sensing his periods of withdrawal. She didn't like the way he could conveniently shut her out, but she never once assumed the responsibility of keeping the channels open by making him talk to her. Instead, she used sex to maneuver her way into his affections. The trouble was, the minute they concluded making love, he'd withdraw again.

As she stared out the window, she found herself missing Quinn. She was still slightly miffed at the way he had brushed her off the night before. It should not have come as a surprise. He had always been very moody, and he was the evasive type. His business and lifestyle called for it.

In spite of his erratic behavior, one fact remained clear: Mallory wanted to be with him again.

It was early evening when she arrived at her motel. After setting down her suitcases, she called Brad at the hospital.

When he answered the phone, she said, "I suppose you're chomping at the bit to leave Baton Rouge tomorrow?"

"That's putting it mildly." The pleasure at hearing from her reflected in his tone. "Where've you been hiding? I've been ringing your room all afternoon."

"I had to go to Baytown to conclude some business," she said evenly. "I didn't think I had to report every time I take a notion to travel."

"Aw, come on, Mal. I wasn't calling to check up on you. I just wanted to make sure you're planning to visit us for a while in New Orleans." His tone was conciliatory because, in truth, he was checking up on her.

"If you don't think you'll get tired of me over the next few days, I think I just might make the trip south," she answered thoughtfully. As long as Quinn was nearby, there was no rush to go home. "Has the crew left already?"

"Are you kidding? They worked their tails off with the Judson well, and it was a tough responsibility. I thought it only fitting that they take a night out on the town and let their hair down, even if I can't go with them."

"I'm sure no one has thought to smuggle a couple of

bottles of beer into your hospital room, have they?" she teased.

"You're not supposed to know anything about that, young lady," he admonished jokingly. "And if you tell Elissa, I'll strangle you."

"My lips are sealed forever." She played with the phone cord. "So, when does the crew plan to leave?" She had to know Quinn's itinerary.

"Quinn said they'll stay and wait for my discharge. We'll go home tomorrow as one big happy family, red-eyed and hung over."

"I see. Well, count me in for the trip, will you? I have to let you go so I can finish packing the rest of my things."

"Aren't you coming to the hospital tonight?"

"I don't think so, Brad. It's been a long day."

"I haven't seen you near as much as I'd like, Mal. It would mean a great deal if you'd take the time for a long visit." There was no mistaking the disappointment in his voice.

"We'll be able to visit on the plane tomorrow." She was evasive, and she knew that he was trying his best to make her feel guilty.

"Yes, but I want you up here tonight."

She didn't like the commanding tone, and wouldn't give in. "I'm a bit travel-weary and need to rest up. I think I'll get to bed early tonight." She was lying, not wanting to grant him the satisfaction of forcing her to go to his bedside. She wasn't the least bit tired.

A few more words were spoken. When Brad understood that there would be no changing her mind, he relented. As soon as Mallory hung up, she gathered her suitcases and the rest of her belongings together.

On an impulse she picked up the phone and dialed Quinn's number at the trailer. It was high time they talked seriously about their involvement. Mallory intended to tell him how it piqued her to be ignored most of the time. She let it ring several times, but there was no answer.

It took only a minute to figure out that the men were probably at some roadside bar unwinding from the ordeal of fire fighting. Knowing Quinn as she did, she suspected he'd stay out with them until dawn, and she wouldn't see him until after their arrival in New Orleans. Maybe not even then, if it suited him.

The thought made her angry. A streak of the old, reckless Mallory began to surface, heightening an impetuous glow that came to her cheeks. It would be up to her to make the next move, and she was more than ready, even if it meant searching the whole town of Baton Rouge for him.

It was about time Quinn Chennault saw that he had met his match in Mallory Steiner. She wouldn't sit still any longer while he did all the dictating and she did all the waiting.

Rummaging through her suitcases, she found a pair of jeans. She slipped into them, smoothing the tight fabric over her shapely hips. A shimmering halter top of pale green and fancy Western boots completed the outfit.

She sat before a mirror and pulled her hair to one side, using a gold barrette to keep it in place. The other side tumbled loosely down a golden, rounded shoulder. A touch of mascara and some lip gloss were her only makeup. She wore no jewelry, content to let her looks do all the sparkling.

Mallory looked sexy and suggestive. That was exactly the image she wanted to project. Just for tonight she decided to let the old Mallory take over, doing as she pleased with no thought to consequences. That included whatever it took to handle Quinn Chennault.

As she drove through the Trend, it wasn't hard to find the fleet of company trucks parked outside a popular lounge. Feeling cocky, she went inside, strolling loose-hipped and bored as she met with stares and wolf whistles.

The dim atmosphere was smokey, noisy, and crowded, and a jukebox blared a popular country tune. Mallory looked around. The club was beautifully decorated with burnt orange carpeting and gold accents. Mirrors lined the walls, reflecting every movement. In one corner was a group of tables. At a far end were couches and low coffee tables for lounging. In the center of the room was a large dance floor, presently filled to capacity.

Cam danced up from out of nowhere and let out a country whoop. "Whoa, babe! Damn, but you look fine!" The deep beat of the music flowed between them. He rocked slightly in time with it.

Mallory's smile was slow, insubordinate. "I know."

He held a beer bottle by the neck and offered it to her. "Care for a drink?"

"Why not?" She accepted, and took a long swallow. The beer was cold and numbed her stomach.

"If you're not out stompin' with anybody, why not join my group? We're havin' a good time." Cam's smile was engaging and appreciative as his eyes undressed her.

"That's what I'm looking for. A good time." She handed the bottle back and let him sweep her along through the crowd.

"Y'all!" he hollered over the music. "This is Mallory. She's one of us."

As the people continued to dance, their acknowledgments ranged from a simple wave to the point of a finger, all accompanied with a smile. Just that easily she was accepted.

Cam led her to a corner of the dance floor, away from the blaring speakers. "You're the last person I expected to see tonight, but I'd be lying if I said I'm not glad to have you here. It's just like the old days."

Always the good-time Charlie, Cam was certainly letting the good times roll as he slipped a possessive arm around Mallory's slender waist. He was handsome, magnetic, and he knew it. The observation amused Mallory.

"It's been a long time since I've let my hair down like this," she said noncommittally. Briefly she scanned the crowd for Quinn. He was nowhere around.

"I'm tellin' you one thing. I meant it when I said I was a stupid fool to ever let something as gorgeous as you slip through my fingers. You look so . . . delicious." He pressed against her for a slight second before relaxing his arm.

Mallory laughed aloud. "You had your chance, baby, and you blew it. Given the circumstances, we both know you'd do the same thing tomorrow."

"Really, Mal, my heart's been breaking ever since we split." He gave her what he thought to be a sincere expression. "We all change."

"All except for you." She was still laughing at the little charade. "Tonight is strictly for fun and games, Cam. Nothing heavy like dredging up the past. *Laissez les bons temps rouler?*"

"If you'll take another drink and have a dance with me for old time's sake." He handed her the bottle. She drank part of its contents before giving it back. He finished the rest, setting the empty container on a nearby table.

Out on the dance floor she stood apart from Cam as a new song played on the jukebox. The music vibrated heavily, and the couple bumped and swung to the beat.

For a time Mallory lost herself in the activity, enjoying the sensation of floating with the rhythm. She and Cam were excellent dancers. Although it had been years since their last time together, their steps still bespoke a certain flair.

Some of the other dancers backed away to give them

room, and Mallory watched as Cam rotated to the tempo. He was vigorous and his superb body never missed a beat. In a suggestive overture he took her in his arms and invited her to follow his movements. They made a striking picture, with his dark good looks complementing her pale blondness.

As she turned in his arms, she looked out at the lounging couches and spotted Quinn. He sat alone in a corner, his tall frame carelessly draped out in relaxation. He was dressed casually in tight-fitting jeans and a plaid shirt opened at the chest to reveal a manly thatch of short raven hair.

Casually he picked up his beer and sipped, squinting and never taking his eyes off the fluid Mallory. He then took a puff of his cigarette, staring her up and down with an unemotional gaze.

Feeling too good to be subdued into second-guessing his unreadable stare, Mallory felt obliged to do as she pleased, and turned it loose. Only when Cam put both arms around her waist and pulled her close did she finally get an objective picture of the situation.

It became precipitantly clear that Mallory had always desired Quinn, that he had, in fact, been that unreachable object placed beyond the bend in the road. Unwittingly she had used Cam long ago, and it had nearly ended in disaster for all of them.

So what would she do about it now? She had made up her mind to have Quinn. She was grown, matured, and had a definite purpose in mind. This time it would end differently.

Swinging her blond head, she pulled away from Cam and lost herself in the bump-and-grind beat of the music. She danced strictly for Quinn, and she'd do what she could to let him know it.

She slowed to the movement of the rock music. Unlike Cam, she kept her rhythm controlled, unhurried. Each time she twirled in a graceful circle, she'd glance to see if Quinn was still watching. He was, but his face remained passive.

With deliberate relish she barely gyrated her hips in a suggestive, graceful motion. Cam caught her waist with a strong arm, and they spun together. If she had to, she'd goad Quinn into a response.

Quinn continued to watch from the sidelines, but he didn't make a move. Slowly his vision raked over the couple and stopped at Mallory's firm, round hips. She swung them rhythmically to the music, smiling at Cam and at their mutual enjoyment of the dance.

Mallory could tell that Quinn was steaming up when his face colored with the beginnings of anger. It wasn't enough for her. She closed her eyes and moved in an even more suggestive fashion. Strobe lighting flickered from the ceiling, reflecting in Mallory's white-blond hair. The hues ranged from red and blue to gold as the atmosphere changed, and she swirled elegantly. She had to make Quinn come to her.

When she opened her eyes she saw that Quinn's eyes were glinting dangerously. A slight flaring of his nostrils gave away the feelings he had tried so hard to hide.

So she'd had an effect on him after all. Now the situation was practically in his lap. What would he do about it?

When the music ended, she stood there, waiting. Tensed and poised for action, Quinn didn't immediately make a move. As a slower song played, Cam eased up to Mallory and started to lead. In a playful gesture he squeezed her and nipped her earlobe as they moved.

By that time Quinn had had about all he could take. Rising slowly, he covered the distance to the dance floor in a loose-limbed saunter and headed straight for Mallory.

He tapped Cam on the shoulder. "This dance is mine."

If Cam had any objections, he kept them to himself

after seeing the murderous look on his brother's face. Gallantly he offered Mallory to Quinn and backed off.

Riled beyond belief, Quinn pulled Mallory to him and impressed a few sexual insinuations of his own. He rubbed against her as he expertly led her across the floor, and let her know that he was thoroughly aroused. A thrill shot inside Mallory from the contact with his potent virility. He even smelled powerful, manly, the scent of after-shave and leather. She closed her eyes briefly and breathed him in.

Daringly she whispered, "Drilling for oil?"

His answer was just as daring. "Only if I think I'll find it."

With a heavy-lidded, provocative gaze, she answered, "You have a habit of taking things for granted. I wouldn't be so quick to count on it tonight if I were you."

They swayed together, their bodies locked tightly.

In a voice that grated, Quinn said, "What the hell are you up to? I'm not made of steel, Mallory."

"That's what I've been banking on." She looked up at his expression, and the sparks flew between them. Her little smile of triumph made him even angrier, and he crushed her in his embrace.

She had managed to make him jealous, and she couldn't help but gloat. "Is something bothering you, Quinn?"

He growled. "No, nothing."

"Then why are you trying to squeeze me to death? Take it easy. I'm not planning on going anywhere." She wiggled in his arms and brushed her breasts tantalizingly against him.

By the middle of the song he had reached his limit. To her surprise, he broke the dance. Taking her arm, he yanked her away from the crowded floor and led her to the cool darkness outside.

"What's with you?" she cried. She tried to pull away, but he was too strong.

"More than you'll ever be able to guess." He picked her up and carried her to his truck.

"I'm not ready to leave." Her protest was not nearly as forceful as it could have been. "Put me down!"

"You should never have showed up here to begin with." He smacked her down in the seat and climbed in after her. "I've just about had it with your little tricks. It's time to put you in your place!"

Her face was a question mark as he gunned the engine and roared out of the parking lot.

"What I did was no trick, Quinn. It's called asserting one's physical magnetism. You do it to me all the time. Why don't you admit that you don't like the way I used mine on you?"

"You're playing games, Mallory, teasing games just like you used to," was all he could mutter.

Try as she may, she couldn't get him to admit that he was insanely jealous. The emotion stuck out all over him, but he'd be damned before acknowledging it.

"You're too much woman for your own good," he growled.

She sat back in silence as he found a side road and stopped the truck. Briefly he hesitated before turning off the engine. Looking her way, he ordered, "Take off your clothes."

She smiled, knowing the situation between them had cleverly reversed itself since the little scene at the lounge. She was now the one who was controlled and nonchalant, while Quinn had a time keeping it together. He may have thought he was giving the orders, but she knew better.

Casually she slipped her halter top down and bared her breasts. "There's no need to be so indignant."

"With you a man can't be any other way." He unbuttoned his shirt and slipped out of it. "What is it you want, Mallory?"

She finished taking off her blouse. "You, Quinn. I want you."

"Sure you do. And you always get what your little heart desires, don't you? By hook or crook, Mallory Steiner has her way."

"And Quinn Chennault doesn't?" she snapped. "Maybe I'm too demonstrative with my purposes to suit you, but you're equally good at angling your own wants in your own way."

"Calculation was the general habit in our past, too, wasn't it?"

As he continued to undress, she slowly slipped out of her clothes and encouraged his little tirade. "I wasn't aware that it was you and I who had a past together."

He ignored the statement. "You're acting just like you did when you were eighteen years old. You spent all your time traipsing around like a little wanton, inviting me to look at you, daring me to touch you."

"That's right, I did. But that was years ago when I was a little girl who tried to be a woman. I never saw you take the bait."

"I wasn't as stupid as you gave me credit for. You were a child, I was an adult."

"Times have changed, and we're both adults now." She sat back and studied him. "I don't think the past is what's really eating at you, but if you want to hide behind it, it's alright with me." Her laugh was husky. She never dreamed she could provoke him so thoroughly, and it was daringly exciting.

He cut off the laugh by brutally covering her lips with his, drawing the very air from her lungs. The kiss was primitive, fiery, as he ravaged her mouth with a relentless tongue.

Mallory responded with a vigor she didn't know herself capable of, breathless from his display of raw emotion. His hands were all over her, weighing the firmness of her breasts and peeling the remainder of her underclothes from her body. The urgency aroused her in a way that nothing else could.

"Quinn," she gasped softly as passion took hold of

her. "I'm not the little girl you remember. I'm a woman, and I knew exactly what I was capable of when I walked into that lounge."

"Then why did you do it?"

"So you'd know that I refuse to settle for anything less than what you can give me."

She didn't understand the inflamed reply because he answered in French, his voice thick with wanting. He pulled her close, hemming her against the truck seat.

The kisses were endless, smouldering, and in the darkness of the cab they clung together, lost in a world that involved only the two of them.

As he raised slightly above her and began the act of love, she knew of a single way to try and make him understand. Her voice was a caress, *"Je desire* . . . only you." Then she gave her very soul to him.

What started as a frantic, frenzied coupling slowed as Quinn's wrath abated. Calmed, he began to earnestly make love to the beautiful woman in his arms.

Mallory accepted him, lovingly wrapped herself around him and drank in every ounce of the exquisite affection that bloomed exuberantly in the dark. Her feelings were changing, expanding, as she tried to interpret the crystalline euphoria that lifted her. His tender lovemaking had set all of the old yearnings free.

At the moment of satisfaction, her reason for existence was finally resolved, complete. She knew for certain that Quinn was indeed the only man she had ever truly wanted.

Unlike the impassioned man of a few moments before, Quinn was now gentle, raining tiny kisses on her face and whispering sweet phrases in his deep baritone. He eased beside her and they lay tightly wrapped in a naked embrace.

Now that he was in a mellow mood, she asked, "Can we talk about it?"

He still insisted on sidestepping a surrender. "There's nothing to discuss."

"But there is." She looked him square in the eye. "It isn't every day that you pull one of those caveman acts and drag me off, you know."

"All right, dammit, maybe it isn't. But I was provoked." That was the closest he would come to an admission. "Cam had his big chance and screwed it up. I don't think you owe him the benefit of another." It was hard to keep from smiling her pleasure at the small concession. "And you can stop grinning like a Cheshire cat. What do you think this is, show and tell?"

Mallory assumed some of the responsibility and came back with, "Maybe not for you, but for me it will be. I want to tell you something that I've never told anyone else."

He propped up on an elbow and nodded lazily. "I'm listening."

"Do you remember the night you decided to spring that little wedding present on me? We went back to your house and found Cam, but that's not the reason I was so angry when I left."

"I don't get your meaning."

"I thought you were taking me to your house so we could make love. Why do you think I snuggled up to you as we drove? I wanted to go to bed with *you,* Quinn, and it didn't matter one way or the other about being engaged to Cam. The fact that I saw the opposite of what I expected made me face the truth. In my own way, I was just as guilty as Cam was."

"You can't go turning things around and blaming yourself for something that probably wouldn't have happened between us . . ."

She put a finger to his lips and silenced him. "We found Cam with another woman. I had every intention of being with you whether I would've succeeded or not. Who was more wrong, me or Cam?"

He sighed deeply. "By now it shouldn't really be of any consequence."

"It is for me. When I left for Houston, it wasn't because of Brad. I was crushed, disillusioned because I didn't figure you'd stoop to such low means."

"Don't tell me that's the reason you maintained a four-year silence, Mallory. I don't deserve all the credit."

"You and I were the biggest part of it. What kept me silent for so long was the fact that I felt nothing for losing Cam. There was no feeling of emptiness. In fact, I didn't feel anything. I didn't know how to care about anyone, Quinn, and I haven't been able to completely sort it out until tonight."

"It seems like you cared a great deal when you danced with Cam. You both made up for lost time." His voice was slightly gruff.

"Cam has never mattered to me one way or the other. It's been you that I've wanted all along. I still want you."

"This isn't the time, Mallory." He didn't try to pull away as she expected him to.

"If it isn't now, then it never will be. Remember when I was eighteen and you refused my birthday present? A pattern developed between us. No matter what I said or did after that, it was as though you put my feelings in a compartment that opened and closed only when it suited you."

"You've never liked the way I've exercised self-control over both of us, have you? Like a reversal of what you did to me tonight?" he teased. "I'm on to you now, so it won't happen again."

It was maddening to have him turn the words back when she was trying so hard to make a serious point, but Mallory kept a cool head and continued. "Even though I've grown a little older and a lot wiser, you're still opening and closing that door, Quinn. I don't like it. What we've done may only be classed as a brief fling, but I deserve more consideration than you've been showing. It's not fair to be together only when you want it. I have rights too."

His look was long and considering before he acquiesced. "You don't know how nice it would've been to give in to you when you were eighteen. But I knew better. You were only a kid."

Her eyes grew large. "You mean you did want me then too?"

"I would've had to be deaf, dumb, and blind not to. Fortunately, I've never been blind to your shortcomings, *mon cher,* and that's what has kept me on my toes these past few days. Still, there's something earthy about you, something that brings out the male in men. You have a deadly combination of brains, beauty, and ambition. I've *had* to put a door between us, as much for your sake as my own." The revelation seemed to come hard, as if he was making himself plainly vulnerable to the power of her charms. "We didn't have the right to be together then, and we really don't now. You want an affair, don't you?"

"Yes. And we have every right so long as we both consent."

"It seems like an affair would see you shortchanged in the long run. You deserve better than what a fly-by-night character like me has to offer. You need roots, security. I can't give them to you."

"I already told you what I need, Quinn Chennault, so don't try putting words in my mouth."

"We could wind up hurting other people, you know." He was referring to Brad and Elissa, and she understood.

At one time she would have gloated in getting even with them, as proven by the affair with Cam. But this was a time to employ logic, not emotion, because Quinn meant something to her.

Mallory reasoned aloud. "While we shouldn't take elaborate measures to hide an involvement, we also shouldn't make any overt gestures at advertising it either. It would stay between you and me, Quinn, where it belongs."

"It sounds as though you've thought through most of the logical angles," he said haltingly.

Quinn looked at her and thought about the past. The old Mallory would have paraded around and displayed an indiscretion like a banner. It was her only way of settling scores and getting back at an overbearing brother. This newer, solid woman was intriguing.

"I plan to return to Houston in a couple of weeks, so it's wise to make the most of what little time we'll have together." It was now or never for Mallory's grandstand play. "Either you say yes and we do it right, or say no and that'll be the end of it for good." Her insides churned as she waited for his answer to the ultimatum.

He pulled her close and held her for some minutes. Until that evening, he had thought the matter of his desire for Mallory resolved. Now everything was turned completely around and he wasn't so sure anymore. "I know where to touch you and what to do to bring your feelings alive. We've learned how to make ourselves want each other. At the same time, I won't know how to just up and walk away from you when an involvement is finished. After all, our lives have crisscrossed for a long time and old ties lay heavily in this decision, for now as well as the future."

She studied his grave expression. "When the time comes you'll just walk away, old ties or not. That's what I plan to do."

"I don't know, Mallory, if this is such a good idea. The worst thing we can do is to keep hanging around in each other's life. This is our chance to break it off completely. . . ." he reflected quietly.

"I'm not any more convinced than you are about the

advantages of breaking it off," she answered. "Neither of us wants that, do we?"

"There's something about you that isn't like other women . . ." he said slowly.

"And you're not like any other man. That's why I think we should go on with it."

"It all boils down to a dangerous fascination between us, a preoccupation with tempting fate. You have to understand that I'm drawn to it just as you are. But that doesn't make it healthy, Mallory. My life has always been in the fast lane. I've stopped only long enough to enjoy a few pleasures before taking off again." It was as if he was apologizing for not being able to include her.

"Will you just cut it out? We're talking about a couple of weeks. No longer," she interrupted. "I don't expect any promises or commitments from you. You keep telling me about how fast and wild you live. You've taken pains to explain it all more than once. So far I've accepted what you've given me without a hitch. I haven't asked for anything more than consideration."

"Haven't you?" He raised a brow. "What was tonight all about?"

The darkness hid her smile. "Tonight . . . was an experiment, slipping into the old Mallory for just a little while to see if she was still there. And it was a desperate bid for your attention."

"Oh, the old Mallory is still there, *mon cher*. And she's ten times more lethal, too. She'll always be there because she's a cornerstone of your personality. Maybe that's what's bothering me." He ran his fingers through the silken blondness of her hair. "You may have outgrown some aspects of the Steiner brattiness, but there are still other facets in there directing you."

"Do I detect a note of suspicion in your voice?"

"No, just caution because I don't know you as well as I thought I did."

"Then I'll help you by laying the ground rules. Call it selfishness, possessiveness on my part, anything you like. I have to be with you right now as much as I possibly can. If it means enticing you to the point of jealousy to make you go to bed with me, then I will. I want everything you have to give me. I need you."

Quinn sat up, shuffled through his clothing, and looked for his cigarettes. "That's what I've been talking about, and why I'm skittish as hell. With you I'm going against everything I believe in, everything I've ever decided for myself. You're the exception to all the rules I've made and followed."

"Then consider yourself the exception to all of my rules as well. We might as well stop trying to ignore the fact that we're in each other's blood, because it's there in front of us. We have to decide what we're going to do about it. Do we keep playing games with our feelings of attraction? Or do we spend them and get it out of our systems? Where do we take it from here?"

Quinn lit a cigarette and let some time pass. He wasn't one to make quick decisions. "At the risk of sounding like I'm making a commitment, which I'm not, I suppose we could concentrate on making the best of what time we have left." He sighed heavily. "But it has to be with the agreement that we'll walk away from each other at the same time with no regrets or criticisms."

"All right. So it's the two of us together for now?"

"Yes. We should sleep with each other."

"Every night?"

"Yes, every night until you have to go back to Houston. We'll make a clean break at that time, understand?"

She nodded. "That sounds fine with me."

He pulled her into his arms, and they embraced. Warm feelings of security filled Mallory to overflowing as she listened to the steady beat of Quinn's heart against her ear. For the time being they'd belong to each other.

Quinn didn't have to know that she was falling in love with him. The day for leaving was far, far away, and she was content to let him think that parting would be as easy as it sounded.

Chapter Ten

The soft vibration of a New Orleans-bound Wild Wells jet was the only sound heard as Mallory sat quietly in a customized lounge. On the other side of the room Elissa busily settled Brad into a wheelchair.

Mallory watched them for a time, noting the soft loving looks they exchanged. After weeks of confinement in a stuffy hospital room they were like children, excited about returning to the comfort of home.

Pulling her gaze away, Mallory stared out the window. The clouds below were fluffy and luminous. The peaks looked like snowy mountains, the valleys slightly darker. She felt as if her life had followed that same natural pattern of highs and lows.

The night before was still fresh in her memory, and surpassed all others. She closed her eyes and envisioned herself on the highest summit with Quinn, reliving it and smiling all the while.

After agreeing to an affair, she and Quinn had gotten

dressed and returned to the lounge for drinks and dancing until after midnight. If Quinn had any second thoughts about the new arrangement, he didn't voice them. In fact, he seemed more relaxed than he had in days. Their togetherness suited him, and he became the ideal of affection and gentlemanliness.

Quinn was an excellent dancer, executing a few moves that even outdid Cam. Mallory adored the feeling of gliding in his arms. There was so much to learn about him, so much to experience.

When the party broke up, Quinn and Mallory had returned to his trailer for a night of love.

A soft, self-appreciating giggle stayed silent inside when Mallory recalled Quinn saying, "You were right about wanting to learn where my skillets are kept. When I'm not using my voracious appetite for sex, I can pack away the groceries with the best of them. Of course, man can't live by bread alone . . ."

With that, he had undressed her and they had made tender, soul-touching love. The gamble had paid off for Mallory, and the happiness she felt was indescribable.

Her only regret was bringing Quinn out of himself by making him jealous. It was an underhanded, manipulative ploy that could have easily backfired. She was lucky that it hadn't. She only hoped that Quinn recognized it for what it was, and that he had completely dismissed the little act as harmless on her part.

At one time Mallory lived and breathed the intrigue of subterfuge. But with getting older she had outgrown the destructive trait. Still, she wasn't sorry that she had played the part of a vamp, making Quinn see that he should commit himself for their short time together.

After awakening early that morning in each other's arms, Quinn had told her he had some business to take care of and some equipment to return. Instead of flying back to New Orleans with the rest of the crew, he and Cam intended to travel by car. The drive would precede the flight, and he'd be waiting for her when Mallory arrived.

She didn't mind jetting back with her family, but it bothered her when Quinn jokingly remarked, "It would look a bit suspicious if we drove to the airport together so early in the morning. That would never do."

They didn't want to hide anything, but at the same time they both knew how narrow-minded and judgmental Brad could be. Quinn was right in not wanting to chance a misunderstanding, because it was none of Brad Steiner's concern. It was agreed that discretion was the only way.

It would be nice not having to sneak around, but Mallory kept her feelings to herself. She had gotten what she wanted, hadn't she?

As Mallory sat back in the comfortable reclining seat and continued daydreaming, Brad clumsily rolled his wheelchair her way. The heavy leg cast jutted out before him like a misplaced mast. He accidentally bumped into her chair. The jarring action made her jump, breaking her reverie.

"Sorry about that," he apologized. "This rig is pretty clumsy, and I don't think we're going to get along at all."

She smiled slightly. "Just be thankful it's only a temporary contraption. You were very lucky this time, Brad."

"I know," he answered. Elissa walked over, leaned a hip against the side of his chair, and listened to the conversation. "I feel like I've suffered punishments in more ways than one during this particular stint in the hospital."

"How's that?" Mallory sat up slowly.

"Well"—he glanced her way but wouldn't look directly into her eyes—"it has been four years since you and I visited, and I thought for sure you'd try to make more time for family than you have."

Mallory looked up at Elissa and then down at Brad. "Three's a crowd. Besides, I'm a businesswoman and I have interests to protect just like you do. We'll have plenty of opportunity to talk later."

Brad was up to something. It wasn't like him to skirt an issue. She waited to see what he was getting at.

In an innocent way he chastised her, trying to make her feel guilty for not spending more time at the hospital. "I figured if we couldn't get together and talk in person, the next best thing would be a nice, long conversation on the phone."

So that was it. Vaguely he implied that he had called her at the motel the night before and she wasn't there.

She shrugged it off. "I had a couple of last-minute errands to run after I talked to you. And a girl has to eat, you know."

Kiddingly he threw back, "For most of the night?"

She tried to sidestep the interrogation, but felt herself tensing up for an argument. She answered coolly, "Dinner was a ten-course meal at a French restaurant."

"Baton Rouge has quite a few nice places. Where did you go to eat?"

"I don't remember, but it was lovely," she lied. He was trying to trick her into telling him what time she finally did come in, but she didn't intend to fall for it. It was as if he wanted to catch her in a lie. His demeanor wasn't angry, just cold with disappointment. Mallory wouldn't give in, and she tried not to let him spoil what was left of her good humor.

The little scene was reminiscent of the old Brad who had once tried to domineer her life and curfew activities. When out-and-out bulldozing didn't work, he'd try other, more subtle tactics. Mallory knew him well enough to spot a ploy on his part. It should have amused her at this point, but it didn't. She had a very important secret she intended to keep, and no amount of browbeating would make her admit anything to Brad. Where she went or how late she stayed out was strictly her affair. She didn't owe him anything.

Feeling edgy as she sat beneath his flinty stare, Mallory inadvertently reached into her purse for a cigarette. Only after she took it out of the package and held it between two fingers did she realize what she was doing.

Before Brad could mutter a comment, Elissa stood and said, "How about having one of your favorite Cuban cigars, Brad? The doctors wouldn't allow it in the hospital. I'll bet you're just itching for a smoke."

"Not as much as Mallory seems to be," he said condemningly.

"When the police grill a person, they're allowed a cigarette. Why not me?" Mallory said recklessly. "What I do or where I've been is my business, Brad. If I want to *eat* these cigarettes, then it shouldn't bother you."

Like many times before, Elissa assumed the role of arbitrator. But today she surprised everyone as she addressed her husband. "I hope you're listening, because what she's saying is the truth. We were in a good mood because we're going home together as a family, just like you wanted. It's a shame for you to spoil it now. You still don't know how lucky we are to have Mallory here with us. Shouldn't we be trying harder to make her feel welcome and wanted?"

Mallory couldn't recall having Elissa take up for her against Brad, and she threw her a thankful look. In her own quiet way, Elissa had reminded him that Mallory could just as easily leave again. He was pushing too hard too soon.

"I . . . think I will have that cigar," Brad conceded slowly. A flicker of suspicion crossed his glance as he watched Mallory put the cigarette between her lips and light it. There was no malice in the action as she ignored him and did as she pleased. He accepted it without qualm.

Grateful for the intervention, but in need of some time to herself, Mallory excused herself. She walked to a baggage compartment at the rear of the plane. She just wasn't up to any of Brad's probing.

Although Elissa had managed to circumvent a brewing argument, it was inevitable that brother and sister would ultimately have words about one thing or another. It was as if Brad was spoiling for it, and Mallory couldn't understand him. Why, when they had everything to look forward to, was Brad pushing for a confrontation? They had agreed to put painful issues to rest, but it was alarmingly clear that the old wounds were still fresh inside for him. How like him to only pretend to forgive and forget.

If only he could be more like her and Quinn—sharing, understanding, and a willingness to calmly work things out. But Brad wasn't like that. He had given orders for much too long and didn't know how to take them.

Mallory had grown out of the habit of listening to anyone except herself, and no amount of love for Brad would see her give in to his demands. What would it take to make him see that she wasn't responsible to him for her actions?

As Mallory sat on top of a large Pullman chest, Elissa came in to check on her, and said, "I hope my husband didn't succeed in unraveling you back there." She sat down next to Mallory.

"Not quite, but he came awfully close." Mallory's green eyes were large as she looked over at Elissa. "I don't want a fight with him. Can't he see that? Why is he so insistent on knowing my every move? It's only serving to push us apart again."

Elissa sighed. "He told me a few days ago that you'll always be his kid sister, someone he has to look out for no matter how old you get. I tried to tell him otherwise, but he's just not listening right now."

"Maybe it's me," Mallory mused. "I'm wearing my nerves on my sleeve this morning, and it shows. I'm just now beginning to see how much of a strain we've all been under. I don't like feeling that I could've gotten into an argument with Brad a minute ago. He still has a long road to recovery and doesn't need any upsets."

"Don't make the mistake of letting him use that to manipulate you," Elissa warned softly. "He was once very good at inducing guilt where you were concerned, even if it did only serve to make you all the more adamant."

The statement made Mallory laugh softly. "Yes he was, wasn't he? I have a long memory, so he won't have that advantage this time. Do you know what it is he wants of me?"

Elissa played with her finely manicured nails. "He wishes to see his sister married and happy. He wants only the best for you, as I do."

"I already have the best," Mallory insisted. "If he'll just stop preaching long enough to see it . . ."

"He will, as soon as I make him realize that you didn't need him in order to get it. He's a little edgy now too, having been in that hospital room all these weeks. He's trying his wings again and wants to roar a little bit. If you're patient, I'm certain he'll calm down."

"I should've told myself that, but I'm too busy trying to show him that my will is still as strong as his."

"If you don't mind my butting in a little bit, I'll get him to accept the truth that you're a grown woman. I don't mean this to sound condemning, but you have been keeping an awfully low profile, Mallory. Some of his complaints are well-founded."

"I've been busy," she said lamely.

"No one has to guess who you've been busy with. It

shows very clearly." Elissa's smile was mysterious. Mallory felt her insides tense, but kept her face blank. "You've obviously been keeping company with a man. A very interesting, entertaining man, I'd say."

Mallory's heart thumped hard in her throat. She was nervous, thinking that Elissa knew Quinn was the one. How could anyone know? Until last night they had taken pains to be very discreet.

"I . . . yes, there is someone," she admitted quietly.

"I thought so. It's a shame we had to leave Baton Rouge so soon. Now you and he can't be together as often as you'd like."

So Elissa didn't know it was Quinn.

Making light of it, Mallory answered, "That's all right. Baton Rouge and New Orleans aren't that far apart. I suppose I'll see him again sometime." She left it at that.

It was a long time since Mallory had thought about the town house in New Orleans. Outwardly it hadn't changed much, but inside it was now nothing short of fabulous.

Elissa had redecorated, and the tones were bold and bright, the motif Oriental. The living room was rich, with tables a blue-green so dark that they looked almost black. Half-moon cornices gave the windows a charming Chinese look. In lieu of draperies were bamboo shades stenciled with priceless mosaics. The floors were of a dark gray marble imported from a special quarry in Italy. The carpeted areas were so plushly done that one tended to sink up to the ankles when walking across them.

Beaming happily, a fleet of servants stood inside the hand-carved double doors and welcomed Brad home. His favorite drink was sitting atop a gigantic custom bar. When he looked askance at Elissa, her approval was a small smile and the arch of a brow.

Mallory admired the town house as the trio sat

comfortably in the living room and enjoyed the immense elegance.

"I'd forgotten just how nice home really is," Brad said appreciatively. "Elissa is quite a decorator."

"I'll say." Mallory lifted her glass in a toast. "Your taste is exquisite. I have just one question, though. How did a dyed-in-the wool Southern lady like yourself ever develop a taste for Oriental surroundings?"

Elissa laughed. "It was a team effort for Brad and me. There was a big fire in Japan, and he sent for me when it was over. We turned it into a little sight-seeing trip. The landscape was so peaceful that I decided to duplicate it in my own home."

"I remember reading about that Japanese fire a year or so ago. It wasn't an oil fire, was it?" Mallory looked Brad's way.

"As a matter of fact it was a poison gas fire, and one of the most dangerous I've ever encountered. That was the time Quinn nearly gave it up for good with a faulty gas mask."

The blood drained from Mallory's face when she learned how close her lover had come to dying. No wonder he was so careful now.

Finishing his drink, Brad called out to one of the servants. He asked if there were any messages from headquarters that morning. When the question was met with a negative answer, he lost control for a moment.

"If I've told my people once, I've told them fifty times to let me know where they'll be and what's going on!" He snapped a finger and issued orders to the servant, who seemed to take it in stride. The master wasn't home an hour and was already asserting his authority.

Mallory gave Elissa a knowing look. The two women stoically witnessed his little fit about undiscerning workers and the need to stay on top of them at all times.

"You're wearing yourself out, Brad." Elissa stopped him when she decided it was enough. "I think it's time you got into bed and rested."

He shook his head. "But I'm not the least bit tired."

"You won't know you're tired until you relax," she insisted. "Your sister probably has a hundred things to do today, and so do I. The doctors gave me strict orders concerning your limitations, and for once I'm going to crack down on you. Isn't that right, Mallory?"

Mallory nodded and finished her drink. Brad was the president of a top-notch organization, but on this particular day he wasn't even the boss at home. Elissa had a way with him that normally involved a great deal of coddling. Not so now.

In spite of strenuously objecting that he was a grown man and could look out for himself, there was no getting around her when it came to his health. It was one of the few arguments he had ever lost to his wife.

Brad looked at Mallory and said, "I hope you're planning on having dinner here tonight. Elissa has a surprise cooked up for both of us."

"I'd like to but I can't." Mallory bowed out gracefully. "There are some prior commitments that need tending to as soon as I leave here." She was thinking of her rendezvous with Quinn, and it felt delicious to keep the secret to herself.

"You're as slippery as an oil-coated monkey wrench," Brad said in exasperation. "I know better than to say I won't take no for an answer. But you will oblige us by temporarily occupying your old room, won't you? Elissa left it just as it was. We've been hoping to see you use it again."

"I'm touched, but I don't know if it's a good idea to move in right now. After all, it's going to take some time for you two to get settled. I'd no sooner move in before having to leave again. That kind of upheaval isn't fair to any of us."

"You really should give it some consideration, Mal."

A slight look of desperation crossed Brad's handsome face. "Elissa and I entertain frequently. We know quite a few eligible bachelors who just might strike your fancy."

"Since when did you start playing matchmaker?" Mallory began to laugh.

"I'm serious about what I'm saying. There's someone important I want you to meet. Who knows? You two just might hit it off. He's the right kind of man. To my way of thinking, he'd make a perfect sire for future generations of Steiner offspring. Of course, no one is rushing you. He'll be a nice ace in the hole when you decide to turn your thoughts to marriage."

Now that Brad was once again on familiar turf, he had fallen back into the old habits. Mallory did little to hide a growing chagrin. It was like forcing an old, worn-out record to keep playing again and again. Her first inclination was to literally scream her frustration at him.

Instead, she explained as carefully as she could, "I appreciate all the consideration you're giving me, Brad. But I'm just not interested. I have no intention of settling down with any man. I also refuse matchmaking on yours or anyone else's part. I consider it meddling, and I won't have it."

"But Mal, it's because I care . . ." He tried to explain.

"I am not prize stock that goes on the block for the highest bidder, Brad. I'm a person who needs the freedom to choose for myself. I love you, and my coming here has proved it. Can't you do the same for me and just leave it at this? My future will take care of itself."

Glancing at the contemptible expression on Elissa's face, Brad knew he had carried it too far.

Putting up his hands in defeat, he backed off and said soothingly, "Sure, sure. There's no rush to any of this. You're still a young woman, and there's plenty of time, plenty of time. Choose whoever you like. Just make sure he's worthy of you, okay?"

"I'd prefer that we just drop it for good," Mallory said firmly. "My personal life will be a closed subject from here on out." She had that determined Steiner look about her.

"Anything you say," he conceded graciously, but they knew he'd get back to it when he figured a way to gain the upper hand. Looking at Elissa, he sighed. "You know, I am getting pretty tired. How's about having my bed turned down and you can tuck me in?"

Elissa smiled warmly. "I'll do that. While you're resting, you can tell me which of your favorite foods you want prepared first."

Mallory felt like an outsider and knew she was overstaying her welcome. Clearing her throat, she picked up her purse and said lightly as she went to the door, "I think I'll leave you two lovebirds to yourselves now."

"What about a place to stay?" Brad piped up.

"I'll let you know where I am as soon as I'm settled." That was the end of any explanations she intended to make.

Later, after Mallory was gone, Brad sat comfortably in the center of his king-size bed. "I don't like the way Mallory shrugged off her responsibilities today. And you backed her up."

Elissa reached over him and fluffed his pillows. "She did nothing of the sort. She just told you to keep your nose to yourself, and I agreed with her."

"But we're her family," he insisted. "And we should come first with her. I mean, we need to keep the lines of communication open for all our sakes."

"Darling, she's been trying to talk to you and you've been trying to talk to her. Trouble is, neither of you is on the same wavelength and refuse to hear what the other is saying. I think it would be wise to give it some time and let Mallory work this out for herself. It's not like she's come home from school. She has another life separate from ours, and she all but said there's a special man in the picture. She deserves the privilege of making up her own mind about the future."

"I guess you're right. I just don't want her to hurt herself . . ." Brad sighed loudly.

"She's much smarter than you think. Look over the last four years and tell me that she made it strictly from blind luck."

He smiled. "You're a sly one, Elissa Steiner. My instincts tell me that you two women have been carrying on a few strategies behind my back. Two against one isn't fair."

"All's fair in love and war," she quipped.

"So it is." He reached up and fondled a breast through her clothing. He had waited far too long to be alone with his wife, and the sight of her doing little mundane, everyday things was oddly arousing.

"Bradley!" She jerked up. "You're a sick man. You need quiet so you can convalesce. And what about that cumbersome cast?"

"What I need will do me more good than any medicine those damn doctors have given me," he said huskily, and pulled her to him. He kissed her passionately as she molded herself readily in his arms. "We'll find a way to work around the cast."

"We really shouldn't . . ." she said breathlessly. "What will the servants think about the lady of the house?"

Brad's eyes turned to liquid emerald as he continued to caress her. "Now isn't the time to be a lady, Elissa. Close the bedroom door. And lock it."

It was the middle of the afternoon before Mallory made it to the headquarters of Wild Wells Limited. Set against the shores of Lake Pontchartrain, it was an impressive building constructed mainly of glass and stone. Nearby was a landing strip and a gigantic hangar for a fleet of private jets. To the other side was a heliport.

The building was sleek and modern. When Mallory entered the plush lobby, she admired the recent redecorating. It was more like a large home than a business, and the atmosphere was easy and relaxed.

Instead of waiting for a receptionist, Mallory strolled through the first open door she came to.

It was a large office, apparently empty. She looked around for just a minute. When she turned to leave, she encountered Cam. He was comfortably draped in an overstuffed chair. He had obviously sneaked into the quiet office for a nap.

Raising a brow, he said dryly, "Looking for anybody in particular?"

"No. Just looking. I didn't mean to interrupt your nap," she said briskly. Cam's insolent attitude irritated her. "I was wondering if anyone was around."

"Oh, we're around all right." He straightened in the chair. "Things have changed since your last visit here. Care for a twenty-five-cent tour of new offices and playrooms?"

"Why not?" She wanted to find Quinn, and joining Cam seemed the easiest way.

As he showed her back through the waiting room, he explained that a second crew of workers was resting as they waited for the next call to fight a fire.

In addition to plush offices, there were a number of recreation areas that offered a pool, video games, movies, any number of diversions that served to relax the crews between jobs. There was even a small cafeteria that catered twenty-four hours a day.

"For someone who spent half the night cutting up, you look better than all of us put together," Cam said appreciatively, his tone softening.

"I feel as fresh as a daisy," Mallory responded insincerely, trying to relax. He seemed to look right through her, and the feeling was unnerving. "I had a very nice time last night."

"Didn't we all? I don't remember much after ten o'clock. Who did you wind up going home with? Who did *I* wind up going home with?"

She didn't like the way he kidded, and felt herself stiffen when he started asking questions. He sensed her withdrawal and stopped their stroll. "Hey, babe, take it easy, okay? You're a little bit high-strung today, aren't you?"

"I . . . suppose I am. I guess I'm not in a joking mood right now, Cam." She recalled the near upset she had had with Brad. She was edgy and defensive with anyone who even remotely irritated her.

It occurred to Mallory that the wrong exchange between Cam and Brad could blow the entire affair to bits, but she couldn't help acting edgy. Did she dare ask Cam to please keep a tight lip about it?

"Mallory." Cam now took it upon himself to straighten out the situation. "Things don't always come crystal clear to me every time, but you don't have to hit me on the head when it comes to seeing things for what they are. Remember, I grew up around you."

Mallory blinked hard. "I don't know what you're talking about."

"I'm talkin' about what's going on between you and Quinn. You still like livin' dangerously, don't you?"

"One evening of dancing doesn't make a relationship." She sniffed, hoping to arrest his suspicions.

"That's funny. It used to." His expression was amused as he reminded her of their first date. When she didn't smile back, he cleared his throat and continued. "Look, I just wanted to pick on you a little bit. Quit getting so uppity about it, will you? You and I were destined to fail as a twosome, because we didn't know how to treat each other. It was just a silly game. I thought we'd agreed there are no hard feelings between us."

"We did," she said curtly. "I told you I don't feel like joking today, especially about my personal life."

"Alright." He put up his hands in supplication. "Then listen to me. What I'm tryin' to say is that I couldn't be happier that you and Quinn are an item. It's really okay by me."

In nervous retaliation she retorted, "I don't need your blessing."

"I know you don't, but I wanted you to know how I feel. I don't begrudge you and Quinn a shot at happiness." There was an expression of genuine sincerity on his face.

"This is certainly out of character for you, Cam Chennault," she said with a touch of awe. She was sorry that she had spoken so harshly a moment before. "You've even got a serious look on your face."

"It's just for the moment." He grinned crookedly and forgave her earlier outburst.

"Yes, everything you've ever done has been just for the moment."

"That's why I'm a Cajun. Today's hardship will be tomorrow's celebration. Ain't nothing goin' to get me down."

They laughed at the obvious truth of his statement, and it put Mallory at ease again.

"I'm sorry," she said softly. "Thanks for the vote of confidence."

"I owed you one." Cam hugged her. "You just be happy, understand?"

Mallory gave in to Cam's good mood and accepted the fact that he was on the level. She nodded. "I'll be happy when I find Quinn. Where is he?"

"Why don't you try the houseboat moored a little ways down the road? That's where he lives now." Cam's eyes twinkled devilishly. He had known all along where to find his brother. He also knew that Mallory had come into headquarters looking for him.

As Mallory approached the houseboat, she saw Quinn on the roof. Wearing black swim trunks, he lay stretched out on a chaise, sunning himself like a big cat. Nonchalantly he stood and leaned against a guard rail. He called down to her, "What took you so long?"

Shielding her eyes from the afternoon glare, she said smartly, "What was the hurry? Don't tell me you've been waiting for me."

"Okay, I won't." He threw back the little barb and stretched. Gracefully he flexed his muscles and stood, intent on going below to help her board. There was no mistaking the undisguised eagerness in his expression as he slid down a ladder and reached a hand out to her. "You look absolutely delicious today, but I can tell you right now that you're wearing too much."

Accepting his help, Mallory looked down at her striped shirt and jeans. "I think my attire is very appropriate, considering this is supposed to be a casual afternoon."

He raised a brow in mock amusement. "So this is going to be one of your playing-hard-to-get days, huh? We're past that, *mon cher.* We promised last night that this affair would be the ultimate, remember?"

"So we did." Her smile was conspiratorial. "Still, a girl can't be too available for a man. I had a few pressing things to take care of. That's what took me so long."

"All of which you purposely set before me?" He put an arm around her shoulders.

"Naturally." She smiled up at him.

"Regardless of what you think, you have to know that I'm a man who doesn't like to be kept waiting." He took her suitcase and led her to the door of the cabin.

She came back with, "And I'm a lady who doesn't like to be rushed."

He laughed good-naturedly. "Touché."

"To be certain. You might as well learn when you've lost a match, because I've won this round."

"Do you think you could find it in your heart to share a swim with a very good loser?"

"I don't see why not."

After they went inside, he put her luggage on a nearby sofa and gestured toward the room. "This is home."

"I had no idea you lived on a houseboat. This is very cozy." She glanced around and liked what she saw. It looked like something Quinn would enjoy. It was a man's home, done in bold blues and aqua, complete with brass nautical accents.

"I had to rush ahead and make sure the house was tidy. I haven't forgotten how you disapprove of the sloppy way I kept the trailer in Baton Rouge," he mocked. "This isn't bad for a bachelor, is it?"

"Not at all." She pretended to check for dust. "But it's quite different from the Tudor mansion you had in the city. What happened?"

"The house was too much for me to keep up after Cam left, so I sold it. This locale is much more convenient to the office. I also find the privacy very inviting. It's peaceful out here on the lake, relaxing when I need it. And here lately I need it a great deal of the time."

"Like you did after the fire in Japan?" Her gaze was level.

"Yes. Brad told you." He said it almost accusingly.

"I'm glad he did. Now I understand why you seem so superstitious. It's a relief to know you're cautious." She went up to him and slipped her arms around his neck. "Everyone needs someplace quiet to unwind. For the next two weeks I'll see that you do."

"You might like to know that I'd give my eyeteeth to be certain we'll have every second of that time together. Let's hope no more fires complicate matters, shall we?"

"I'll personally see to it." She lifted her face, and he kissed her tenderly.

She had spent the night before in Baton Rouge wrapped in Quinn's embrace, feeling the protective solace that only he could provide. She felt it again as he held her close.

He broke the kiss and looked down at her. "Maybe I'm speaking out of turn, but I sense that something is wrong. Did anything happen today?"

"I never could hide my upsets from you, could I?" Although Mallory was relaxed, Brad was still very much on her mind. She couldn't help but fret over what went on that morning. "Nothing is seriously wrong, Quinn. At least, nothing that I can't handle."

"What is it? Do you mind sharing it?"

"I think you already know." She chewed her bottom lip.

He nodded. "Brad."

"Uh-huh. We had a little bit of a row this morning. I don't know what it'll take to get through to him that I'm no longer the person I used to be. He has no right to expect anything from me."

"Being family, you both should expect certain things of each other. But knowing Brad like I do, I suspect he wants to be king." Quinn reached down and picked up her suitcase. He motioned that she precede him into the bedroom at the rear of the houseboat. "Was there fighting?"

"There could've been, but I wouldn't allow it." A hand on the small of her back guided her in front of him.

He set the suitcase down on the bed. She opened it and searched for a swimsuit. When she looked at him, her eyes were luminous with a worry she thought was hidden. "Brad called the motel for most of the night, and I wasn't there to answer. I guess he wanted me to admit that I hadn't stayed in and gone to bed like I said I would."

"It doesn't sound as serious as it could be." After Mallory took off her blouse, she pulled up her hair and turned her back to Quinn. He unclasped her bra. "What did you give him in the way of an explanation?"

"I said I had a long dinner." She slipped off her bra and turned back to him. "He wanted to know where I'll be staying over the next few days. I told him I'd let him know as soon as I get settled in. This is going to be harder than we'd thought, isn't it?"

"Not as long as he stays at home recuperating. If it comes down to supplying a residence, just rent a motel room and leave it at that. I'll have the answering service at the office route all your calls from that number to mine. No one will be the wiser. It's easily solved."

She looked relieved. "I'm not going to lie about my dislike of having to sneak around. I almost told Brad that I don't care what he thinks. Then I thought about you. He'd never have the first inkling of understanding where our affair is concerned."

"Wouldn't he?" Quinn's expression was thoughtful.

"Of course not." Mallory unsnapped her jeans. "I'm practicing discretion as much for you as I am for myself. You two have a twenty-year friendship hanging in the balance. I'd never try to come between you, even though he would do his best to come between us."

"That's noble of you, but you've got it backward, sweetheart. I'm doing this for you. Brad wouldn't understand *your* part in it. Our friendship certainly won't be on the line because of it."

She put a hand on her hip. "I beg your pardon?"

"You don't know how it is between your brother and me, Mallory." He sat on the edge of the bed and tried to explain. "I don't feel the least bit guilty about being with you. Brad and I have a healthy tolerance for each other that somehow you can't earn from him. You and I both know he would blame you, just as he did when you were involved with Cam. Would you care if he did?"

"Yes, but I thought you'd have more cause to worry than I do. I shouldn't have bothered. I forgot that you always land on your feet." She gave him a hard look and said with pretended indignation, "And now that you've mentioned that so called 'tolerance' you men have . . ."

"It's a fact of life, *mon cher.* Nothing personal against the gentler sex, of course."

"You men are all alike." She lifted a shoulder and shrugged it slightly. Hooking her thumbs in her jeans, she slipped them down her hips. She stood there wearing panties, her naked breasts thrust out proudly. "And we women are the ones who take all the risks."

Although she made light of it, inside a little worry etched itself against the brightness of the day. Quinn was taking Brad's interference too lightly to suit her. She didn't want to think about it right now.

Quinn reached out and put his hands around her waist, drawing her close and inviting her to lay on top of him as he eased back on the bed. "You've got that right. We men are little more than selfish beasts."

They tousled for a few minutes, laughing and playing on the bed. Quinn was very eager for Mallory and saw little reason to hide it. He slipped a hand inside her panties and tried to arouse her.

She eased away. "We've got plenty of time. Let's swim for a little while and get the kinks out from the trip, okay? I'm still high on last night."

"Whatever you say." He saw the need to humor her. "But I won't wait long."

They sat up together, and he watched as she slipped into a skimpy bikini of bright orange. She took a brush from inside her suitcase and quickly brushed her hair back, tying it with a rubber band. "I'm ready."

Outside, the afternoon was warm as they climbed atop the houseboat and looked down into the blue-gray waters of the lake. Mallory was the first to dive in. Her slender body formed an arch as she glided through the air and disappeared beneath the waves. Quinn followed, and they broke the surface at the same time.

In slow, measured strokes they swam a few yards away from the houseboat. It was a lazy mood, with the water working as a calmative for Mallory's frayed nerves. On the return to the deck she did a leisurely backstroke, her arms graceful as she lifted them out of the water and propelled herself.

As they neared the deck, Quinn reached out and pulled her to him. With a deft hand he slipped the bottom of her bikini off and they went underwater.

She came up sputtering. "Hey, no fair!"

"I told you I wouldn't wait long." His smile was engaging. Pushing her against the side of the houseboat that faced the lake, he began to touch her in a way that said more than words ever could.

She giggled. "Quinn, it's broad daylight!"

"Who cares? Nobody can see anyway." His kiss was wet, tantalizing. "Don't you know variety is the spice of life? Come on, Mallory, loosen up."

"You asked for it." Her expression was sardonic as she reached down and pulled his swim trunks off. She gathered their swimsuits and threw them overhead behind her. They landed with a thud on the porch.

Quinn imprisoned her against the boat, putting an arm on either side of her. As they began to make love, she read an expression of sudden urgency in his need for her.

After a few minutes, he complained, "This water is slowing us down. Let's go indoors."

Taking care not to be seen, they eased over to a ladder on the side of the vessel and went to the bedroom to finish the loveplay. The afternoon turned into evening and then night.

This time when Mallory made love with Quinn, she tried to pack a lifetime into every sensuous minute. As glorious as their times together were, there could well be an end to it. She intended to store up enough memories and affection to last the rest of her life. But would it be enough?

It was after dark when she slipped out of bed. Quinn was breathing regularly with his back to her. Quietly she went out on deck and stared at the glimmering moonlit water. She puffed slowly on a cigarette and thought about herself and Quinn.

No matter how she sized things up, it was going against the grain to sneak around for any reason. She was a grown woman, answerable to no one. More than anything, she wished that they could go public with the relationship. But part of the agreement with Quinn was that things would have to remain just as loose and easy to walk into and out of as they had always been.

She had no right to get possessive, angry, or resentful, because this new situation was all her own doing. That meant no complaining to Quinn or changing the rules again. She knew he wouldn't stand for it.

She was giving everything she had, laying it all on the line for him. Why, then, did she feel confined? Restricted?

The answer was plain. An affair just wasn't going to be enough. If she tried to declare her feelings, it would undo everything she had accomplished so far. She was desperately in love with Quinn and would do what she could to get him. The accomplishment seemed near impossible, though, because Quinn Chennault was his own man and had his own ideas about fidelity.

From the looks of things, Quinn also held many aces: his friendship with Brad, a maddening charisma over Mallory, his freedom. He was too shrewd for tricks.

Why did she bother staying when all the cards were

stacked against her? Because she cared so much. And she couldn't stand the thought of losing Quinn. If this was part of the price she had to pay, she'd willingly accept it.

In the meantime, she had two short weeks to make him fall in love with her. But how?

Chapter Eleven

The next morning Mallory awoke to the delicious smell of coffee brewing. She opened her eyes and smiled at the sun-filled room. She couldn't remember a time when she had known such happiness, such completeness. She wanted the feeling to last forever.

Quinn called out as he pushed the door open with a foot, "It's time to wake up, sleepyhead. It's almost eleven o'clock, and it's a beautiful day."

Still barefoot and wearing his pajama bottoms, he carried a breakfast tray lightly laden with two cups of brimming hot coffee. He pushed the door closed behind him, smiling at Mallory as he offered a cup to her.

"This is lovely." Mallory sat up. She was wearing his pajama top and rolled up the sleeves to expose her arms. She accepted the coffee and sipped slowly, saying, "May I expect this every morning?"

He gave her a comical grimace. "Are you kidding? You're spoiled enough as it is. The first day on my houseboat you're considered company. After that, you're a habit."

She laughed. "In other words, it's going to be up to me to rise early and see that you have coffee, right?"

"We'll compromise and take turns." He winked and picked up his cup.

She could tell something important was on his mind by the preoccupied look on his face. When he didn't introduce the subject, she said, "So, what are we going to do today? Is there anything special you have to take care of?"

"Not really. But I think you do." He took another swallow and let her stew for a couple of seconds. "I've been doing some thinking about the situation between you and Brad."

"Oh, that." Her tone was sullen.

He sat on the side of the bed. Hooking a finger beneath her chin, he lifted it and made her look at him. "Yes, that. I'm not a light sleeper. I think Brad was the reason you had to prowl around last night."

"Well you needn't have wasted your sleep, because I often get up at night with insomnia. Didn't we agree yesterday that Brad will be taken care of?"

"That's what I want to talk to you about. I think you should play it straight with your brother. It isn't right to feel that you have to hide everything and lie to him. It puts you in a very precarious position, and that bothers me."

"What a switch." She drew her knees up and sat against the headboard of the bed. "Yesterday I was trying to protect you. Now you want me to go to him and bare *my* soul? You want me to tell him that I'm carrying on with his best friend?"

"Not exactly. But I can't forget the expression on your face when you told me about the near argument you two had. You could tell him that you've met someone, so most of your evenings will be tied up. That way you'll be able to give him more time than he's been getting. It might get him off your back, too." His face was a question mark.

"Oh, I see. It's sort of like being a half-virgin, right? I'll tell him I'm in the backseat of a car, but I'm not doing anything wrong. Brad can have one piece of me and I'll save the other part for you. Sorry, but I like the feeling of staying whole and in control."

He turned away. "Dammit, Mallory, don't put it like that. I was too quick, too careless yesterday when I said I have no feelings about sneaking behind Brad's back. Of course I do, and I think you do too. We have too much respect for each other not to feel something in the way of remorse for deceiving him."

She leaned close to Quinn, suddenly apprehensive. Was he trying to tell her that he had cold feet about the affair? "Brad's forcing us to do it this way because of his stubborn, overbearing Steiner ways, don't you see? What's the matter with leaving things the way they are? Don't you think I'm worth it?"

He looked at her for a long moment. "You're more than worth it. That's why I'm trying my level best to think about you. I just figured you deserved better . . ."

"And let's not start that again, shall we?" She was determined not to let the relationship take a step backward, especially for Brad's sake. She had argued with herself the night before about having to rely on subterfuge with her family, and had decided that any price was worth Quinn. It was time to take another chance. She played a trump card. "If you're talking about backing out so soon, say so."

"That's not what I'm saying. What I'm looking ahead to is the possibility of repercussions. Neither of us has been thinking clearly since this whole thing started. I just don't want to see anyone get hurt."

"And you think I do?" she demanded.

"No, of course not. But I hurt you once before and I don't intend to do it again, accidentally or otherwise."

He reached out and put a warm palm against her cheek. "I want very much for us to be together, *mon cher*. But I can't shake the feeling that something black may be on the horizon."

"Well I hope it's not smoke," she teased. "Because this is one fire you just might have to miss." She kissed him softly. "I'm touched that you want to protect me. And the fact that you're concerned means you do have a conscience after all. Look a little harder, Quinn. We're both grown-ups now. I can take any knocks that come along. Can you?"

"When you look at me with that challenging light in your eye, it does something to me, Mallory Steiner." He put their cups on a bedside table and stretched across the bed, pinning down the top half of her body.

They played for a moment, and then his kisses became serious, expectant as he reached below the pajama top and toyed with her breasts.

About that time there was a noisy commotion in the living room. Releasing his grasp on Mallory, but leaving an arm around her, Quinn tried to sit up. "What the hell was that?"

Before he could get up to investigate, the door to the bedroom swung open with a thud. Clumsily Brad pushed his way in, his laughter boisterous and carefree as he bellowed, "Some people should own clocks, partner. If I can make it to work today, so can you. It's about time—" He froze on the spot when he encountered the guilty, dumbfounded expressions on the faces of the couple before him.

Time stood still as Mallory tried to comprehend the gravity of the shock. Obviously Brad had thought to surprise Quinn by getting around on his own, but it was he who stood there white-faced and stoney.

Feeling an illusory sense of time and place as trauma mercilessly trapped her in invisible chains, Mallory stayed as she was. Helplessly she watched her brother's face turn from white to crimson as his anger mounted.

Quinn sat up and shook his head as if to clear it. "It looks bad, I know, but I can explain . . ."

Brad ignored him. His eyes burned into Mallory's. "Get your damn clothes on. You're coming home with me!" It was all he could say.

There was something in his tone that prompted Mallory to come out of herself and take a good look at what was happening. The illicit feelings of being caught in *flagrante delicto* were replaced with the indignation of having her privacy impinged upon. With as much dignity as she could muster, she answered, "Don't you know how to knock before entering a room? This is someone's home, and you have no right to just barge in."

"I told you what I expected of you. Now do it!" he bellowed louder.

Quinn put out an arm in an effort to steady Brad's trembling. "Look, man, we can talk this out over coffee . . ."

"Like hell we can!" Disregarding the crutches beneath his arms and resting his weight on the cumbersome cast, Brad did his best to make a fist. He took a swing at Quinn. The agile Cajun ducked as the momentum of the action made a swishing sound in the air between them.

Having missed the target, Brad was temporarily pulled off balance and fell back heavily against the door. When Quinn tried to help him, he ground out, "If you come near me, I'll make damn sure not to miss this time." He struggled and stood again, looking at Mallory as she slowly got up and wrapped a sheet around her bare legs.

"Are you going to get dressed or not?" he said through clenched teeth.

"When I'm good and ready. And even when I do, I

won't be going anywhere with you." Mallory was determined not to give in to him.

Brad was furious. "I may be sporting a fifty-pound cast, but if I have to, I'll dress you myself."

Quinn tried to step in on Mallory's behalf. "You're too upset right now and don't mean half of what you're saying, Brad. We all need some air and some time to let our tempers cool."

Mallory put a gentle hand on Quinn's arm. "I think maybe you should go on deck and give Brad and me a few minutes alone, will you? This is something we have to settle between ourselves." She looked back at Brad. "It's been coming on for a long time."

Quinn nodded slowly, reluctantly reaching for his pants and slipping them over his pajamas. "If you say so." It was apparent that he didn't want to leave Mallory alone. "I'll be up top if you need me."

Pushing his way past Brad, he went out the door without saying another word.

Mallory unwound the sheet from around her body. Quinn's pajama top reached halfway to her knees, so she felt it was no longer necessary for any pretenses at modesty. Her anger was boiling as violently as Brad's. The encounter she had been dreading was suddenly upon her.

"So this is the thanks I get, huh?" Brad said. He leaned heavily on the crutches and hung his head. "I really thought you had changed into something better than this."

"Better than what? A flesh-and-blood woman who has feelings and rights just like you do?" she spat out. "I don't owe you any thanks for anything, Brad Steiner. Nor do I owe you explanations for my actions."

"Don't you? Who busted his butt working the oil fields for years? Who risked his life to feed and clothe you all that time? I did."

"Nobody said you had to do that. I was content with what I had before we moved to New Orleans. And don't go making it sound as if I was the one you did everything for. We both know you were the one with the wanderlust, the need to be a big man. Well you're not so big that you can order me around!"

"You really made it easy not to give you orders, didn't you? Ever since that first day, you've treated Elissa like a stranger, pushing her away and refusing to learn anything about being a real lady." His tone was biting.

"I know all there is about being a lady without benefit of Elissa's counsel. What you wanted was for me to be a doormat, like your wife and every other woman you try to dominate!"

"So now you have to sling mud at Elissa, do you?"

"I didn't bring up her name, you did. Since the last time I was here, Elissa and I have come to a mutual understanding. We're better friends than we've ever been. She accepts me as I am. Why can't you?"

"I'm sure she'd change her estimation if she caught you wallowing in bed with Quinn Chennault."

"Quit making it sound like something cheap and filthy," she rasped. "It's not like that at all!"

Ignoring her words, he looked around the small bedroom. "This is quite a lovenest. Much better than the sleazy hotel rooms and parked cars you and Cam had, isn't it?"

Mallory sucked in her breath at the harsh insinuation. "None of that was necessary."

"Oh, but it was, sister dear. It wasn't enough to have one Chennault brother. You had to go after the other. I'd just like to know how you managed to lure Quinn into bed. He knows you for what you are, just as everyone else probably does by now."

"Stop it, Brad!" she warned him in a near-hysterical voice. "You have no right to say any of these things to me!"

"I have every right because I'm your brother, the man who raised you. When I think of all the fancy schools I spent a fortune on so you'd be a well-educated, polished lady. Instead you came home a high-classed tramp!"

"And this is what you're reduced to, name-calling? You say I haven't changed? Well you haven't either. You're still the same hypocritical, judgmental, narrow-minded bastard you always were. What irks you the most about me is that I won't let you play God and order me around like you do everyone else."

"You've never acted like you have the good sense to know what to do. Someone had to do it for you!"

Defiantly she reached for her purse and pulled out a cigarette. After lighting it and taking a deep puff, she answered, "I've been taking care of myself for a long time without your so-called guidance. I can do it now, too. You've done everything you could to subdue me, even going so far as to take away money that rightfully belongs to me. You don't like the fact that I can assume command as easily as you do. You always said I was more Steiner than you. Is this what you meant?" Her eyes narrowed to angry slits. She didn't give him a chance to answer. "I wonder . . . are you angry because it's Quinn who's in my life now? Would you be making the same kind of scene if it had been that lah-de-dah businessman you wanted to fix me up with?"

For a brief second he looked tired, drawn, as if he might concede the argument. The look was replaced with one of renewed vexation. "I only want what's good for you."

"I'm tired of hearing that line, Brad. Can't you think up a better one? For the first time in my life I feel a sense of joy, a sense of direction that I never felt before. I know what I want, what I've always wanted, and you're doing your best to try and take it away from me. Why can't you just accept me, and let me get on with living?"

"Because my truths and your truths should be the same, Mallory. I'm fiercely proud of our heritage, our position in society. I do what I can to protect it."

"From what?"

"From gossip-mongers, people who'd like nothing better than to see us destroyed and in ruin. I have many friends, but I've also made some enemies along the way. It seems that my biggest enemy exists within my own family."

"Only in your mind, Brad. You still haven't answered my question about Quinn. Are you upset because it's him?"

"I did answer. You found a way to lure him is all I can figure."

"In other words, it's all my fault?" She took another puff.

"More or less, yes."

"Since I'm bearing the entire burden of responsibility, I have something important to say to you. Listen well, because I'll only say it once, Brad. All my life you've preached the necessity of good family ties and a promising future with the 'right' kind of man. But when it comes to the help, or people you consider undesirable matches, there are a different set of rules to live by. We can work with them, eat with them, have them in our homes. We can even sleep with them if we're careful not to get caught. But don't make the mistake of marrying them. We're the upper crust and must remain so at all costs, right?"

He was slow to reply. "The part about sleeping around was unnecessary, but in essence you're right."

"Oh, I see. Having affairs applies only to you?" Pertly she ground out the cigarette in an ashtray.

"To all men, Mallory. If you didn't have such ridiculous ideas about your place as a woman, I think your life would run much smoother."

"Well, excuse me for having a few ambitions of my

own! I think that's where you and I have split on the issue, Brad. To me, men and women should be on the same levels, or at least allow each other the respect of trying to be. That's the bottom line as far as consideration and rights are concerned. And what do you know about my relationships? Only what you read in the papers and hear from close acquaintances, I suppose. That's a pretty sketchy basis for such a strong judgmental response."

"I don't want to get into this, Mallory. It's not the problem."

"In a sense it is. You've conditioned yourself to have levels, divisions in every part of your life. It involves less time spent putting people into categories for when you need them. You've tried to force me to take the same, lopsided outlook as you do. If I don't agree with what you say, I'm automatically wrong. Period."

"Just keep trying to rationalize. And put the entire blame on me, will you?" he said defensively. "Kick a man when he's down and can't properly defend himself."

"You didn't seem to be having any trouble starting this fight. If you're so helpless, why are you coming at me so hard and using the big guns, Brad?"

"You always could argue better than I could. Go ahead and split hairs, Mallory. See what it gets you."

"I'm not trying to do that. But you're making it awfully difficult to meet you halfway. And that was as far as I had intended to compromise."

"You don't know what it is to compromise." He eyed her suspiciously. "If you did, maybe you could commit yourself to a decent relationship and stop acting like an alleycat with my best friend!"

"All right. I'll do just that." Her expression was set.

"What are you saying?" He knew enough not to trust that tone of voice.

"Only that I have some news that might make me a

halfway honest woman in your eyes. I've discovered that Quinn Chennault is more of a man than anyone I've ever met."

A slight smirk curved the corners of his mouth. "I wonder what you're using as a gauge?"

"Let's not get nasty, shall we?"

"And let's not forget that it was Quinn who had the unmitigated gall to take you back to his house four years ago to show you what your beloved Cam was up to. It was damn cruel of him. Do you consider that the mark of a caring man?"

She paled slightly. "No more cruel than some of the things you've tried. He has since explained himself, and we've worked it out. I'd venture to guess that you would've been the one to do the ax job, had you thought of it first."

"I probably would've," he admitted reluctantly. "I'd do anything to steer you off of a collision course and keep you from hurting yourself. Other men just want to use you."

"You make me sound like a helpless mental case. I'm a competent woman, and no amount of taunting will make me change my opinion of Quinn."

"Nobody's trying to. I just want you to face the truth. If I gave the word, Quinn would drop you like a hot potato. Don't you realize you're little more than a diversion for him? One of many women he keeps handy? Of course, with your classy looks, I can't blame him for taking what you dangled in front of him."

The words stung. He could tell by the expression on her face that they had hit home.

"Well, here's a truth *you* better start facing right now." She shook her finger at him. "I'm so in love with Quinn that it's eating me alive. I'd marry him in a minute if he'd have me. Why? Because he's a *real* man and he answers to no one but himself. You've never been able to push him around and you can't do it now.

He won't take the first order from you. At least, not where I'm concerned!"

"Wasn't it enough to try getting me back by using Cam? You were the one who wound up getting shot down, not me. Don't pull those old threats again, okay?"

"This isn't a threat, this is a promise!" Her eyes shot fire. "I didn't have to come back, but I did because I felt that we needed each other. I also needed Quinn, but I couldn't see it right away."

"Now you're saying that I'm not a necessary ingredient to your future happiness, and he is?"

"You could be, if you'd stop acting so childish and listen to me. I don't need either of you in order to survive. Why can't I have both of you in my life?"

"Because it isn't right!" Brad snapped.

"Just because you *say* something is wrong doesn't necessarily make it so!" she snapped back. "If you push me too hard, I'll leave and you'll never see me again!"

"Don't say things you'll regret later," he warned softly. "You're pushing me into a corner."

"I can't have any more regrets than I do now, Brad. Elissa has tried to talk to you; I've tried to talk to you. Even Quinn has tried in the past. But you won't listen. If you don't stop tampering with my life, I'll go away and never come back!"

Angrily Brad chewed his lip. The expression on Mallory's face was lethal. She would do exactly as she said. There was nothing left to discuss. He'd have little luck trying to force her into doing as he said.

"If that's your final word, then you can't leave soon enough to suit me," was all he muttered. Clumsily he turned and opened the door, pushed his way out, and never looked back. "I just hope you know what you've done to all of us."

He was gone for only a few minutes when Mallory realized her legs were trembling. They threatened to give way beneath her. She fell heavily on the bed, knowing he'd never understand no matter how many times they went through it.

She felt a tightening in her chest and allowed the first of many tears to come. Damn Brad and his arrogance! Why couldn't he be like other men? Why did he set himself up in a position where there could be no backing down, no compromise? He sat there as judge and jury, all the while insisting that he truly cared.

Many times she had asked herself if it was she who was wrong. She knew she wasn't. She couldn't live under a tyrant no matter how hard she tried.

Quinn would be coming inside shortly. Mallory didn't want him to see her crying. Quickly she ran to the bathroom and dabbed her face with cold water. If she felt the need to cry, there would be plenty of time later to indulge. For now, she had to be strong because that was what he expected of her.

She heard the front door open and close. On feet that padded as softly as a big cat's, Quinn came up the hallway. His demeanor was a mask of grave concern.

"*Mon cher,*" was all he said as he walked into the room and sat next to her on the bed.

"I thought women were the only ones who were supposed to have intuition," Mallory said thickly as she avoided his stare. "I told you I could take a hard knock."

He pulled her into his arms and eased her back on the bed. For a long time they lay side by side, saying nothing. Although she didn't make a sound, she fought hard to keep the tears at bay. She felt cold, lost, and would have fallen apart if it hadn't been for Quinn's strong support.

"It didn't go very well," he said softly, breaking the silence.

"Didn't your premonition tell you as much? I would have more luck getting through to a brick wall than Brad."

"He's hurt, disappointed in both of us."

"He was abusive. I've been hurt too, but that's no reason to excuse his hateful accusations." Her voice was flat, emotionless.

"Is there anything I can do, Mallory? I'm as much at fault in this as you are."

"No, there's nothing left, Quinn." She pulled away from him and sat up. "We wasted our time worrying about sneaking around. And you were right when you said Brad would blame me for everything."

"What did he say?"

"He said I'd lured you into bed. The old Adam and Eve scheme."

Quinn sat up also. "No one can make either of us do anything we don't want to do. Our arrangement was made by mutual consent."

"That's what I tried to tell him. He used every dirty little tactic he could to turn my feelings around. They were the ploys of a desperate man. He said everything he could to hurt me. He'll never have the satisfaction of knowing this, but he accomplished what he set out to do."

"He shouldn't have succeeded." Quinn lifted her face with his hands and gently kissed her lips. "It wasn't right for you to send me out and face the old lion by yourself."

"I can talk back better than you can." For a brief second an old fire flickered in the depths of her eyes.

"I want to know what was said about me," Quinn ordered softly.

"No you don't. Not really," she said resolutely. "It's enough that I told him you're more of a man than I've ever known anyone to be. And we're together because we want to be." She was careful to omit the part about wanting to marry Quinn.

"Did he happen to include the old phrase about not wanting you to marry beneath your station?" His eyes turned dark with a slow burning vexation at Brad's crassness.

"Doesn't he always?" She was immediately sorry for answering without thinking.

"Yeah, I can remember his ranting and raving about Cam, and how much of a poor match he'd make for you. Well, I'm not trying to sell myself as any kind of goods, but I think it's time Brad takes a hard look at how the other half feels. Once and for all, your brother needs to know exactly what position he holds. It won't be the pretty picture he's been looking at for the last twenty years."

Quinn went to the closet for a shirt and shoes.

"What are you talking about?" Mallory's brows drew together with undisguised worry.

"You had your turn trying to drum some sense into him. Now it's mine."

"Maybe you shouldn't . . ." she said slowly. "It's not worth the pain for any of us."

"If it hadn't been you, it would've been something else working as the catalyst for the showdown we must have. Don't worry. I've always been able to get him to see most things my way. It's time he and I cleared the air about you."

Her brow raised sardonically as she fleetingly thought that she'd like nothing better than to see Brad Steiner face someone his own size. If anyone could take him down, Quinn Chennault could.

She immediately felt guilty for such treacherous thoughts, because Brad's undoing would have to be at Quinn's expense. Instead, she said aloud, "I'm not worth this kind of a risk."

Ignoring her, Quinn headed for the door and said over a shoulder, "I'll only be a few minutes. Wait here for me."

Mallory's green eyes clouded as she hugged herself and did as she was told.

Chapter Twelve

In an angry, uneven gait, Brad hobbled into his office and slammed the door behind him with a crutch. After the stalemate with Mallory, he had mixed feelings about her and Quinn. Foremost in his mind was the disappointment of betrayal. He had suspected that his sister was playing with dynamite again, but had had no concrete evidence before today. How he wished he'd never gone to the houseboat.

When he looked around the room, he didn't see the decorative, colorful murals of the fires he had fought during the years. All he saw was Mallory, and everything that had been built for her. She had foolishly chosen to throw it away for a few nights of stolen pleasure with a man totally out of her league.

Brad damned her for being so difficult, for acting more hardheaded and independent than she ever did before. He never could get her to see anything his way.

He was a fool for not putting two and two together in

Baton Rouge. Both Quinn and Mallory had always been conveniently absent at the same time. He should have known something was up then. He never suspected, because he had trusted them both.

He headed toward an open bar set on a fancy credenza and reached for a bottle of bourbon. He put the cork between his teeth and opened the bottle as he reached for a glass. Instead of pouring the whiskey, he threw the empty glass against a nearby mural and watched it smash into a hundred little pieces. He put the bottle to his lips and drank from it, oblivious to the fiery sting as the liquor went down his throat. In seconds his insides were numb. That was what he wanted.

Taking care not to fall, he balanced on crutches and eased to his desk, settling in his chair. As he took another long swig, the door to his office opened and Quinn Chennault sauntered in. He acted like nothing out of the ordinary had happened.

Brad eyed him critically and didn't say anything at first. Instead, he finished the swallow and put the bottle down on his desk. Complacently he rocked back slowly in his chair and studied the man he thought he knew so well, the man to whom he had entrusted his very life.

Quinn glanced around the office. Obviously Brad hadn't thrown any fits because all the furniture was still in one piece. Should he risk taking it as a good sign? He decided he would.

Quinn went to the bar and said, "Mind if I siphon off some of your whiskey?"

"Why not?" Brad said quietly. "You've helped yourself to everything else that belongs to me."

Ignoring the barb, Quinn poured himself two fingers of whiskey. He turned around to face Brad, and drank half of it in one gulp.

With a caustic expression, Brad said, "You really took a chance coming here like this."

Quinn finished the last of his whiskey before making a reply. "That's what my life is all about, taking chances."

"I can believe that," Brad said thickly and reached for the bottle again. "You took advantage of me, Quinn. You're the last person I would have thought would do it."

Quinn tilted his head. "I've taken advantage of no one."

"That's debatable," Brad said between swallows. He winced as the last one went down. "When I asked you to take care of Mallory, you took me literally."

Taking a deep breath, Quinn said, "You have to understand—"

Brad exploded. "Oh, I do understand, boy do I understand!"

With his aggravation showing slightly, Quinn crossed the room and stood at the foot of Brad's desk, facing him directly. "It's time you and I squared some things away, Brad. We have to clear the air."

"I think it's a little late for talking." Brad bristled.

"It's never too late." The statement was met with a hard look as Quinn plunged in. "Because of the compromising way you discovered us, I feel it's necessary to explain about my involvement with Mallory."

Brad reached over to a cigar box, took out a Cuban cigar, bit off the tip, and lit it. He puffed expansively and let the smoke curl around his face. He squinted. "I'm listening."

"This was something that Mallory and I didn't plan, but it was meant to happen. We've all been friends for a long time, Brad, and you have to believe that I'd never do anything to intentionally hurt you."

"Up until about an hour ago I would've fought to the death for that one belief. Now I'm feeling deeply wounded. It's not easy to accept."

"Again, I tell you we didn't plan this. Here lately you and I have been under one hell of a strain with our work. You seem to be gung-ho, going after every dangerous thing you can."

"And you seemed to be too cautious. It wasn't my fault that you had a leaky gas mask in Japan."

"Maybe not, but after almost twenty years in this business I let my guard down for a few minutes. It nearly cost me everything. Look at what happened to you at the Judson site. We've both been careless, and we're getting to the point where our work is something that's just a matter of course. We don't approach fires like the dangerous jobs they really are."

Brad chewed thoughtfully on the cigar. "So what does that have to do with Mallory?"

"Maybe, in an oblique way, that's how things began with her and me. Through carelessness, a good kind of carelessness. Somewhere along the line it changed to caring."

"You may have changed, but has my sister? Men have always been a matter of course with her. Since you're older and know her track record, I was relying on you to keep her in line."

"That's why we have to work it out. I've come to understand her, and so should you." Quinn rested a leg on the corner of Brad's desk. "Do you love your sister?"

"That's a stupid question if I ever heard one," Brad answered flatly. "Of course I love her. I love her dearly."

"Then quit trying to strangle her. You're killing what feelings she has for you."

"Mallory has feelings? For me?" Brad laughed harshly. "She sure has a funny way of showing it."

"She said the same thing about you. From the way I see it, you're two opposing forces that can't find common ground. The reason you can't find it is that you're both spitefully proud."

"I've made an effort . . ." came the defensive answer.

"I've watched you try to squelch every natural urge, every healthy emotion that Mallory has ever had. She has such depth, such warmth. She's a very caring person, and has shown it by making the first effort at bridging a four-year gap. She didn't have to come back here to see you. You have to let yourself believe that her feelings are genuine."

"Right now all I know is you went behind my back and took advantage of her. You wanted her here for yourself. That's the real debate. Let's stick to it."

Exasperated, Quinn reiterated, "Yes, I did want her here too. You probably won't believe this, but before you came into the bedroom, Mallory and I were discussing the fact that we shouldn't keep things from you."

"Oh, is that what you're trying to tell me I walked in on? If it is, how convenient to bring it up now. And if she was going to tell me the same story, she would've done it with a great big self-satisfied, vengeful smile."

"Not this time, Brad. You expected her to be blatant and wanton, but she's not. She kept our affair very quiet in order to protect you and Elissa. That in itself should tell you that she's changed some. Don't you remember how destructive she was with Cam?"

"She may have altered a bit, even mellowed," Brad snarled, trying to cover up fleeting feelings of belief in Quinn's argument. "But I still stand the same as I always have. All I've ever wanted was for Mallory to marry well, to find a husband who's worthy of her and the Steiner money. Is there anything wrong with that?"

"No. I think it's very noble."

"It looks like Elissa and I can never have children, so Mallory's sons would someday inherit this dynasty I've built. It's important that her children are acceptable. They have to have the right kind of sire to do that, to uphold our heritage and our name."

"I can buy that. What, in your estimation, is the right kind of man to father children with Mallory?"

"He has to be upstanding, his heritage has to be pure, untainted of scandal. He has to be able to take care of her in the style to which she's accustomed."

"I have to agree with all three points." Quinn nodded. "Anything else?"

"Yes. Most importantly, he has to love her."

Quinn stared down at the empty glass in his hand and toyed with it for a moment. He felt an old fury trying to come to life, but he controlled it as he painstakingly set the glass on the desk. He looked at Brad with a strange expression in his eyes, and said, "There's another bone I've been meaning to pick with you for years. Now's as good a time as any. When you objected to Cam and Mallory's involvement, I stayed on the sidelines and gave you moral support. We both knew that Cam was immature. He wouldn't have been the right kind of husband. A man is supposed to be good to a woman and take care of her. My brother fell short of the mark."

"At least we agree on something!" Brad picked up the bottle again.

"I'm not finished yet. I want to tell you a thing or two about siring, and you better take it to the bank. *I* am pure-blooded and can trace my family tree all the way back to the first landing at the Acadian coast, even further if you want to go to our origins in Canada. A man's bloodlines shouldn't be measured in dollars and cents, Brad. It's what he is, as well as what his people were. Where do you get off thinking that Cajun is less than what you think the Steiners are deserving of? Many's the time this Cajun has saved your life and literally pulled your tail out of the fire."

"So what bearing does this have on our conversation about Mallory?" A light of realization began to dawn in Brad's eyes as he slowly answered his own question. "You're acting like you've decided to put in your own bid for my sister."

"Am I?" Quinn's expression was quizzical. "Everything seems to have turned in that direction, hasn't it?"

Taken aback, Brad sat there for a moment. "You're a bigger fool than I am to even think of it!"

"Maybe. But the point remains that you owe me for plenty, Brad Steiner, and it's time for me to collect."

"Just because you've saved my life more than once . . . . What do you want? My half of the business? More money?"

"I've got all the money I could ever use. If we quit today we'd both have enough to live on for the rest of our lives, and then some. I'd never dream of asking for your half of Wild Wells, because you love it more than life itself. In fact, it *is* your life."

"Then what is it you're after? Name your price."

"You already did. It's Mallory."

Brad's face turned beet red. "You're out of your mind! You can't be serious!"

"I'm very serious." Quinn never cracked a smile.

"No!" Brad roared loudly.

"It would appear to me that Mallory isn't really yours to give anyway. We're talking about her as if she was a chattel instead of a person. I was asking out of courtesy, nothing more." He never lost the rigid control that directed him.

"I . . . I need to think about this." Brad sighed tiredly. He knew he was defeated, but he didn't want to give in.

"All right. You've got sixty seconds." Quinn glanced at his watch.

"You have to give me a chance to decide."

"No I don't. You forget that I can't be brought to heel like one of your helpers, Brad. I happen to be the other half of Wild Wells, the working half right now, and I have as much power as you do. I've never asked your permission for anything and I won't start now."

Gruffly, Brad bleated, "Won't you grant me anything?"

"What for? So you can try some underhanded trick to make me change my mind? I know you too well. My head is set where Mallory is concerned. Accept it here and now, Brad."

Trying unsuccessfully to harness his chagrin, Brad sputtered, "So now your true colors are finally coming through. Am I going to have to knock your block off in order to prove that I have rights where Mallory's future is concerned?"

"No, but it's a shame you feel you have to revert to threats in order to make a point."

"I picked you up off of a dirty oil derrick. I took you home to my family, I gave you half of a business. This is what I get in return. What would you know about real class?"

"I know plenty. You taught me. I can make Mallory happy. I can give her everything she's accustomed to. Most of all I can give her love. Are you listening? I'm in love with Mallory. If I want her to, she'll come with me."

Quinn watched the play of emotions on Brad's face. Quietly Brad said, "I've never asked anything of you before, but I'm asking you now. Don't rush my sister into anything, please? Leave Mallory alone until she and I can work out our problems?"

"I've always tried to do what's right for you and me, but this is something I can't and won't consider, partner. I want Mallory. I'd be old and gray if I waited around for your sanction of her lifestyle."

"I'm not accustomed to having my orders disobeyed." Brad's voice was dangerous. It was his last, desperate stand. "You can't claim her."

Quinn shook his head sadly. "How ignoble for a man of your stature to grasp at such flimsy straws. You don't mean to browbeat me. It's your pride talking now, Brad. For the first time in your life you're going to have to swallow it and realize that Mallory is right and you're wrong."

"My pride would see you burning in hell before letting you have her!"

The force of the denial surprised Quinn. He looked hard at Brad. "Do you know why you don't want Mallory to marry? There'll never be anyone good enough as far as you're concerned because you want to keep her for yourself!"

Brad picked up the bottle and reared back to throw it at Quinn. "You son of a bitch! I ought to . . ."

"It's a shame to see that's all you have left, Brad. Physical force is the bottom line, and even that isn't effective any more."

Shaking visibly, Brad fought the urge to follow through and throw it at Quinn. Slowly he put the bottle back down on the desk. The truth was slowly sinking in. Defeat settled like a dark cloud on his face.

He sighed loudly. "Just do what you will. You're both intent on ruining your lives, but I won't let you ruin mine. As of this minute I no longer have a sister—"

Quinn interrupted. "Don't go declaring things that you can't take back later. I don't see how two people in love could be ruining anything."

"You just are," Brad hissed. "Look, you're the two who are cutting out, not me. I don't owe you any explanations for my reasons."

"You're cutting us out as well as yourself. Get down off that high horse and think things through, man."

"There's nothing to think about. It's all been decided for us."

"You're wrong. There's plenty—a twenty-year friendship, a business, the future. There are lots of things to think about that hang in the balance."

"Maybe there are, but right now they don't mean much." Brad stubbed the cigar in an ashtray. "Mallory's children were my one hope for the future, and that single hope is now dashed. That probably makes you very happy. If it's my blessing you want, don't hold your breath waiting for it."

"What about Wild Wells? Without me it's nothing. You're not willing to trash it too, are you?"

"Why not?" Brad bluffed. "If I backed out, you're the one who would wind up with nothing."

"Not so, buddy. I've always had everything I ever wanted. You're the one who's still searching."

Quinn patiently waited for a sign. Brad knew that all he expected was the offer of a hand, and the angry words and accusations would be forgotten and settled. Part of Brad wanted to reach out to him, but his arrogance kept him rooted to the chair. In his heart, he knew that Mallory would never find a better man than Quinn Chennault. He just wouldn't admit it out loud.

After a fair interval, Quinn drawled, "I feel like hell that it's come to this. I love your sister, and we belong together. She could do a lot worse, you know."

When Brad wouldn't meet his gaze, Quinn knew it was time to leave. Noiselessly he walked to the door. He glanced back briefly and saw that his friend still hadn't moved.

"I thought we had a stronger friendship, Brad. I still do."

"So did I," came the hollow reply.

"Your convictions about the old Steiner blood are deeply ingrained. I can understand how you might view me as an upstart, but I'm not. Let's put things on ice for a while. You'll know where to find me when you're ready to patch our friendship back together. But the deal will have to include your total acceptance of my marriage to Mallory, or it's no go."

Brad turned away. It was true that Wild Wells was his life, and Quinn was the only person who could stop it from going down the drain. The very point Brad had stressed about Mallory needing family had suddenly hit home with him as well. Still, he refused to put aside his egotism and surrender. He didn't know how. He watched as Quinn quietly closed the door behind him.

Mallory relaxed on the deck of Quinn's houseboat. She was dressed in gray slacks and a soft pink blouse, both of which Quinn had once admired as flattering colors on her.

She stared at the placid lake and thought about the happenings since her return to Louisiana. She was at a crossroads. The very things she had worried about the night before had blown up in her face. She still felt the shock of Brad's unexpected visit. The folly of deceit had taken care of itself, but at what price? She still wanted Quinn, and wondered if she had any more to lose by coming right out and declaring her feelings for him. She should tell him once and for all that she was in love with him. She feared a strong rebuff, and right now her bruised feelings couldn't take another jolt, expecially from Quinn.

For the first time, she was afraid, uncertain. Quinn's visit with Brad could either make or break the love affair, and she expected the worst.

Things looked bleak as she envisioned her life without Quinn. Did she have the right to feel sorry for herself if she did lose him? He never gave her anything substantial to pin her hopes on. All he had agreed to was a brief affair. She couldn't expect more than that. She felt in her heart that, given a few more days, she could find a way to make Quinn fall in love with her. Was it too late? It seemed to be, and a black depression tried to claim her.

She jumped at the sound of an approaching car, and saw Quinn drive up. Slowly he climbed out and made his way toward the houseboat. For a moment Mallory savored the pleasure of watching him walk in a graceful saunter that told the world he had supreme confidence. He approached the deck and climbed aboard, never once looking at Mallory until he was almost beside her.

She was glad to see him, but she read nothing in his expression as he slowly looked her over. His eyes were silvery, distant, and traveled from her head to her feet and back up again as if seeing her for the first time.

She eased out of the chair and stood. Her expression was puzzled as he continued to make a thorough assessment of her.

"You are a very beautiful, desirable woman," he said softly. "So beautiful that a man can't help but want you no matter what it costs him."

Mallory walked over to him. Sliding her arms around his waist in an embrace, she rested her head against his chest. They stood close for a few silent moments.

"I was becoming so frightened," Mallory admitted meekly.

He stroked the softness of her blond hair. "What were you afraid of, *mon cher?*"

"I thought maybe you weren't going to come back." She looked up at him. "I don't want to hear about what went on between you and Brad, and yet I do."

"What we hashed out isn't the important thing right now. What is important is what's going to happen to us."

He broke the embrace. They walked to a side of the houseboat and leaned against a guard rail. Quinn contemplated the lake as it met the sky. The houseboat swayed gently in rhythm to the natural movement of the choppy water. It was a calming, peaceful sensation.

He turned Mallory's way and said, "I never thought I'd find myself in a position where everything I have, everything I am, is at stake. It's as if all I care about is flashing before me: my relationship with Brad, our association in business, the affair you and I agreed to. I've laid every bit of it against my desire for you."

"You always said you were a man who liked to take risks," came Mallory's solemn reply. "You think I haven't chanced anything? I've been wondering if the stakes were too high for you."

Quinn tilted his head questioningly. "Are they too high for you?"

Mallory smiled confidently. "You're worth any price, and I'll gladly pay. My only regret is that Brad was hurt by it. Any pain he experiences is his own doing. I'm no longer going to feel guilty about what he does or doesn't expect of me."

"My sentiments run along the same lines," he admitted. "Sometimes it's hard to live up to a bigger-than-life image that others often have of us."

"Then let's not. No matter what's happened in my life, I've always known that I could be myself with you. You know the ins and outs of my personality better than I do." She put a hand over his. She added as an afterthought, "Best of all, you act like you care about us, in spite of walking a shaky tightrope. That's everything to me."

"It's more than my desire for you, Mallory." He turned her to face him. "I find it little to gamble when I think I can have you."

"I've been yours all along. Didn't you know that?"

"I do now. I've desired you for as long as I can remember. All the feelings stayed inside, and I haven't dared reach out before now."

"Why didn't you say anything?"

"I kept my silence for both our good. There's always been an allurement about you, a fatal fascination that still may threaten us. You're right, I do know you well, the faults as well as the virtues. Up to now my fascination has been an unwilling one. The fact that I practiced self-denial is the only thing that has kept me from totally succumbing to your charms."

"You're not perfect either." She blinked and pretended mild offense. "You're like the great stone face who won't give away the first emotion. You're a tough man to figure out, Quinn Chennault."

He grinned slightly. "Until now, neither of us has

been ready to handle more than a physical relationship. I think there should be something else, don't you?"

Was Quinn declaring himself? Mallory gave him a long look. "I don't know if I quite grasp what you're getting at. Do you mean we'll go ahead and spend these next two weeks together like we agreed?"

"Right now a lifetime wouldn't be long enough to suit me." His eyes sparkled devilishly.

"For a man who lives the here and now and can't promise any tomorrows, that's quite a loaded statement," she chided.

He knew she was toying with him. He got right to the point. *"Je t'aime,* Mallory, *je t'aime."*

"I . . ." She couldn't believe her ears, and said coyly, "I don't understand French. Would you mind translating?"

He threw back his head and laughed deeply. The sound carried across the water. "You delightful little tease! If I allow it, you'll string me out until the last minute. I said I've fallen in love with you."

Her eyes were large and liquid. For a minute she thought she might cry. She was both excited and touched at the admission. "I was afraid to hope that you'd ever say it, Quinn." Her voice was shaky. "I love you too, so much that words can't describe what I'm feeling. It started surfacing when I saw you at the hospital. I didn't know how to handle it at the time. God, I think I'm dreaming again!"

"Again?" he prompted.

"Just call it feminine intuition. I'll tell you all about it later."

He pulled her close and kissed her passionately. "You're not dreaming, *mon cher*. We're both very real. And so is the feeling between us." He kissed her again and again, making her breathless. "I love you, Mallory. No matter what happens, you can always count on it."

"I will, Quinn, I will!" She offered her lips again.

He scooped her up in his arms and carried her to the door of the houseboat. "Just in case you have any doubts, I intend to prove it, woman."

She giggled and reached for the door, opening it so they could go inside. He carried her down the hallway and into the bedroom. After he laid her on the bed, he stood and undressed. Mallory eased back and watched him.

"Say it again, will you?"

He raised a brow. "I love you, my dear little spitfire. Now, are you happy?"

"More than you'll ever know. I still think I'm dreaming."

"You won't be in a minute." He took off his shirt. Wearing his slacks, he knelt on the bed and removed Mallory's clothing piece by piece.

As she lay beneath his gaze, wearing nothing but transparent lace panties, his eyes traveled over the golden curves of her figure. She was feminine, perfect, with her flaxen hair flowing out on the bed like a shimmering fan. He kissed her nose, her lips, the tips of her breasts, her navel; even the soft pillow of her pelvis didn't escape the warm ravishment of his lips.

Mallory felt like a goddess as Quinn worshipped her beauty. Between kisses he said, "I'm a rich man and can support you well."

"That's very generous, but I can take care of myself. I don't want to be kept. Isn't it enough to know I'll be available whenever you want me?"

He looked at her hard. "The supply will never keep up with the demand. I'll settle for nothing less than marrying you. I want you as my wife, by my side all my life."

An infinite tenderness filled Mallory as she cupped Quinn's face and kissed him softly. "Wow, you really know how to pack a punch!"

"Don't you want to get married and make babies??

Maybe you don't want to marry me. We could just make babies instead." His smile was slow, assured.

"It's not that, and you know it!" She laughed. "I don't know if I'll be able to acquire a taste for your lifestyle."

"Ah, too fast for you, huh?"

"No. Too slow." Mischief was plainly written across her face.

"If you don't give in, I'll drag you off again like I did that last night in Baton Rouge." He continued the banter.

"You can't force a willing soul, Quinn. Yes, I'll marry you. I'll share your name and have your children." Her voice lowered to a serious level. "You're all I've ever really wanted. I was afraid to admit it to myself because I thought I could never have you. When did you realize you loved me?"

"I wasn't completely certain until today. When you and Cam got together, it threw a curve my way and made me give up the notion of wanting you. I had stood around, wondering if you would ever grow up. You fooled us all and chose him."

"Only because I thought I couldn't have you, Quinn. Somewhere inside I had convinced myself that Cam was a good second. I was settling."

"A Steiner settling?" He chuckled. "That's a first."

"It's true!" she insisted. "On the night of the fire, Cam came up to the porch and we talked about the past. I realized then just how little I cared for him, and why our breakup wasn't painful. I never loved him. My love and wanting has all been for you. Want to know something else?"

"What?"

"If I had to, I intended to make the memories of these last few days with you stretch over the rest of my life. If I couldn't have you, I wanted no one."

"I would have never let you go again," Quinn said

tenderly. He paused. "My time came when I had to make a declaration in Brad's office. For days I've lived with the fact that I was treading on dangerous ground. I've had enough trouble without borrowing more. But when I thought of you, I knew I'd be an empty man without you. I had to tell him how I really felt."

"How did Brad take it?"

"More or less the way you expected. I banked heavily on the fact that he and I have twenty years invested in each other and he'd listen to me. You were the realistic one in predicting that he wouldn't."

"He didn't give you a chance at all?" Her voice was emotionless.

"No."

"Why not? Is it because he thinks he's the only person who's allowed happiness? He has everything he could ever want. Why has he always been so jealous of me?"

"I think he cares too much for you," Quinn said carefully. "You see, you're all he has. Just as you depended on him when you were a child, he's seen fit to depend on you as a man. Don't ever count on his owning up to it, though. He hides behind all that bluster about your heritage and your good family name staying polished."

"I don't understand. He has Elissa. Isn't that enough?" Mallory turned on her side and faced Quinn.

"Evidently not. Have you ever watched how he babies her and how she coddles him? It hints at a strong protectiveness in both their characters. You haven't been just his sister. You're the child he and Elissa lost hope of creating. And you're the only living link to a family he no longer has. Your brother is a very lonely man, Mallory."

"That didn't give him the right to treat me the way he did. Lots of people are lonely, but they remedy it with kindness, by reaching out." Pain clouded Mallory's green eyes. "There have been times when I've felt like Brad has treated me as less than a person."

"I know. I felt the same way in his office. That crusty armor around him is so thick that it's a prison. The only person allowed in or out is Elissa. And even then she has to beg admittance. He's inflexible and doesn't want to accept the truth no matter who tells him. I did what I could to set him straight."

"Then you told him everything about us?"

"The entire truth. It's his option to accept or deny, and he's pretty upset about it. Especially since I gave him no quarter. He'll need time to come around. If he doesn't, well, that will be his problem." Quinn played with a soft strand of her hair. "It's no longer a secret that I love you. I want to tell the world."

Exultant, Mallory felt like laughing aloud. She had feared losing everything, but Quinn had defended her to Brad and had admitted that he loved her. Knowing her brother as she did, she suspected he was probably throwing a royal fit at that very minute. It wouldn't hurt to let him smolder for a little while in that self-made prison before working out some kind of a truce. Brad would eventually listen to reason. Quinn would see to it.

Mallory sighed. "Brad Steiner can dish it out, but he can't take it. In a way, it's good that he got what was coming to him."

Quinn propped up on an elbow. "We should pity him for being so damn shortsighted."

"Perhaps." She smiled. "All that matters to me is that I'll be a Chennault after all."

Quinn didn't think he had heard right. "Would you pass that by me again?"

"Brad is going to be very lonely now," she explained. "Even more so when he sees us happy together. You know what I mean."

"Unfortunately I do, and I don't approve of your

selfish attitude." Quinn slowly withdrew. She didn't readily understand why.

"What's wrong? I just made a simple statement." She sat up, suddenly worried. The look on Quinn's face was anything but pleasant. "You and I love each other, and no one can stop us. We have the right to be together if we want to. Brad will see that eventually, but it will hurt him at first. That's all I meant."

"Is it? I'm not some trophy for you to wave under Brad's nose. If I marry you, will you be my wife or will I be just your husband?"

Mallory's brows drew together. "What kind of a silly question is that? Husbands and wives, wives and husbands. There's no difference. Quinn, you're upsetting me and not making any sense."

"You're making the kind of sense I don't like." Still wearing his slacks, he picked up his shirt. "I thought you had changed, had matured enough to put down the contention with Brad. I was wrong. You want to marry me so you can get back at him."

"That's not true!" she insisted. "Just because I came out with an innocent remark—"

"Innocent hell! You slipped up and said what you were really thinking." Quinn was livid, and the unholy light in his eyes made a shiver of dread pass through Mallory. "It's still a power struggle with Brad, isn't it? A little more sophisticated, perhaps, but a game for power nonetheless."

"That's a lie! You've got to listen to me!" she insisted. "You're acting exactly like Brad, drawing conclusions from a thoughtless statement. You won't give me a chance to explain what I meant!"

"All I have to do is look over what's happened since this morning. I'm not so certain that it wasn't an elaborate setup."

Mallory sat up straight. "In what way? Do you think I made arrangements for Brad to find us together?"

"No, but after the blowup you and he had, you

played me like a real sucker. The hidden tears, bringing out the protectiveness in me so I'd go to Brad and fight for you."

"That was none of my doing!" Mallory exploded. "Stop twisting it around to sound like that! You went to Brad of your own accord. I begged you not to."

"Of course you did. It would've looked pretty fishy had you encouraged me to go." By this time Quinn was so enraged that he couldn't think straight. "For days I've been agonizing about everything that's gone on between you and me. I sacrificed twenty years for you, and gave up the best friend I ever had, even if he is a bigot. All you can say is you're glad you can get even with him."

Mallory began to cry softly. "How little you really do know me. I thought you had looked inside me, understood, but right now you have even less insight than Brad. I've changed, Quinn. I still may be headstrong and outspoken, but I wouldn't deliberately set out to hurt anyone. Least of all you. What reason would I have?"

"Turning on the tears a bit early, aren't you?" His eyes were cold, hard. "You had a score to settle with me. I hurt you badly four years ago, remember?"

"No!" she screamed.

"You planned well, *mon cher,* drawing me in and making me admit my passion for you. You waited until I was vulnerable and then you managed to strike back. Well, you've more than evened up the tally."

"That's not true, and you know it! You're upset with Brad, and you're blaming me! I never planned anything, Quinn. I came back for the good of all of us."

"Sure, sure." He wouldn't look at her.

"My brother has proven that he'll never change. He said something to make you turn against me like this. What was it?"

"I have a mind of my own," he said flatly. "I don't need anyone else's impressions."

"Then start thinking for yourself, dammit!" Mallory felt that she was fighting for her life. "Right now I hate Brad for trying to make things tough between us. But I love you for caring enough to face him for me." She couldn't stop the angry tears from flowing down her cheeks. "Don't misconstrue my words, please?"

"With you hate means love, Mallory." He slipped on his shirt and went to the door.

"Don't you dare walk out, Quinn Chennault!" If he left, Mallory feared she'd never have another chance to reason with him. "We haven't finished!"

"Now who sounds like Brad? You two are more alike than I'm comfortable with. I can't and won't spend my life battling in a triangle. I finally won the war in my head and wanted to make a go of it with you. It's impossible because you're still fighting yours."

"Where are you going?"

"Outside to put some space between us. I don't like the feeling of being played for a twenty-four-carat fool." The door slammed behind him.

For a long time Mallory sat in the middle of the bed and tried to piece together the jagged edges of a life that was suddenly turned topsy-turvy. She had spoken without thinking, and it was enough to drive Quinn away forever.

Hours later Mallory sat outside on the deck, listening to the crickets and frogs sing to the sunset. There was no further word from Quinn, and she began to lose hope that he'd return. She sipped a drink of bourbon and Coke. How many did that make? Two? Three? It didn't matter. The alcohol had little effect on her nerves.

In the twilight she saw a man approaching from the roadway. Thinking it was Quinn, she jumped up and ran to the boarding ramp. "I knew you'd come back! You must listen to me!" she called out happily.

When he came closer, she realized it was Cam. "I take it Quinn isn't here right now?"

Mallory nodded slowly, feeling silly for the childish display of emotion. "He . . . had something to take care of. I . . . was waiting for him."

She went back to her chair and sat down heavily.

Cam followed. "I just wanted to tell him that it's all clear at headquarters. A relief crew is lined up for tomorrow morning." He was uncomfortable, shifting from foot to foot. "Mallory, I don't mean to be a buttinsky, but is somethin' wrong?"

"Why, no. What could be wrong?" Glumly she sipped her drink and stared down at the floor.

"Babe, did you and Quinn have words?"

"You really shouldn't be a buttinsky," she warned softly. "I can handle this myself."

He nodded. "I know you can. But you look so lost and hurt that I can't help thinking—"

"Do me a favor and don't think!" she snapped. "Just get off my case, will you?"

"Alright, alright." His tone was placating.

She bit her lip, but the tears came anyway. "Oh Cam, I've made such a dreadful mess of everything! With just a few stupid words I've managed to turn Quinn completely around."

"What's going on?" He sat next to her on a chaise.

"He wants to marry me and I want to marry him. Only he thinks I want to marry him to get back at Brad. It's not true. I love him dearly." She sniffed.

"Hey, that's great! You'll be my sister-in-law."

"No it's not great, because it'll probably never happen. Quinn won't give me a chance to explain."

Cam took out a handkerchief and gave it to her. "Look, Quinn is the most levelheaded, straight-thinking man I know. Here lately he hasn't been himself and this . . . this shortsightedness started in Baton Rouge. You're not to blame if he's harboring a mistaken assumption right now. If you give him some thinking time, he'll come back and want to make up."

She stopped crying and said in a childlike voice, "Do you really think so?"

"Sure. Remember the night we all went dancing? Even then he wasn't himself. Of course, I couldn't blame him for horning in on my time. It didn't take a genius to figure out that sparks were flying between you two. And you worked that out with a little loving and a little smooching, didn't you?" He smiled broadly. Mallory had to laugh at the comical way he expressed himself. "Now you just dry those tears and get inside. The mosquitoes will eat you alive if you don't. You want some company until Quinn comes back?"

They walked together to the door. "I think I'll be all right now. I have the feeling that Quinn and I will be up for most of the night talking. I better get some rest before he comes home."

"You do that, babe."

"Cam?" She looked up at him. Her face was shining with a grateful light. "Thank you."

They embraced as he accepted. "You're more than welcome."

In the dimness Quinn approached the houseboat. He had walked for hours, thinking about Mallory and Brad. He damned himself for letting Mallory use him, if she had indeed intended to do that. At the same time he still loved her. Maybe he had been too quick in accusing her of trying to get back at Brad. Maybe it hadn't been a setup after all.

The painful feelings from the argument with Brad were still churning badly inside. He hadn't given himself time to deal with them before admitting his love to Mallory. Was he sorry for saying he loved her? No. He had said it and couldn't take it back. He didn't want to take it back.

As he walked toward the gangplank, he thought about talking it out with her. When he looked up, he saw Cam in the doorway, embracing Mallory. They stood there in each other's arms, talking and laughing, oblivious to the fact that he was only a few yards away. Jealousy made Quinn bristle inside as the churning grew stronger.

Quinn tore his eyes away. Slowly he retraced his steps back to the road. He had no intention of breaking in on the tender embrace. Mallory could play all the games she wanted, but it would be at her own expense from now on.

Chapter Thirteen

For a day and a night Mallory waited at the houseboat for Quinn's return. When he failed to show up, she took the hint and left. The hardest thing she had to do was pack her bags and walk away. But she did it. She moved back to Houston and spent the better part of a month trying to patch up her shattered life.

As she stood at the window of her third-floor penthouse, she looked out at the Houston skyline. It was a beautiful city, busy and noisy, bursting at the seams with frenetic activity. At one time the Houston pulse had pumped her lifeblood. She had loved the tense, electric atmosphere. Now it seemed disquieting, almost maddening as she tried unsuccessfully to make the transition back from the appealing tranquility of the delta.

Mallory's thoughts strayed to the day she and Quinn drove around South Louisiana. Life was lazy, peaceful, as she had slipped easily into the comfortable bayou rhythm.

For countless years she had traveled, always bound for one place or another. Now she knew she was tiring of the pace, and she gave serious thought to eventually settling down somewhere alone. With its verdant landscapes and peacful sunsets, Louisiana was the perfect place to mend a broken heart. But not for Mallory, because all her memories had originated there.

Had things worked out with Quinn, her life would now have meaning. They would probably be settled somewhere in New Orleans. If she felt a need to travel, she could accompany him to oil fires. But things hadn't worked out, and she was the biggest loser of all, giving up a brother as well as a lover.

The nights were endless as she asked herself why a thousand times. When she did find sleep, her thoughts flew to Quinn's houseboat. In her dreams she would relive the times they had spent alone making love. She always woke up depressed, sometimes tearful. The toughest acceptance of all was the fact that she'd never again feel total security, that sense of belonging Quinn had always managed to impart with a simple embrace.

Although Brad had made no attempts to contact Mallory, Elissa let her know that a channel would remain open any time there was the need to talk. Mallory often called Elissa to see how things were going, and to check on Brad. It was upsetting to learn that Wild Wells Limited had temporarily closed their operation. Brad stayed in a blue funk, unwilling to discuss his problems with anyone. He quietly waited while his leg healed, so he could go back and salvage the business.

When it did come about, chances were he would wind up folding after the first few weeks. It took years learning to fight oil fires and building a reputation as the best. No one but Quinn Chennault could assist him in handling it the right way and completing the famous team.

What little Elissa heard of Quinn was not enough to

talk about. He was somewhere in Europe, and had not made much of an effort to contact family or friends in Louisiana. He had simply resigned, dropping out of sight for parts unknown.

It was as if three lives were isolated, placed in suspended animation, and there was nothing anyone could do to release them.

Mallory felt guilty, helpless. Had she not returned to Baton Rouge to mend fences with Brad, none of this would have happened. Too late she had learned that the pursuit of Quinn Chennault was not worth the high penalty the three of them were forced to pay. It was a haunting regret.

One evening she was on the phone chatting with Elissa.

"Is Brad doing any better?" Mallory asked, knowing the answer beforehand.

"Somewhat. The cast comes off in another few days and he'll start physical therapy. I've enjoyed having him around, but it has been trying." Elissa's voice was wistful.

"If anyone deserved to gain from this unfortunate experience, it should've been you. For years you've sat back and let Brad do all the traveling. Now you've had the chance to keep him to yourself and it's been a labor."

"You can say that again. He's been restless, so unhappy most of the time. I can't seem to get any response from him like I used to."

"I don't understand," Mallory said.

"He's been acting strange over the last couple of days, as if he's expecting something, and he won't tell me why. Last night he started talking about taking a short vacation, but he hasn't decided where to."

"Humor him. Maybe you two need to get away for a while."

"What Bradley needs is his family," Elissa said resolutely. "Quinn hasn't tried to make the first contact. I think that bothers Brad the most. I told him I'm keeping in touch with you, but he acts like he's not interested. If I could just think of some way to get y'all back together . . ."

"I know." Mallory sighed. "But there isn't. I made my bed and I have to lie in it. This is a rare situation where the three of us have equal, irreparable hurts that go too deep to heal. It's like a domino principle where one collapse ultimately causes another. I'm thankful I can at least talk with you. It gets lonely out here sometimes."

"Do you think, given time, you might try to come back?" There was a flicker of hope in her voice.

"I can never come back, Elissa. Brad gave me a choice, and I made it. We were all gambling heavily and lost too much to ever make it like it was before. I've hurt my brother badly, and Quinn nearly crushed every feeling I have. It's all I can do to look at myself in the mirror sometimes, much less face anyone."

"You stop acting like it's all your fault, Mallory. We've been over this before and I told you that everyone shares equal responsibility. In spite of it all, you still love Quinn very much, don't you?"

"Yes, and it hurts all the time. I wonder, does it ever stop or lessen?"

"If I could answer that, I would," came the kind reply.

The doorbell rang and Mallory concluded the call before answering it. When she opened the door, Quinn Chennault stood in the hallway. He was dressed in a conservative three-piece business suit. Patiently he waited for an invitation to enter.

Shocked to see him again, Mallory was temporarily at a loss for words. As she stood there trembling, he said, "I've come up to this door at least five times in the last two days. But I couldn't ring the bell. Please don't make this tough by slamming the door in my face."

"What do you want?" she said briskly.

He gazed down at her with those irresistible, flashing indigo eyes and muttered in a soft Louisiana drawl, "I think you already know the answer to that, Mallory." He walked inside uninvited.

"I don't know anything anymore." She swallowed hard. "And you don't have the right to just walk in and out of my life like you own it." It was an effort to keep up a haughty pretense. Vanity was all that kept her from faltering.

Oblivious to her words, he glanced around the apartment. It was posh, delicately designed in muted rose and gray tones. "This is a nice place. Soft, feminine, just like you."

"What do you want?" she repeated shakily, feeling resentment rising like bile in her throat.

His expression was subdued, but his eyes were alive with a light of determination. "I've spent a great deal of time thinking about us."

"Good for you. I haven't had the chance. I've been too busy," she lied. He looked better than she remembered. She felt the need to protect herself against his penetrating, soul-searching gaze. "In fact, I was on the phone when you rang the doorbell. I was making plans for tonight. Whatever it is you have to say, make it quick, because I have places to go."

He sighed. "After the argument at the houseboat, I carried pretty hard feelings. Maybe if you had tried to call or drop a line . . ."

"*You* wanted *me* to drop a line?" she asked incredulously. "Don't flatter yourself! I waited around for two days, and you never showed. You walked out on me, not the other way around!"

"I knew I wouldn't hear from you, because it's just not your style. I forgot you're Brad Steiner's sister and just as stubborn as he is," he continued patiently.

"I think it's you who has the monopoly on stubbornness," she concluded quickly. "At least Brad half listens to what someone has to say before he passes judgment. I wasn't given the courtesy of getting a word in edgewise the last time we were together."

"I know, and I'm sorry." He shook his head in defeat. "This is going all wrong. I should say what I came here to say and be done with it. I was a stupid, insensitive fool for letting you go like I did, and I regret it."

"Is that why you set off in another direction and left everything behind?"

"Yes, it was necessary for a while."

"You know, you could've written to me as well."

"I've come here to talk to you in person instead. I had to get away and do some serious thinking. So many things were closing in on me too fast. I needed time to sort them out."

"Why couldn't you have told me this at the houseboat? I would've gladly given you all the room you wanted."

"Why do we do any number of crazy things when we're hurt and confused? I was raw inside when Brad finished with me, and I turned around only to blame you for everything. The two people I love most in the world were driven apart by ridiculous prejudices. I just served to drive the wedge deeper. I tried to pretend otherwise for your sake, but we're talking about the kind of guilt and disappointment that eats a person alive. If that's not enough to confuse a man about his motives and priorities, what is?"

"Please, Quinn, this isn't doing us any good now."

"Do you know what it's like to want something so badly that you can't think of anything else? To have it within your grasp, knowing that you'll have to destroy something equally precious in order to get it? Before taking a step that serious, you must feel that the reward is well worth the sacrifice, because it's something you intend to keep for the rest of your life. That was how I felt about taking you into my world and making you the center of it."

She couldn't bear to look at him any longer. He was, after all, a flesh-and-blood man who had swallowed his pride to admit to a serious, damaging mistake. He had also confessed to suffering the same tortures she had faced over the last month.

Traitorous recollections began to filter in and out of her mind as she fought to forget how it felt to have his arms around her. "It's over and done with. You saw to that. If you're asking for my forgiveness, you've got it." She checked her watch. "Now, if you don't mind . . ."

Quinn ignored the gesture. "You know, *mon cher,* no matter how much distance I put between us, no matter how much time went by, I couldn't escape the fact that I'm madly in love with you. I also won't forget that I faulted Brad for being arrogant. You were correct a minute ago when you said I had him beat."

"And I can't forget that you accused me of playing games and using you. I didn't do that." She watched his face carefully.

"I know that now. This should've been ironed out on the night of our argument. After I cooled down, I went back to the houseboat to talk with you. When I saw Cam standing in the door, and how comfortably you seemed to fit in his arms, something snapped inside."

Her eyes grew large. "You saw us? Why didn't you say anything to let us know you were there?"

"Because I was jealous and wanted to believe that you had used me. Seeing you with Cam reinforced that belief."

"You wanted a reason to leave me," she admonished.

"I suppose. It set me back a bit to admit that I didn't know as much about Brad and you as I thought I did. I knew deep down that the argument with Brad wasn't a setup. I just couldn't get it out of my mind what you said about being a Chennault, of Brad being lonely. It sounded so much like the old spoiled Mallory . . ."

She looked down at her hands as they nervously clenched and unclenched. "You don't know how many times I've regretted that statement. I figured Brad would need to stew for a little while, that's all. Together we could've made him see how right it was for us to marry."

"That's why I'm here. If you can find it in your heart to forgive me, I want to try again and make it work for us this time." His eyes were the softest blue she had ever seen.

Slowly she shook her head and said, "I don't think I care to tempt the fates again. You once said what drew us to each other was a dangerous fascination. We were playing with fire and thought how grand it was to get away with it. We . . . tried unsuccessfully to make it more than it really was." She couldn't believe she spoke so calmly about a matter that shook the core of her soul.

"Is that what you really think?"

"I have to if I want to survive. You wouldn't believe me when I showed you my vulnerability. I don't intend to be hurt that way again."

"Then my words have all been for nothing?"

"They have." There was a note of finality in her voice.

"If you want me to go, I will," he said thickly.

"Yes, please go." Her eyes begged him to stop the torture and leave her alone.

He cocked his head to one side and studied her. "No. I'm staying."

She felt anger overwhelm her. "Damn you! You no longer have the right to stay! Get out!"

"No, Mallory." He made a move toward her.

"Just . . . stop right there, Quinn. Please, don't come near me," she begged in a tiny voice. She could feel herself wavering.

"I can't stay away any longer," he groaned. He

pulled her into his embrace and covered her mouth with his. The kiss was hungry, passionate. As he savagely commanded a surrender, she responded against her will. His caress was melting, lingering, and Mallory was pulled along with the tide.

"I'm in love with you, Mallory, and you love me. We belong together. Try and deny it now," he challenged tenderly.

"Oh, Quinn," she sobbed softly. "Don't do this to me! Haven't we all paid enough? Why are you holding me like this?"

"It's the only way I know to make you see the truth. Sure, we've hurt each other. And there may be more times when arguments and misunderstandings will threaten to tear us apart. That's why we have to have faith in each other and remember that we should stick together. *Mon cher,* I need you!"

She looked up at his face, at the angles and planes she had touched so many times. The wanting in his eyes was almost tangible, and she gave in to it.

"I do love you so!" She kissed him again, clinging to him and drawing on his strength to support her. Inside she felt like a parched, dying desert. Quinn was a life-giving rain. For long, lonely weeks she had yearned for the security of his embrace. All self-protective barriers fell away as she held him tight.

"Tell me again, Mallory. I have to hear it again," he whispered in her ear.

She answered him huskily. "I adore you, Quinn. I haven't stopped wanting you for one single second. I've been so lost . . ."

He broke the words with another kiss, muttering against her mouth. "Never again, *mon cher.* I swear, never again."

He spoke the truth, and she accepted it as she filled with a happiness that made her glow. "Where do we take it from here?"

"Back to Louisiana where we belong."

She hesitated. "I know it's not going to be easy, but we'll have to find a way to cut Brad out of our lives if we marry and live together."

"He'll never be out of the picture, Mallory, and we can't sleep three in a bed. Remember that quaint little French church we visited one day?" She nodded. "We're going back so I can make an honest-to-goodness Cajun bride of you. That should make peace with your family once and for all."

"But how?" Her eyes clouded for only a second.

"I won," he said resolutely. "Brad broke down and got in touch with me. He's ready to mend fences if we are. In fact, he's at his office right now, waiting for my call for help."

"Help with what?" she asked.

"He agreed to be best man at our wedding. That is, if I succeeded in convincing you to marry me. If you didn't listen, he was going to reason with you and insist that we get married." Quinn's grin stretched from ear to ear.

"Oh, Quinn!" she squealed, and jumped into his arms. "Tell me you're not lying!"

"What do you think?" He laughed exuberantly. "We have some plans to make. That is, if you can break your date tonight."

Mallory put her head down and meekly admitted, "The date I told you about was really a conversation with Elissa. She's been wonderful about keeping me abreast of all the news." Her brows drew together in concentration. "Wait a minute . . . she said that Brad talked last night of taking a short vacation. Was he referring to our wedding?"

"That's right. Two days ago Brad admitted to me that he can't possibly hold off the three of us at one time. We've given him no choice, and he's going to accept us once and for all. He intends to surprise Elissa with the news after I call him. They'll be waiting for us in front of the church tomorrow. Do you believe me now?"

"Yes, with all my heart." She smiled her love at him. "I know you're sincere about loving me, because you've practically moved heaven and earth to prove it. And I can see forever in your eyes."

"You'll see it every day, *mon cher.* I promise." He weighed his next words. "You once told me you could acquire a taste for my lifestyle. Do you still mean it?"

"Of course. My brokerage business can be handled from anywhere in the world. There's no reason why you and I can't be together all the time. Every day, every minute will count, even when you're fighting oil fires."

"Not anymore. When we do get things back together at headquarters, I'll be a member of the board on a consulting basis only. That'll mean a great deal of traveling for us while I check out the fires for my crews. Let some other jerk risk everything he has. I'm going to be too busy flying planes and making babies with you." His laugh was deep, resonant. "How about picking up your briefcase and let's get this show on the road? People are waiting for us."

She took him by the hand and led him to the bedroom. "One thing at a time, my darling."

"You're talking my language already. I promise not to dictate to you like Brad did, but I'll be damn demanding in our bedroom, do you understand?"

"Totally." She smiled up at him, saying sweetly, "I hope you know what you're doing, because you've just made a commitment to embrace the biggest fire of your life, Quinn Chennault."

"Yeah," he drawled slowly. "But I'll be damned if I'll put this one out!"

READERS' COMMENTS ON SILHOUETTE SPECIAL EDITIONS:

"I just finished reading the first six Silhouette Special Edition Books and I had to take the opportunity to write you and tell you how much I enjoyed them. I enjoyed all the authors in this series. Best wishes on your Silhouette Special Editions line and many thanks."

—B.H.*, Jackson, OH

"The Special Editions are really special and I enjoyed them very much! I am looking forward to next month's books."

—R.M.W.*, Melbourne, FL

"I've just finished reading four of your first six Special Editions and I enjoyed them very much. I like the more sensual detail and longer stories. I will look forward each month to your new Special Editions."

—L.S.*, Visalia, CA

"Silhouette Special Editions are — 1.) Superb! 2.) Great! 3.) Delicious! 4.) Fantastic! . . . Did I leave anything out? These are books that an adult woman can read . . . I love them!"

—H.C.*, Monterey Park, CA

*names available on request